Wasted on the Young

Wasted on the Young

Thomas E. Coughlin

Fitzgerald & LaChapelle Publishing

Written and produced in the United States of America

ISBN: 978-0-9666202-7-6

Cover Design: Lisa Atkins, Pelham, NH

Cover Model: Nicole Poirier, Wells, ME

Cover Locations: Mousam River and Parsons Beach, Kennebunk, ME

FIRST EDITION

Fitzgerald & LaChapelle Publishing
814 Elm Street, Suite 401
Manchester, NH 03101
Phone: (603) 669-6112   Fax: (603) 625-1450

Acknowledgements

Gary and Diane Leech of Congdon's Donuts, Dick Varano of Billy's Chowder House, Kennebunk High School including Susan Cressey, Bruce Lewia and Joe Foster, Sue Lashua, Deborah Rubero, the Kennebunk Free Library, the Brick Store Museum in Kennebunk, Rosalind Magnuson and her book, Trunks, Textiles & Transits, Doug & Eddie Bibber and especially to Mary and George Moore who allowed me to use their oceanfront cottage as the model for Emma Lipton's home.

Dedication

For Elaine...again

Part 1

1

October 15, 1973

The early morning sun squints above the trees while an out-of-state delivery truck coasts down Route 1 toward a cement bridge spanning the Mousam River. In the next instant the driver presses down on his break pedal and hears the sound of cascading water, while taking in the quiet main street of Kennebunk's upper village. The outsider is reminded of his whereabouts, an idyllic country town in the southern corner of the state of Maine. He pauses momentarily while his eyes take in all the makings of a Norman Rockwell magazine cover including the surviving nineteenth century mill building, the well-ordered procession of shops along the town's main street and the white church steeple towering majestically above the community. It is the physical manifestation of everything his society and culture has worked toward over the past two hundred years, he thinks. It is the farthest thing from the setting for a young girl's nightmare as one could imagine. However, for sixteen year old Emma Corman, it is.

"Time for the two of you to be getting into the shower," called out a too familiar voice from the bottom of the stairs. The command elicited an audible groan from the far side of the bedroom wall.

"It's Emma's turn to shower first," affirmed the thirteen year old from the far bedroom.

"In the event my idiot sister has forgotten, I got up and showered first all last week," argued Emma Corman from the warmth of her bed.

"Mother, we alternate mornings. That's the arrangement," countered the younger girl.

"Mother, inform my moronic sister once again that I showered first last Friday and we alternate. Please explain to her what the word *alternate* means."

"But, Mother, it's a new week," added the thirteen year old. Becky was the baby of the family, three years younger than Emma. It was also generally agreed that Becky was the prettier of the Corman girls. "Nature gave Becky the looks and Emma the brains, and the universe remains in balance," theorized Bertrand Corman to his wife on numerous occasions, but always out of earshot of his daughters. Mr. Corman was a professor of

Sociology at a small, nearby college and prone to lend his learned insight whenever possible.

"Emma, would it kill you to get up first and shower?" asked Harriet Corman from halfway up the stairs. Even through the bedroom wall, Emma picked up on her sister's muffled laughter. Recognizing that she was fighting a losing battle, Emma ripped the blankets back from her warm body and lowered her feet to the floor in search of her slippers.

Moments into her shower Emma felt the grip of anxiety gather in her stomach. Her weekend of refuge from school was over and in two hours she would have to face another dreadful week in the company of classmates. She had not seen this stressful condition materializing a month and a half earlier but it sprang on her a few days into the school year. Her junior year at Kennebunk High School had started much like her prior two, with one major exception. In her freshman and sophomore years, Betty Harmon had been her constant and only companion, a friend, study mate and confidante. As underclassmen, these two intellectual rebels had sat on the sidelines and quietly found fault with all of the ordinary and mundane aspects of high school life. However, life at Kennebunk High changed for Emma in September after Betty and her family relocated to Massachusetts. Somehow, and for no reason clear to her, Emma found herself on the receiving end of the wrath of Whitney Crowninshield, an angel-faced overachiever blessed with all things genetics and providential fate could provide. Born into one of Kennebunkport's better families, Whitney did not just have her family's wealth and social standing behind her, but also brought an amazing intellect and exceptional physical beauty to the table. Immensely popular with students and faculty alike, she was the last person anyone wanted for an antagonist. Whitney's newborn animosity for Emma manifested itself during the first week of this school year. Both were enrolled in the college program and shared a number of classes. This gave Whitney easy and frequent access to Emma and she took full advantage of it. One of the Kennebunkport girl's favorite tactics was to simply stare at Emma for an extended period, silently taking in every detail of her face and body. During these periods of humiliation Emma most times found herself tongue-tied and in awe of the young woman's beauty and demeanor.

"I was hoping to give you a few beauty secrets. You know…accentuate the positives. Unfortunately for you, Corman, there are no positives. You're a mess…no redeeming qualities," pronounced Whitney smugly to onlookers during week one. Emma had not replied. As she saw it, no counterattack was possible. Whitney was near perfect in face, body and mind. Emma knew she would only be mocked if she even tried to find fault with her tormentor. That one-sided exchange during the first days set the tone for the school year and for the relationship between the two young women.

After descending the stairs, Emma turned into the kitchen and saw her father hunched over his morning newspaper. Bertrand Corman was a man of average height and weight with a sad, drooping face perched atop a thin, yet flabby, body. Across the room, her mother stood over the toaster and waited on two slices of wheat bread. Harriet Corman was a petite woman whose thick brown hair often dropped down over her face. She had been pretty in her youth, but the passage of time had now reduced her to the sort of woman a stranger's eyes were apt to pass over in a crowd. The sixteen year old slid her petite body onto a chair at the table beside her father. His eyes moved upward from the newspaper.

"Oh, Emma, I'm glad you're down early. I've got to talk to you about the phone bill. I just got around to opening last Saturday's mail. Emma, you're spending much too much time on the phone with your friend in Massachusetts. Our bill's gone through the roof. Now listen to me: one call a week and no more. Do you hear?" Emma shook her head in frustration.

"Daddy, I really miss Betty."

"Then put a pen to paper and write. We're not millionaires," he answered decisively.

"It's not the same." He locked eyes with her.

"Limit yourself to one call per week and preferably on the weekend," he insisted before dropping his eyes back to his paper and closing the discussion.

The Corman family lived in a well kept but modest home on Mechanic Street. Emma and Becky walked to school every day, but seldom together. Kennebunk High School and the junior high were located approximately three quarters of a mile away, and while many juniors at the school were already driving themselves to class, Emma was not among them. The Corman sisters emerged from the house together on this morning but Becky quickly made her way in the direction of Fletcher Street while Emma lagged behind. She dreaded the idea of returning to school on this Monday, not knowing what sort of physiological torture Whitney could have dreamed up for her over the weekend. One hundred feet up the road she had already conjured up an alternate plan for the day. She actually played with the idea of passing right by the high school and making her way up the road to the Maine Turnpike. She could turn this day into an adventure, she thought, and hitchhike her way north to Portland. She would grab a ride from a young Jack Kerouac type and spend the day sipping on coffee and listening to music in the city. She entertained herself with this mental fluff for a few, brief moments before dismissing it.

By the time Emma turned onto Fletcher Street she had already returned to the here and now. Her spirits fell away as an all-too-familiar anxiety returned and began to fester deep inside her, a feeling foreign to her until her junior year in school. It was an apprehension born of the anxiety she had observed on the faces of others, mostly boys, in the past. She remembered studying the appearance and actions of young men who found themselves paired up to engage in a fist fight after classes, far away from the eyes of any school officials. On two occasions she had followed the throng of high school students, mostly male, to a predetermined location for the battle. It was not the confrontation that drew her but rather a close-up study of the participants. There was always some degree of false bravado from one or both of the gladiators, but she looked more deeply at her subjects and always caught sight of the fear and anxiety hidden just beneath the surface. It was at these times that she appreciated being a female and not subject to the laws of the jungle. However, Whitney Crowninshield had changed all that and exposed her to the same fear and anxiety present in the eyes of the unfortunate boys who did battle. Only the nature of the bruising was different.

The walk from her front door to the high school was about seven tenths of a mile and took approximately twenty minutes. On this October morning, sunny with a brisk wind coming in off the ocean, she gazed apprehensively at the extended, two-story, brick structure that was Kennebunk High School and walked tentatively over the extended lawn toward the building's entrance. Emma thought back to her freshman and sophomore years at Kennebunk High and the absolute joy she felt coming to class every morning. Of course, those were the years spent in the company of her life-long friend, Betty Harmon. She tried to console herself with the thought that, just as those times had passed, so too would these.

Emma ascended the stairwell to the second story, her eyes trained on the floor, and turned up the hallway toward her homeroom. Lifting her head, she took in the sight of the dark brown lockers lining the long corridor. In her years as an underclassman, she had never noticed the dreary shroud cast over the hallway by this shade of paint, but on this morning, it pounced on her senses. A quick glance at her watch told her she was only a few minutes early. That was good. It only gave Whitney a few minutes to mount any form of attack on her. Turning into homeroom, she was relieved to see Mr. Foster standing by his desk. Shifting her eyes, she noticed Whitney seated in the second row, the blonde's eyes already trained on her prey. "Perfect hair, perfect face, perfect figure and, alas, perfect attendance," thought Emma. The word, perfect, was not an exaggeration when applied to Whitney. So flawless were her features that she was able to wear her blond hair quite short. It gave the sixteen year old a somewhat adult appearance. With this more mature look and her faultless diction, she seemed already prepared to take her place in a board room, even at her tender age. Mr. Foster, their homeroom teacher, shot Emma a warm smile, stepping aside and letting her pass. She returned the smile, albeit timidly, and scurried past him to her desk. The knot in her stomach grew in intensity as she seated herself, a mere three feet from her blond nemesis, and placed her chemistry book on the desk. A voice crackled over the loudspeaker and called the student body to the Pledge of Allegiance. The class lethargically rose to its feet in unison and listlessly recited the words. About a half dozen students, including Emma, still placed their hands over their hearts during the recitation. Patriotic words were followed by a string of announcements revolving around an almost endless list of clubs including the ecology club, the language club and the math and science clubs. It was near the close of this day's proclamations when Emma picked up on the attention she was receiving from Whitney. The beautiful junior was turned in her direction and was doing what she did all too often this school year…scrutinizing her.

"The dishrag! That's what it reminds me of…my mother's old dishrag," she forcibly whispered back to Mandy Cowger. "My mother keeps this mangy dishrag under the kitchen sink. She only takes it out when something particularly repulsive has to be scrubbed. It finally dawned on me: mom's dishrag and Corman's hair are the identical, revolting color," explained Whitney behind one of her fashion model smiles. A moment later Emma felt her hair lightly manipulated by the girl seated behind her while a smattering of subdued laughter sounded from the back of the room.

"Something you wish to share with the entire class, Miss Crowninshield?" asked Mr. Foster sarcastically.

"No, Mr. Foster, sir."

"Then eyes and shoulders to the front," he insisted, causing the young woman to rotate in her chair away from Emma.

"Now look what you've done, Dishrag," growled Mandy from behind in just above a whisper. The track star and close ally of Whitney reached forward and yanked on Emma's dull, brownish black hair. At that moment the bell sounded and students were called to their first classes of the day.

Emma hung back and lethargically assembled her books and papers while her fellow juniors made for the door. Mr. Foster was just finishing up an attendance sheet when Emma passed by his desk.

"Emma, correct me if I'm wrong, but there seems to be something going on under the radar back in your corner of the room. Care to enlighten me?" She stopped but only half faced the teacher.

"No, Mr. Foster, I'm fine…things are fine," she responded, but without conviction.

"Eye contact, Emma, give me some eye contact here." Foster was young, in his thirties, with a broad smile and compassionate face. Emma looked down on the man and flashed him a weak smile. "I don't want to see you withdrawing into a shell, because that's what it looks like from where I'm sitting. Is everything okay at home?"

"I'm fine, Mr. Foster, really. I just really miss my friend, Betty, that's all. You remember Betty Harmon?" The teacher nodded.

"That's right. You two were practically attached at the hip, if I remember correctly." Emma gave a shrug and dropped her eyes. "Give it time, young lady. You'll find yourself another kindred spirit," he assured her.

Emma loitered behind the mass exodus of students on this day, first taking the time to prune any and all excess papers from her notebooks and desk and then by meandering lethargically up the hallway to her locker, where she painstakingly sorted and rearranged everything stored there. This Monday had been a particularly difficult one, she thought, with Whitney and her crowd bearing down exceedingly hard on her. The day had started out with an attack on her personal appearance but switched to matters of personal hygiene by noontime. Seated close by Emma during lunch period, Whitney and Mandy staged a public scene and questioned her cleanliness. In voices that reached many seated in the converted gymnasium, they railed against her feminine hygienic practices with snide and catty innuendos. "There's this great new invention, Corman, it's called soap and water," sniped Whitney during the episode. The attack had driven Emma from the gym and outside to finish her lunch alone behind the school building. Now, she stared into her locker and tried to drive all thoughts of the incident from her mind. Glancing down at her watch, she saw that nearly twenty minutes had passed since dismissal. Hopefully, Whitney, Mandy and the rest of their crowd will have vacated the building and school grounds, she thought.

The staircase at the end of the building was quite deserted when she descended from the second floor and exited onto the spacious lawn at the front of the school. Emma had already decided not to go directly home on this afternoon. Instead she would visit a spot by the river where she and Betty had often gone to talk about all things pertinent to growing up. It was here where she and her friend had first confessed their thoughts regarding the future, life at home, changes in their bodies, the young men of Kennebunk High and, of course, sex. It was on the banks of the Mousam

River where each girl had learned, thanks to the honesty of the other, that their thoughts about young men at night in bed prior to sleep were not abnormal or strange. Emma thought back to a particular Friday afternoon in their sophomore year when their sexuality had been the only things on their minds and they had discussed what intimate acts they would consider doing and with whom. The exercise in total frankness had pushed the girls to grow more and more uninhibited on this day resulting in outbursts of uncontrollable laughter. It was on occasions like this that the bonds of friendship had been tightened between the two young women.

A few students remained grouped on the grounds at the front of the high school while Emma passed diagonally across the green lawn in the direction of the village. She knew that a visit back to her special spot on the river would not be the same without Betty, but she craved the magic of her special place nonetheless. If anything could help wash away the negative effects of this nightmarish day, the sight and sounds of the river could, she thought. A half a mile up the road, she joined Storer Street and walked in the general direction of Rogers Pond and the river. This route brought her past buildings surviving from the village's proud manufacturing era. However, little manufacturing activity remained in town. The Kesslen Shoe Company was the lone exception and occupied the three-story mill building crouched above the river. Reaching Route 1, she glanced up Main Street toward Bowdoin's Pharmacy. Her instincts told her that Whitney might be somewhere in the vicinity of Bowdoin's if she had not already returned home to Kennebunkport. She flitted across the roadway and continued down Water Street for a few hundred yards toward Rogers Pond. This pond, a swampy body of water about the size of a football field, sat back from the road practically on the lip of the Mousam River. Emma meandered toward the sound of moving water, past the stagnant pond, and climbed down the embankment to the gurgling, fresh water. The river here flowed with a certain enthusiasm and was perhaps one hundred feet shore to shore. She had visited this spot with Betty during dry summer months, when the boulders at mid stream were easily reachable on foot. That was not the case on this afternoon with water depths approaching two feet. Content to rest by the side of the waterway, she found a dry spot and took a seat by the river.

Emma spent the first moments at her special spot merely absorbing the sight and sounds of the Mousam. She folded her legs in front of her in a Native-American fashion and closed her eyes. It was then that a reality crystalized in her mind: she was alone in the world, unconnected with family and void of any friends in the here and now. There was no one for her to turn to for comfort or relief. How great it would be to not have to awaken the next morning and face a new ordeal at school, she thought. She wanted a certain end to her life as it was now unfolding. An image of her standing on the side of Route 1 hitchhiking came to mind and she entertained it. Why not head south and lose herself in Boston? Did she have the courage to take such a critical step? She remained by the river for the next two hours and felt her spirits decline while shadows lengthened and the sun descended toward the western horizon.

The color of the foliage on Mechanic Street was peaking on this day as Emma made her way toward home. The Corman residence was a small, two-story house with an expansive front porch and sat about halfway between Fletcher Street to the north and Storer Street to the south. The slender teenager entered the house and found her mother and sister in the kitchen.

"Oh good, you're home. I need you to go to the IGA and get bread and milk," barked out her mother.

"I just got in. Send Becky," insisted Emma.

"No. Your sister's been home all afternoon and helping me for the past half hour. No, young lady, you're going." Emma let out a long sigh and approached her mother. Harriet reached into a cookie jar, plucked out two one-dollar bills, and handed them to her elder daughter. "Get me a gallon of milk and a loaf of Sunbeam Bread."

"Are you sure this'll be enough?"

"It had better be or they've seen the last of the Cormans. Oh, and I'll be expecting change," she added. Emma bit her tongue and started the long walk back toward Main Street. She took a series of back streets on the errand, increasing her odds of avoiding any and all classmates from school.

Mr. Corman arrived home at the stroke of six and the family was seated around the kitchen table by six- fifteen. Harriet served spaghetti and meatballs on this night and was only mildly surprised when Emma insisted on only a small portion.

"Your appetite has not been good as of late," commented Mrs. Corman, while extending her daughter a curious look. "My God, your blouse and skirt are practically hanging off of you," she added before taking another mouthful of food. Emma shrugged her shoulders and played with her food. "I ran into Mrs. Bibber at the bank this afternoon. She asked about you. She asked if everything was okay with you. I'm guessing she noticed your loss of weight."

"Maybe Emma wants to be a model and she's trying to look like Twiggy," scoffed Becky.

"God, you're such an idiot," shot back her sister.

"No fighting at the table," injected Mr. Corman before reaching for a slice of warm bread. For most of the next fifteen minutes, the majority of the conversation came from Becky, who reported that she found an anonymous love note in her desk that morning. Both parents insisted on seeing it and saw it was innocent enough, containing nothing more than sentence after sentence of childish adoration.

"Oh, I almost forgot, Emma, you received a large envelope in today's mail. Were you expecting something?" asked her mother. A surprised look broke over the teenager's face.

"No, nothing," she answered. With the evening meal drawing to a close, Harriet retrieved Emma's package from the hallway and brought it to the table. She placed it down in front of her daughter and prompted her to open it. Hesitating for a moment, she stared down on the mailing before tearing open the packaging. Seconds later Mrs. Corman let out a gasp when the image of a sparsely dressed man and woman emerged from behind the wrapped paper, the cover of the November issue of *Playgirl Magazine*. Bertrand Corman stared across the table at his daughter in disbelief. Becky exploded into a fit of nervous laughter.

"Have you totally lost your mind?" cried out the shocked mother. "I've held my tongue for the last couple of months while you've moped around the house and complained about having no friends and being bored, but this is totally over the line. I can't believe you'd have the unmitigated gall to have this trash mailed to our house! What is going on in that head of yours beyond the brooding and the isolation up in your room?" Emma was finally emerging from her state of disbelief.

"I have no idea why this was mailed here. Daddy, you must believe me," she implored. Mr. Corman snatched the magazine from the surface of the table, removing it from the sight of his daughters.

"I want to believe you, Emma, but how could such a thing happen?" He glanced down at the mailing sticker on the magazine wrapping and saw his daughter's name, address and zip code clearly displayed. Emma was now in tears.

"Daddy, I just don't know."

"Upstairs to your room…and don't come down until you're ready to own up to exactly what's going on," insisted her mother. The shaken parents watched as their daughter bolted from the kitchen and scrambled upstairs, weeping uncontrollably, before barricading herself behind her bedroom door. She collapsed onto her bed and buried her face in a pillow. From between fits of sobbing, she could hear her parents on the first floor discussing their problem child. She let out a low moan as the events of the day passed through her mind. It had been a horrible day, perhaps the worst day of her life, she thought. From downstairs came the sound of the telephone ringing. Perhaps it was Betty calling from Massachusetts, she thought. Seconds later, Becky was called down to the phone. Eventually, Emma's tears were replaced by a sensation of nausea. She raised herself from the bed and became lightheaded. Her forehead was heavy with perspiration. She stumbled from the bedroom and made her way to the small, upstairs bathroom. Sensing what was necessary, she moved to the pedestal of the toilet and hung her head above the bowl. Following two unsuccessful attempts she managed to purge her stomach of its contents. She flung her head back and drew in a deep breath. The nausea in her stomach was gone. She rose to her feet.

"Are you okay, Emma?" her father called up from the bottom of the stairs.

"I'm okay, Daddy."

Emma made her way back to the bedroom on wobbly legs. Hesitating at the door, she finally walked to her record player, clicked it on, and dropped the needle onto a forty-five. The air was filled with the scratching sounds of a few hundred previous plays before a melody became audible.

In a little while from now,
If I'm not feeling any less sour,
I promised myself to treat myself
And visit a nearby tower,
And climbing to the top
Will throw myself off...

"Shut off that depressing song and think about what you've done wrong," called up her mother from the base of the stairs. Emma crawled out of bed and lifted the arm of the RCA Victor from the Gilbert O'Sullivan forty-five. Turning off the unit, she returned to the comfort of her bed. The school week was only a day old and she already longed for the weekend. She remembered a possible quiz in English class but had neither the energy nor the inclination to study for it. Emma was just drifting off to sleep when the creaking of her bedroom door brought her back to consciousness. Opening her eyes, she spied Becky's pretty face staring down on her.

"Life with you is turning into such a bummer," declared the thirteen-year old. "Emma, you're such a spaz," sniped the angel-faced teenager before quietly closing the door.

Emma was last to appear at the breakfast table on Tuesday morning and received a cold shoulder on arrival. She returned the favor, barely speaking to her parents and sister. Her father attempted to break the ice by venturing up to her bedroom prior to leaving for work. He walked in to find his eldest daughter seated on the edge of her bed and staring at the wall. He eased himself down on the mattress beside her.

"If your mother and I seem to come down on you it's only because we care so much about you," he explained tenderly. She nodded her head. "We are so proud of our brilliant and pretty daughter that we just don't want her to get sidetracked for any reason. You have to admit, you haven't been yourself for the last few months. Is there anything we can help you with or that you need to talk over?" She shook her head no.

"I'll be okay, Daddy," she answered weakly. He planted a kiss on the top of her head and sprang to his feet.

"I told Mom I wanted meatloaf and mashed potatoes for supper tonight. I know it's your favorite."

"Thanks, Daddy."

"I want you to have seconds. You're getting way too thin. I know it's the rage and it's the slim girls who seem to catch the guy's eyes these days, but you'd still be a looker with another ten pounds on your bones," he joked. She looked up at him and flashed a grateful smile. Kind words at home were hard to come by in recent months and her father was the only source of them. Harriet Corman put a premium on appearances and popularity, which put Becky above Emma in her eyes. However, Emma took some consolation in her father's attention, no doubt earned over the years by her excellent grades and perceived intellect.

2

Emma descended the stairs and made her way out the front door. With her peripheral vision, she caught sight of her mother sitting at the kitchen table. She exited the house without uttering a word. It was overcast as she stepped off in the direction of Fletcher Street. Again, she timed her walk to coincide with the start of the school day. She needed to minimize her time spent within hailing distance of Whitney Crowninshield. Emma noticed the grass was damp as she completed the last leg of her walk, the spacious front lawn of Kennebunk High. It was a few minutes before eight o'clock when she turned into her homeroom. Mr. Foster was not seated at his desk.

"Good morning, Dishrag," sounded a half dozen voices led by Whitney. The salutation was followed by laughter and then a few sounds of disgust by classmates. *"For God's sake, knock it off,"* and *"Give it a rest,"* echoed through the room as some people in attendance were clearly put off by the greeting. Whitney glared to the back of the room at any would-be defenders. "Did the three hundred pound woman you stole your jeans from put up a fight?" she continued. Emma dropped her head and moved across the front of the room to her desk. She was seated only seconds before Mr. Foster burst into the classroom with his patented level of energy and quieted those in attendance.

Emma managed to stay out of Whitney's line of fire on this Tuesday morning. Chemistry and Trigonometry classes passed without incident and she was making her way toward study hall when she felt her personal space being invaded. She turned to find Benny Fadden leaning into her, his face only inches from her own. Fadden was the nearest thing Kennebunk High had to a class clown. Loud and physically unattractive, he wormed himself into the social fabric of the school by being its unofficial jester. Fadden could always be counted upon to shout out an off color comment or scandalous observation at the most inopportune time and always at someone else's expense. His humor was seldom clever but did often elicit laughs, thanks to his high, whiny voice and the round, pimply face from which it emerged.

"I have it from good sources that a certain brainy broad is looking for a boyfriend," he whispered in her ear.

"Better recheck those sources, Benny," responded Emma while

speeding up her steps. He choked out a repulsive laugh and kept pace with her.

"It's the quiet ones that have all the pent up energy. They're the ones who surprise everyone and are hell on wheels in the sack," he jested in a low voice. Emma pulled her arm from Fadden's grasp and made her way into the stairwell. The aggressive junior remained in pursuit and stopped her progress on the first landing.

"Are you going to deny telling your friends about your passionate feelings and the need for a boyfriend to help you deal with those feelings?"

"Telling my friends? What friends? Who the hell are you talking about? Get out of my way," ordered Emma, while attempting to push Fadden aside. He responded by burying his face into her neck and inhaling. Revolted by his actions, she grabbed at his oily hair and pulled him off. Her bold rejection brought him out of his passionate advance. Anger registered on his face as he stepped back and scanned the stairway for witnesses. There appeared to be none.

"You smell like my grandmother," he snarled, any trace of his passion from seconds earlier having vanished. "What am I doing wasting my time on a scrawny, little sweat hog like you? I don't care if you would be easy," he added. Emma brushed by Fadden and scurried down the stairs to the ground floor, flustered by both his words and actions. Making her way to the cafeteria, she purchased a tuna salad sandwich and carton of milk and retreated to the sanctuary of the campus grounds. She walked past the line of pickup trucks at the rear of the school in the direction of Veterans Field and slowly regained a measure of her composure. She wondered what had prompted Benny Fadden's advances. She barely knew him and they did not share a single class. She remembered her thoughts from the morning before, the inclination to head to the turnpike or Route 1 and make her way to Portland. She reconsidered her daydream but thought of the hell there would be to pay on her return. Lifting the sandwich to her mouth, she realized her hand was shaking from the accumulating stress. Moving by the baseball field backstop, she walked toward the distant tree line, a full two hundred and fifty yards away. The isolation from the other students had a calming effect on her. She timed her return to the high school building to coincide with the start of her American Literature class.

Whitney was preoccupied, flirting with two boys in home room prior to dismissal on this day, sparing Emma the burden of dealing with her acid tongue. She hung back after the final bell to allow Whitney and her inner circle ample time to visit their lockers and make their way out to their cars. She had the company of Mr. Foster for the first ten minutes or so and then found herself alone in the room. A few more minutes passed and the hallway grew quiet. It was a full twenty-five minutes after dismissal when she finally closed her chemistry book, rose to her feet and left home room. She walked the twenty feet down the hall by the parade of brown lockers to her own, unlocked it, and began organizing what she needed to bring home.

"What's this I hear about being rejected by Benny Fadden?" roared Whitney into her ear, causing Emma to let out an exclamation of surprise. "I go to bat for you, Corman, and you screw it up! It's clear you can't get a boy interested in you on your own so I did what I could to introduce a male into your life," explained the Kennebunkport girl, her face only inches from Emma's.

"I have no interest in Benny Fadden," countered Emma meekly.

"Shut up! If I want any shit from you, I'll squeeze your head. Anyway, I handed Benny to you on a silver platter and what did you do? You screwed it up." The beautiful teenager's words gave rise to more than one snicker. Emma realized she was surrounded by Whitney's entourage of friends. Among the group was Keith Gorman, a boy she had carried a crush on since freshman year. "It seems Benny only had to get within two feet of you when he picked up on your one of many personal hygiene problems. You smell, Corman. You're pathetic and I, for one, am tired of biting my tongue and not telling you about it. Well, that's over, because I'm tired of your body odor and I'm tired of knowing each and every time you're on the rag. You're a disgrace to the junior class and a disgrace to the school," snarled Whitney to a chorus of laughter. Emma's eyes filled with tears as her head dropped forward. Reaching out, Mandy Cowger made contact with Emma's books and sent them tumbling to the floor. She collapsed to her knees, her eyes blinded by tears, and lethargically began retrieving her books. Mandy reached down to continue the torture but was stopped by Whitney. Apparently, the sight of a classmate kneeling before her was enough to satisfy her sadistic cravings. "Let's leave her alone and let her think about our constructive criticism," declared Whitney. Emma watched through teary eyes as Whitney's black pumps stepped back and the group moved away down the hall. She remained on both knees, gathering up the three books she needed to bring home, and collecting paper tablets containing the day's notes. She was about to rise to her feet when a hand came down gently on her shoulder. She cringed. She looked up to see Barbara Yager, a classmate, standing over her.

"Don't listen to her. Emma, you don't smell. I'd know if you did, we have two classes together and I sit right behind you in one of them. She's just trying to mess with you. Whitney's a bitch and she just seems to love making a lot of us miserable. I know; freshman year it was me." Emma stared up into the face of the Kennebunkport girl and extended her a grateful half smile. "Count your blessings. I live on the same road as she does," explained the teenager.

"I don't know what I've done to make her hate me so much."

"It doesn't take much. You get really good grades and Whitney doesn't seem to like any competition," theorized Barbara. With all of her paperwork assembled and clutched against her chest, Emma rose to her feet.

"Could I ask a favor of you, Barbara?" The long-haired junior gestured to her to continue. "Would you mind if I just hung around with you and your friends a little…at lunch and maybe after school?" The girl gave a pained expression and dropped her eyes.

"It's not that we don't want your company or anything like that, but I'd rather not do anything to cross Whitney and maybe get myself back on her shit list," she explained. Emma nodded her understanding. "As I said, I've been in your shoes and I wouldn't want to do anything to cross her and wind up taking any more of her garbage." The two juniors left the building together. Barbara offered her classmate a ride home, but Emma declined. Crossing the lawn, she picked up on the sound of the Kennebunk Rams running drills on the football practice field. Her mind flashed back to the confrontation in the hall and the insults fired at her. She had seen Keith Gorman standing in the crowd of Whitney's friends. He had heard the disgusting comments about her cleanliness. She could shrug off the humiliation from others even entertaining the possible truth of such an insane accusation, but not from Keith. She had secretly longed for him since freshman year, with no evidence of any interest on his part. She would need to talk with Betty before bed tonight. Her world was coming down on her and she needed consoling. Reaching Fletcher Street, she walked by her neighborhood and made her way to the town library, where she found silence in the Reference Room and immersed herself in homework and studying.

Emma quietly slipped downstairs while her mother and sister sat in the next room in front of the television. She bit her tongue and withheld comment when she heard the familiar wisecracking of the Hee Haw cast blaring out from the living room. She took the phone from the hallway table and slumped down to the floor. She dialed the out-of-state number and waited as the call was redirected southward through phone lines to Massachusetts. The fifth ring was interrupted by an adult voice.

"Hello," sang a woman on the other end.

"Hello, Mrs. Harmon. I was wondering if I could speak to Betty. It's Emma."

"Emma, dear, I thought it might be you. I'm afraid you're out of luck, at least for tonight anyway. Betty's over at a girlfriend's house studying for a history exam. I'm afraid I don't expect her home for another hour and a half," explained the woman. Emma felt a wave of disappointment descend on her. "I can tell her you called and maybe have her call you back tomorrow night."

"Is she with that girl from down the street?" she inquired. Mrs. Harmon laughed into the phone.

"Actually, she's with Jill from school, but there're also a couple of boys thrown into the mix. It's well chaperoned, that I'm sure of," she added quickly.

"Boys? Really?"

"That's right. Our shrinking violet is turning into quite the little social butterfly these days, thanks to Jill Hilliard." The woman waited for a response from the other end of the phone line. Following four or five seconds of silence, Mrs. Harmon broke the uncomfortable quiet. "Emma, I'll tell Betty you called. I'm sure she'll return the favor tomorrow night." Emma returned the phone to its cradle and processed the woman's words: Betty had moved beyond their friendship. Betty needed and had found a new friend in some faceless girl named Jill Hilliard.

The pressure growing from conditions at school was becoming unbearable. She decided to speak to her father. She knew her mother would only chastise her for being weak if she confided anything of her predicament at school in her. She had long found fault with Emma's socialization skills or lack of them. All this would do was validate her mother's criticisms if she learned of Emma's dilemma, she thought. She sought out Mr. Corman and found him seated beneath a reading lamp in the living room, his eyes staring down through reading glasses at a *Life Magazine*. Kneeling beside the man she whispered her request.

"Daddy, is there any way I can speak to you in private? There's something I really need to talk over with you." The man stopped and made eye contact. "Daddy, can we go out in the kitchen and talk—"

"Bertrand, *Hawaii Five-O* is coming on," sang out Harriet from across the room. His eyes moved to his wife and then back to Emma.

"Can it wait, Kitten? I don't get to watch too much that I really like on my own television. *Hawaii Five-O* is almost the lone exception. Can this wait?" Emma nodded a reluctant yes and pulled back from her father. He rose, walked halfway across the room, stopped and turned. "This doesn't involve a pregnancy or any such thing, right?" He spoke loud enough for her ears only. She shook her head in a decisive no. He smiled back at her and joined his wife and younger daughter in the far end of the room.

Emma climbed the stairs and returned to her bedroom. She flicked on the overhead light and sauntered over to her record player. Glancing down at the turntable, she saw the familiar Gilbert O'Sullivan forty-five resting atop it. She turned the 'on' switch and set the record in motion. She slowly raised her eyes and focused on herself in the bureau mirror. She was plain, she thought, plain and dull and friendless. She stared long and hard at herself. Why couldn't she have been born with the face...and the hair...and the body of Whitney Crowninshield?

It seems to me that there are more hearts broken in the world

That can't be mended, left unattended

What do we do? What do we do?

Raymond O'Sullivan understood. That was Gilbert O'Sullivan's real name. She had read it somewhere in a magazine or newspaper. He knew what a painful ordeal it could be just waking up in the morning and facing another day. She considered going to someone at school, perhaps Mr. Foster or Mrs. Bibber, and telling them what she was going through. No doubt they would act on her behalf, but then what? Did she dare cross Whitney? The remedy could prove more painful than the problem, she reasoned. Through all of her inner debate, she knew that one thing was beyond question: she could not continue living her life in this manner. Emma turned from the mirror, collapsed onto her bed, and for the first time in her life considered the unthinkable.

3

Emma opened her eyes to a darkened room on this fall morning. Daylight was growing noticeably shorter with every sunrise. She had not slept well, awakening over and over through the course of the night. Her alarm clock told her it was ten minutes before six. She decided to avoid the hassle with her sister and made her way to the bathroom and shower. A peak into the mirror confirmed her suspicions. She had darkened circles under her eyes from the lack of any restful sleep.

It had already begun to rain by the time Emma set off for Kennebunk High. She reminded herself that it was Wednesday, halfway to the weekend and some relief from the nightmare that was her junior year of high school. Armed with an efficient raincoat and an umbrella, she managed to reach the school in dry clothes. Having lost track of the time since leaving the house she arrived in homeroom a few minutes early. Her eyes were trained on her trigonometry notes when a hush came over the classroom. A few seconds passed before she lifted her eyes out of curiosity. Instantly, the cause for the silence came into focus. Standing at the front of the classroom at Mr. Foster's desk was a young male, his back turned to the students. Emma's mouth dropped open as she took in the youth's proportions. Standing somewhere in the vicinity of six feet, eight inches in height, the transfer student towered over Mr. Foster, his broad shoulders and back literally erasing the teacher from view. An amused Whitney turned to her friend, Mandy.

"Someone call *York's Animal Farm,* clearly they're missing a gorilla," she wisecracked. The comment caused Emma to chuckle.

"What are you laughing at, Dishrag?" Whitney asked behind a scowl.

"Oh, Christ, that has to be the kid my mother heard about," whispered Mandy to her friend. "He's a friggin' criminal! He's straight out of reform school. He beat up his father and sent him to the hospital. His mother doesn't even want him in the house anymore. I think they put him in a foster home down here," reported Mandy. Wide-eyed, Whitney turned from her friend and looked back to the front of the room. A few seconds passed before Mr. Foster addressed the students. It was then that the new kid slowly turned toward his new classmates. Emma stared up at the youth in a mild state of awe. The stranger had pronounced simian features, a fact that made Whitney's gorilla comment all the more clever. His mildly pock-marked face was framed by a swirl of unruly, auburn hair which succeeded in making his appearance all the more threatening. His eyes were hard, while his mouth seemed bonded into a permanent snarl.

"Class, this is the newest member of Kennebunk High, Finian Cromwell. He's come to us all the way from Jonesport," announced Mr. Foster. "Interesting name you have there." The new boy glanced back at the man.

"I have an Irish grandmother who bribed my father," he muttered back to Foster. The teacher smiled and instructed young Cromwell to take a vacant, front desk.

"You will be in need of a lot of leg room, young fellow," he explained. The oversized youth followed the man's directions and took a seat.

Emma's mind took flight, influenced by the appearance of this imposing stranger, and she imagined herself confronted by this mammoth human being on an abandoned dark street. For a second she envisioned his huge hands wrapped around her throat, mercilessly choking the life out of her. She glanced up to the back of his head at the front of the room. That would and could not happen, she thought. A second later she forced her mind back into reality.

"Holy shit...that is one ugly bastard," proclaimed Mandy to her surrounding classmates.

The arrival of Wednesday's lunch period brought Emma a new crisis. Outside the windows of Kennebunk High School the water poured from the roof, down the gutters and along the walkways, turning the latter into rivulets. On Tuesday she was able to take her food and drink outside, far away from the influence and scrutiny of Whitney and her friends. On this day there was no such option. She joined the cafeteria line, all the while her eyes scanning for Whitney and Mandy. She spotted Barbara Yager and a few of her friends spread out by the stage but honored the girl's wishes and did not impose upon them. Finally, with meal and tray in hand, she made her way to the hallway and climbed the stairs to the second floor. The stairwell and classrooms were unusually dark, thanks to the cloud cover outside. Reaching the top story of the building, she slipped into the nearest darkened classroom and placed her tray down on a desk out of the line of sight of hallway traffic. After sprinkling seasoning on her meal, she stood up to remove her sweater. It was then, while casually glancing to the back of the room, that she spotted Finian Cromwell seated in the far corner, his head bowed over reading material of some sort. He did not raise his eyes or acknowledge her presence in any way. Flustered, she considered picking up her food and leaving but decided against it. For the next ten minutes the room remained nearly silent, the only noise coming from the sound of

Cromwell turning the page of his magazine. Finally, the quiet was broken when the voices of Whitney and Mandy filled the hallway and bled into the classroom. Emma held her breath and hoped they were only passing by. Fate was not smiling on her this day. It was Mandy who stepped through the door and announced her find.

"You can stop looking, Whitney, Dishrag is down here," she called out. Within seconds there came the sound of scampering feet. Whitney entered the room with an air of authority and locked eyes on her prey.

"Did you actually think you could hide from us, you disgusting little mole?" Emma raised her eyes to Whitney and, incredibly, could only think of how beautiful she was.

"Do you goddamn mind? I'm trying to eat my lunch in peace," roared Cromwell from the back of the room. His voice was forceful and smothered in a thick Down East accent. The two intruders had not spotted him when they entered the room seconds earlier. They both stood dumbfounded for a moment before Whitney spoke up.

"This is none of your business," she insisted.

"When it interrupts my lunch…it's my business." Whitney stared a full ten seconds at the seated giant, clearly weighing her options. He did not blink.

"Okay, let's leave Mister Sensitivity alone. You, out in the hall," ordered Whitney. Emma went to gather her belongings but was stopped short by Cromwell.

"Never mind her. I just want you two to clear out. It only got loud when you got here," he explained. There was no compromise in his tone of voice. The two young women stared coldly at the new boy but moved toward the door.

"See you in homeroom, Dishrag," sniped Whitney before glaring at Cromwell a final time. Emma sat motionless at her desk until the sound of the two girls' voices could not be heard from the hallway. She swiveled her chair sideways and looked back at the imposing teenager. His eyes had already returned to his magazine.

"I can leave you alone if you want," she suggested timidly. He did not raise his eyes from the page.

"You're no bother. Finish your lunch," he answered through a thick accent. She weighed her options, neither of which were particularly pleasant, and went with the lesser of the two evils. She remained at the desk in the company of a boy with a violent past in a state of complete vulnerability. Ten minutes passed before she assembled the remnants of her lunch on the tray and stood to leave.

"Enjoy what's left of your lunch period," she muttered en route to the classroom door.

"The school needs a real cafeteria," he growled as he shifted his eyes up to her from his reading material. Emma nodded her head in agreement and scurried out the door.

Emma was expecting the worse at dismissal time. Therefore, it was a pleasant surprise when Mr. Foster practically chaperoned her to her locker and then offered Emma a ride home to Mechanic Street. Rain was still falling quite heavily as the car rolled down the driveway and out onto Fletcher Street. They were engaged in meaningless chit-chat when the vehicle came up behind the towering figure of Finian Cromwell as he plodded toward the village. He was not dressed for the precipitation, his denim jacket and pants saturated after absorbing so much of the pelting rain. His unruly, auburn hair was soaked flat against his head.

"I feel bad not offering the kid a ride but, if I did, I'd have to offer everyone one," he explained. "Tell me, Emma, what's your take on our newest student?" She glanced sheepishly across the front seat of the car at the popular teacher.

"He's quite intimidating. He's so big."

"That he is. That can be a blessing and a curse," added the man. "Tell your dad we're long overdue for a beer up in Biddeford." The car slowed to a halt in front of the house and Emma thanked her teacher for the ride before scurrying onto the extended front porch.

Emma barricaded herself in the bedroom until she was called down to supper at six thirty. John Chancellor had just signed on the nightly newscast when Harriet ordered the television turned off and the family took their seats in the kitchen. Mrs. Corman served the pot roast and brown potatoes to her husband and daughters and joined them at the table while classical music wafted into the room from a hallway radio. There was practically no conversation for the first ten minutes of the meal as each member of the family applied their full attention to dinner. It was only after Mr. Corman claimed a second helping of potatoes that his wife reported what she had heard in the village that day.

"I got a real earful from Dottie Hoffman at the IGA today," said Harriet to her husband while running a slice of bread over her gravy covered plate. "You're not going to believe what they're allowing to move into town these days."

"Harriet, why do you listen to that old gossip?" Bertand asked.

"Dottie might be a gossiping, old biddy, but she keeps her ear to the ground and doesn't let anything get past her," answered the woman. "Apparently, Kennebunk High will be getting a punk straight out of reform school in the next few days. According to Dottie, he was sent away for beating up his father up in Jonesport. He sent the poor man to the hospital. The family threw him out, even his mother wanted nothing to do with him, and he's been cooling his heels at the Youth Center in Portland. Now, somehow and for some reason, he's been brought down here. No one knows if he's someone's foster child or what. Dottie says she caught a glimpse of him yesterday in front of Kesslen Shoe and he's the size of two men."

"Oh, my God, I know who you mean, Momma!" The brief description had activated Becky's memory. "He walked by our school after class. I was out by the road and got a good look at him. Momma, he's huge. I mean really, really tall...and really ugly. He's scary looking. He stared at the girls when he was walking by and a few of them let out with a shriek."

"Based on your description of the young man, that doesn't sound like a wise thing to do," commented Mr. Corman. A look of heightened concern spread across Harriet Corman's face.

"Emma, did you come in contact with this hooligan while you were in school?"

"He's in my homeroom," answered Emma matter-of-factly. "Oh, Daddy, Mr. Foster says hello and wonders when you two can go out for a beer. He gave me a ride home from school in the rain." Her father looked up from his plate and focused on his elder daughter.

"It has been a while. Tell him I'll give him a call by the end of the week."

"Am I the only one in the family who has the common sense to be concerned about this thug?" exploded Harriet from her end of the table. "I want you to keep your distance from this white trash. Do you understand me?" Her orders were directed at both daughters. Emma turned to her mother.

"His name is Finian Cromwell and when he first reported to Mr. Foster, a number of the girls commented on how much he looked like a monkey...a gorilla, to be precise." Emma's words caused Becky to giggle, but triggered horror to register on Harriet Corman's face. Emma knew better than to mention the incident at lunch to her mother.

"More delicately stated, he has simian features," voiced Mr. Corman, without raising his eyes from the table. "I always thought Mick Jagger had simian features," he added nonchalantly. Her father's observation caused Becky to laugh.

"Compared to Finian Cromwell, Mick Jagger looks like Robert Redford," stated Emma.

"Compared to Finian Cromwell, Mick Jagger looks like David Cassidy," added Becky. Their mother was not amused.

"I don't want either one of you going anywhere near this filthy monster," she insisted. Both sisters assured their mother that they would stay far away from the violent stranger from Jonesport and rose from the table. Becky immediately made her way back into the living room and turned on the television set. Emma peeled away from the family and climbed the stairs to her bedroom, where she closed and locked the door before pulling out the notes from her American Literature class. She flipped her textbook open to a James Baldwin short story. Her eyes widened when she looked down at the cover page to Notes of a Native Son. She stared down and took in a grotesque message literally carved into the page: *YOU'RE NOT ONLY UGLY BUT A FILTHY LITTLE WHORE.* A charge of nervous energy grew in the pit of her stomach as she continued to gaze down at the message. It was not enough that her enemies had transformed her time at school into a living hell but now they were invading her home life, she thought. First, they had the Playgirl Magazine delivered to the house and now this. Emma stepped back from her desk and burst into tears. She raised her hands to her face and noticed they were shaking violently. It was becoming too much and it only seemed to be getting worse, she thought. She drew in a long breath in an attempt to regain some measure of composure and stepped across the room to her record player. There was no need to search for what she desired to hear. It was there on the turntable.

In a little while from now
If I'm not feeling any less sour
I promised myself to treat myself
And visit a nearby tower
And climbing to the top
Will throw myself off...

Emma played and replayed the Gilbert O'Sullivan record no less than a dozen times this night. She retired to bed early. The pillow case felt cool against the side of her face while she surveyed her life and considered her emotional state. She had sometimes thought about the condition called depression, having heard it discussed. They had a neighbor a few years earlier that had to be institutionalized by her husband when her condition had worsened. She remembered her mother speaking ill of the woman, calling her weak and not right in the head in the first place. Incredibly, she felt a connection with that unfortunate woman who was taken away from her family. The family moved from Mechanic Street a few months later and no one had ever learned of the poor woman's fate. She counted the hours until she would have to face Whitney. It was less than eleven hours away. She was nearly asleep when a realization popped into her head: Betty Harmon had not returned her call from the night before. Betty had found new friends in Massachusetts. More than ever, Emma was convinced she was alone.

4

Emma stared across the bedroom on this Thursday morning and dreaded the start of a new day. The familiar sound of a neighbor's car engine turning over told her it was five-thirty or so. Mr. Schofield's work schedule was consistent if nothing else, she thought. She had just tossed and turned her way through a night of brief interludes of sleep punctuated by vivid and unpleasant dreams. In one dream she had been pawed and manhandled by Benny Fadden. In another she had thrown herself at the feet of Whitney Crowninshield and pleaded with her to call off her vendetta of cruelty. She lifted her head from the pillow and felt lightheaded from a lack of restful sleep. Her circumstances at school and the lack of a meaningful friendship were now taking a toll on her mental and physical state. Listlessly, she pulled her robe from the metal hook on the back of the bedroom door and slipped into it.

Downstairs in the kitchen, Emma spooned out the coffee grounds for the Mr. Coffee machine and started the morning's breakfast in motion. A few minutes later, she felt her father's hand give a squeeze to her shoulder as he made his way over to the coffee maker for a dose of caffeine. It struck her that this might be a good time to initiate some discussion concerning her ongoing situation at school, but this was cut short by the appearance of her mother in the doorway to the kitchen. She did not have the stomach for any critical analysis by her mother on the matter of her lack of popularity or social skills and dropped the idea of making mention of it at this time.

"Don't expect anything more than cereal and toast this morning. We'll have pancakes this weekend, but first I have to make it to the market and do some more food shopping," explained Harriet. "Emma, when you're through with breakfast, why don't you shower first and let Becky get a little more beauty sleep."

"Oh, God forbid if I should ever need a little more beauty sleep!" lashed out Emma.

"You're already up!" voiced her mother forcefully. "And on the subject of beauty, sleep or otherwise, I don't think that's somewhere you want to go for your own good." The message was unspoken but still conveyed: your sister is a beauty and you are not.

Emma arrived on school grounds no more than five minutes before the opening bell. She turned the corner into her homeroom and saw Mr. Foster seated at the front of the room. Glancing downward she saw Finian Cromwell's long legs extended out from under his desk, causing her to walk in an arc around them. He stared menacingly at the blackboard. The morning Pledge of Allegiance from the main office began just as Emma reached her desk. She stole a glance over at Whitney and thought of the demeaning dream involving her from the night before. Catching her in the act, the beautiful blonde answered with a spiteful smile, the kind used to unsettle a victim and warn them of some future calamity.

The morning classes passed without incident. Emma decided that morning to prepare her own lunch and avoid the line and assembly at school. When lunch period arrived, she picked up her peanut butter and jelly sandwich from her locker and made her way outside. This October day was windy and cold in southern Maine, but the isolation to be had on the edge of the school property was not something the warm building could offer. Emma spent her lunch break with her back against a chestnut tree, out of the wind and away from any potential detractors. Covered with goose bumps and her face red from the cold October air, she re-entered the school building. Climbing the stairs to the second story, she turned into the hallway and observed a small group of classmates clustered near her locker. Fortunately, she had her full compliment of afternoon textbooks on her and was able to scoot directly into American Literature class and avoid the mob down the hall.

Over the course of the day, Emma learned that there was to be a general meeting of the faculty of Kennebunk High School directly after dismissal in the gymnasium. Students were advised that teachers would not be available for consultation after school on this day and that any questions or concerns should be brought up sometime prior to dismissal. Arriving back at homeroom, Emma observed Mr. Foster collecting paperwork from atop his desk in an effort to facilitate a quick exit at the closing bell. Her strategy for leaving school on this day became clear when Whitney advised Mandy in no uncertain terms that she needed to be home as early as possible and that she would not put up with any lagging around on the premises. Emma decided to delay her departure from homeroom until the hallway was relatively quiet, knowing her primary antagonist, namely Whitney, would be halfway to Kennebunkport before she ventured out of the room.

Emma glanced up at the classroom clock and could not believe her eyes. Twenty-five minutes had passed since dismissal. She had started reading a Jack London short story, *To Build a Fire,* and completely lost all grasp of time. She hurriedly assembled her books and made her way out into the hallway. It appeared deserted. She walked up the hall past countless drab brown lockers until she reached her own. Playing with the lock, she finally gained access and swung open the door. Suddenly, she was aware of something closing in on her from behind. While turning to discern the problem a hand made contact with the side of her face and forced her forward. She cried out when her cheek made contact with the back wall of the locker. From behind came juvenile laughter while she felt her lower body being wedged between the metal walls. She struggled, but additional hands further constricted her movement and she found herself facing away from the light and her attackers. From the flood of catcalls and laughter behind her, she thought she made out Mandy Cowger and Benny Fadden's voices. Emma was now crying uncontrollably.

"Close the door. Lock her in," called out a male voice. The door slammed shut with a clang and a roar of laughter went up.

"You can't leave me locked in here," implored Emma through sobbing. Her words were followed by another eruption of laughter. A second later the locker door swung open and she felt something being mashed into her face.

"Here's a snack, Dishrag," squealed a male voice. She took it to be Benny Fadden's. Immediately, she picked up on the smell of egg salad. His actions prompted another chorus of laughter and the door slammed shut again. Emma slumped down part way to the locker floor.

"You can't do this," she muttered feebly.

"Stop your whining, you pathetic little nothing. The cleaning crew will be up here by four and you can go home to your mommy," whispered a voice through the ventilation grooves. It was Whitney. "Don't even think of running to anyone at the school and blowing the whistle on us. This is nothing compared to how bad we can make it," she warned.

"She won't say anything. She knows how bad we could really screw her up," snarled a male. The voice belonged to Keith Gorman, the young man Emma had carried a torch for since freshman year. Keith had witnessed this whole humiliating nightmare, she thought. The crowd of voices began moving away as a stunned Emma sat wedged inside the locker. Then, a single set of footsteps could be heard hustling back in her direction.

"Hey, Emma, is there any chance of me borrowing your homework?" Benny Fadden whispered through the air holes. His words were followed by weeping from within. Fadden burst out laughing and banged loudly on the locker door, the metallic sound piercing her eardrums.

"Enough," called out Whitney from down the hall and he scampered away to rejoin the group.

Slumped inside her locker, Emma reached a decision. She could no longer bear her life as it was, and was now considering an exit strategy. The hallway outside the locker was deadly quiet. It afforded her time to think and she devised a plan. It did not have to be today or tomorrow, but soon. She would visit the drug store. There were painless and bloodless ways to check out. Beyond her parents, maybe even only her father, no one would care.

Approximately five minutes after her tormentors had filed down the stairwell and away from the building, a single set of footsteps could be heard moving in her direction. Emma listened as the lone figure walked deliberately up the hall and stopped in front of her locker.

"Is someone in there?" asked a deep voice with a thick Maine accent.

"You know damn well there is," she shot back. For the next few seconds there was the sound of someone fiddling with the handle and lock to the door. Then, there came a few seconds of silence before the deafening explosion of steel and metal. The locker door swung open and Emma looked up at Finian Cromwell. He stood, towering over her, the locking mechanism still in his hand.

"What? Did you have a guilty conscience?" He tossed the door handle on top of the lockers with a resulting crash and extended his hand down to her.

"Get away from me. You're no better than the rest of them," she snarled. She noticed part of the egg salad sandwich still clinging to her blouse. She snatched it from her clothing and flung it at him, hitting him on the shoulder. He had no outward reaction. He turned and started walking toward the stairwell. "I'm not forgiving you. I'm not forgiving any of you," she called after him. He continued to the end of the hall and disappeared down the stairs.

Emma had carried a five dollar bill in her purse for emergencies since junior high school. On the walk home this day, she decided take the first step in her new life plan. Still shaken from the incident at school, she continued past Mechanic Street and made her way down to the village. She had already ruled out going to Beaudoin's Drug Store. There were too many teenagers on or around the premises and word might make its way back to her mother. In addition, there was no way she wanted to run into anyone from Kennebunk High. Reaching Main Street, she made her way to Fiske's Pharmacy, the drug store of choice for senior citizens, and purchased a bottle of sleeping aids.

Emma was stretched out on her bed in a pool of darkness when she picked up on the theme song for the *Carol Burnett Show* from downstairs.

She did not move a muscle. Mired in disinterest for everything, she continued to relive the humiliation suffered at her locker earlier in the day. She tortured herself with thoughts of Keith Gorman witnessing the confrontation and doing nothing. How stupid she must have appeared, crammed into her locker with the remnants of an egg salad sandwich clinging to the side of her face, she thought.

"Carol Burnett is on," called up her mother from the bottom of the stairs. "You've already missed the opening." Emma knew she was in no mood to put on a plastic smile and watch television with her parents.

"It's okay, Momma. I'm going to skip it tonight," she answered, projecting her voice through the bedroom door. Simultaneously, the hallway telephone rang and her mother picked it up on the first ring. Emma's mind raced with anticipation, thinking it might be Betty calling her back from the night before. It was not. Instead, Becky was called in from the living room. It was a call from a boy and far from her first. She was still in junior high and already drawing attention from the opposite sex. Understandably, the sound of her sister laughing and cooing at the bottom of the stairs did nothing to raise her spirits. Her mind caromed back to the incident at the locker. She thought of Finian Cromwell. For an instant, when the door flung open and he was standing there she thought he might be back to do her serious bodily harm, perhaps even kill her. He could snap her neck in an instant, she reasoned. There was a trace of cruelness in his eyes. That was unmistakable. She let out a sigh. If he had only done her in back in the hallway, then her ongoing nightmare would be over and she would be at rest. Anticipating another restless night, she remembered the bottle of sleeping pills. That would help her drift off. She reached for the bottle and stopped, reminding herself of the reason they were there. They could not be squandered two at a time. A full bottle was integral to her exit strategy.

5

Emma found herself awake and staring up at the plastered bedroom ceiling at three o'clock. The upper village of Kennebunk, Maine rested in total silence at this hour. Her mind was already racing ahead to her coming day at school. She attempted to block it and everything else out that constituted her life. It was much too painful to relive the events of the previous day. Her mind wandered to the matter of her own sexuality or lack of it. She thought of all the romantic relationships in the world and then to all in her small corner of the planet. She was sure there was no boy who felt anything approaching love for her. At the same time there was Whitney, who probably commanded the sexual daydreams of eighty percent of the male students at Kennebunk High. She envied Whitney for a myriad of reasons, but none more than her breathtaking beauty and pure sexuality. There was no doubt in her mind, Whitney Crowninshield could sensually conquer and take possession of most any teenage boy in the school. Emma knew she would trade her high intellect for even a fraction of what Whitney possessed. What did it feel like to know you could reduce a member of the opposite sex to a state of utter helplessness? Even at the tender age of sixteen, she had witnessed men brought to their knees by a female, ready to sacrifice their fortunes, families and lives even just to bask in the good graces of some wily woman. She was convinced Whitney could select any boy at random from the junior class and, with anything beyond a token effort, put him completely under her power, a marionette to be manipulated as she pleased. She was just as sure that she herself possessed not even a fraction of the Kennebunkport girl's sex appeal. How often had she observed young males staring in a trancelike state at Whitney? How she yearned to be the cause for even a fragment of that adoration in a boy's eyes. Unfortunately, Emma knew she never had and, in all likelihood, never would. This realization and thoughts of another day of classes allowed a new shroud of depression to descend on her and block her from any substantial sleep.

Emma was shaken awake by her sister the next morning. She had nodded off just after five o'clock and was now running behind schedule.

"I've already showered. You're going to miss breakfast if you don't move your scrawny behind," wisecracked Becky before shuffling downstairs. Exhausted, Emma rose from her bed, her eyes barely open, and staggered in the direction of the bathroom. Peering into the mirror, she picked up on the dark circles crested beneath her eyes. She realized she looked as poorly as she felt. Dabbing cold water on her face and eyes she took a deep breath and prepared herself for another horrendous day. Becky was already putting her breakfast dishes away when Emma plodded into the kitchen and joined her parents at the table.

"Emma, I've already advised your father and sister that I will not be here for supper tonight. So, you will have to fend for yourselves. Your aunt is coming by and picking me up later today and we'll be making a day of it, including dinner in Portland," said Harriet. "There's soup in the cupboard and plenty of cold cuts in the fridge. You can do without a hot meal every once in a blue moon." Emma nodded and filled her cereal bowl with Kix. She did not mind having a quiet night at home with her dad, cold cuts or no cold cuts. As was now her custom, she loitered around the house as long as possible before setting out for school. Predictably, she reached the grounds of Kennebunk High School with little spare time before the opening bell. Entering homeroom, she felt the eyes of half her classmates follow her across the front of the room, one exception being Finian Cromwell, whose attention was focused on a brightly colored sheet of paper resting on his desk. As she approached her desk, Whitney whispered something for public consumption.

"And the smell of egg salad wafts into the room," she chanted. Her words prompted sporadic laughter but also caused Mr. Foster to raise his eyes from the book on his desk. He scanned the classroom with a critical glance before returning his attention to the book.

There was a bright spot in Emma's schedule on Friday mornings. Fridays meant Public Speaking with Mrs. Bibber, a class populated with seniors and sophomores, as well as juniors, and where a college prep student like herself competed with business and general studies students. She enjoyed this particular class for a number of reasons. First, she enjoyed it because it was one of the few she did not share with Whitney Crowninshield. Second, she loved Mrs. Bibber as a teacher and human being. Third, it was a subject that she could clearly see impacting her life in the years after high school. Emma entered the first floor classroom and received a smile from her favorite female teacher. Joanne Bibber was a woman just entering middle age, her warm, pretty face framed by a head of perfectly groomed salt and pepper hair. Emma took her seat at the front of the room and watched as her classmates sauntered in one by one. She was flipping open her notebook when a tall figure appeared in the doorway. Passing through the entrance, Finian Cromwell ducked his head and made eye contact with her. She looked away, withholding anything that might pass for an acknowledgement. Cromwell lumbered up to Mrs. Bibber's desk and handed down some form of paperwork. The teacher glanced up at him and smiled amiably. Emma eavesdropped, listening as Mrs. Bibber explained what the class was working on at present and how soon he would be expected to carry out an assignment. Lastly, she instructed her new student to claim a desk, encouraging him to choose something that could accommodate his long legs. Cromwell took a lazy glance around the room and focused on the desk next to Emma. She dropped her head and listened as the six foot, eight inch, seventeen year old walked in her direction and then collapsed into the next desk.

Even the presence of Finian Cromwell could not detract from her enjoyment of Public Speaking class. The current assignment called for a two-minute introduction of some famous person. Emma had volunteered the preceding week and, based on Mrs. Bibber's observations, had done quite well. Now she was able to sit back and watch others suffer through the experience. On more than one occasion she glanced over at Cromwell and took him in at close range. He wore his hair reasonably long, not Beatles' length, but well over the ear. She looked closely at it to see if it appeared clean. It did. She wore a plaid skirt this day and thought she observed him glancing down at her exposed calf. She responded by shifting her legs away from him. On another occasion she stared at his huge hands resting on the surface of the desk and envisioned his clenched fists reigning punches down on his unfortunate father. She remembered her mother's warning: keep a distance between you and this criminal. That was not going to be as easy as she first thought it would be.

When everyone else was making their way to the cafeteria, Emma searched out someone from the maintenance crew and reported her broken locker. Meanwhile, the dry autumn air allowed her to leave the building at lunchtime and slip away toward Veterans Field and the far tree line behind school property. She drew small consolation from the approach of the weekend. Her afternoon classes proved uneventful, which pleased her. Whitney was distracted by discussions with her friends about their weekend itineraries and Emma was largely ignored. This continued through to homeroom where Whitney, Mandy and company crowded around a *Portland Herald* and discussed the specifics of a dance scheduled for later that weekend in Saco. When Emma saw the crowd of popular kids hanging back at the school, she quickly decided to vacate the building and start for home.

Exiting the high school, Emma was greeted with a rush of unseasonably warm air. She crossed the lawn and turned up Fletcher Street, where she caught sight of the towering figure of Finian Cromwell a couple of hundred yards ahead of her. She had decided to visit her peaceful spot on the Mousam River on this afternoon, not knowing how many more temperate days southern Maine would enjoy before the onslaught of winter. It had not been a bad day by recent standards. She did not like the idea of having the Cromwell boy in Public Speaking class, but it was tolerable. Her book pack dug into her shoulder as she walked in the direction of the village while a steady stream of vehicles from the school sped by her. The roadway had gone quiet for the better part of a minute before a single vehicle sped up from behind her. Emma did not surrender to the temptation to turn and satisfy her curiosity as it grew closer. A second later, she felt a sting on the side of her face as an object made contact with her cheek.

"Something to help wash down your egg salad, Dishrag," screamed a male voice from inside a convertible. His words were followed by a chorus of gasps.

"What did you do that for?" called out a female. The car roared off up the road as Emma dropped to one knee and tried to process what had happened to her. On the ground by her side was a small carton of orange juice. It was partially opened and gushed out some of its contents. She reached her hand to her face. It was wet. On examination, it appeared to be a residue of the juice. The skin beneath her left eye stung from the impact of the missile hurled at her. She cried out in pain and humiliation and hobbled to her feet. She had begun to sob as she continued up the road. A few seconds later came the sting of her salty tears on what was apparently an open wound. She let out a wail but there was no one within earshot to extend her comfort of any kind. She turned her face away from the roadway, not willing to share her humiliation with the world, and scurried homeward.

Emma entered the house and made her way to the downstairs bathroom. It was there that she was able to closely examine the wound on her upper cheek. Looking in the mirror she saw that the skin was broken, but the laceration was no more than a quarter of an inch in length. There was swelling under her left eye with darkening already surrounding the puncture. She walked to the refrigerator and removed a handful of ice cubes from the freezer. The pain from the wound was now throbbing and was accompanied by a headache. She wrapped the ice cubes in a facecloth and applied them to her swollen face. Emma broke out into a new fit of crying and climbed the stairs to her bedroom. Life had become unbearable, she thought. She was unwilling to face any more of it. Kneeling before her bureau she reached in beneath her blouses and pulled out the bottle of sleeping pills. It was time. She tore a piece of paper from one of her notebooks and made her way downstairs to the kitchen. There, she scratched out a note to her parents.

Mom and Dad,

I've accepted an invitation to spend the night with a friend from school. Her name is Barbara Yager and she lives in Kennebunkport. She is very nice. I'm sorry about the short notice. I will be home by noon tomorrow. I love you very, very much.

Emma

The plan had been worked out for a couple of days, but even she was surprised at how soon she was going to put it into action. She would take the entire bottle of pills this evening on the banks of the river and drift off into eternal sleep. The note, she hoped, would keep anyone from looking for her until it was too late. The thought of being found with her dress draped over her head struck her. She changed into a pair of jeans and covered her blouse with a bulky, woolen sweater. She did not want to attract any attention on her walk down to the Mousam. Emma closed the front door to the house with a heavy heart, knowing it was the last time she would lay eyes on her home.

Hidden behind a pair of large sunglasses, Emma followed Storer Street down to the village, crossed Route 1, and continued along Water Street. The run of rapids, her favorite portion of the Mousam River, was just above Rogers Pond. It was there she had already decided to spend her last few hours in this world. It took her just under a half hour to make her way from her house to the edge of the river. It was just after three thirty when the sixteen year old reached the edge of the water and took a seat on the extended root of a tree. She was pleased to see few people in the immediate area. At present there was only a single car parked over by the pond and that was well over a hundred yards from her position. The gurgling sound of swiftly passing water blotted out even the rustle of leaves in the trees as the horizontal sunlight danced and sparkled off the surface of the river. She reached up and touched her cheek. The small cut was beginning to scab over. Back at the house she had seen a patch of black and blue blossom under her left eye. She replayed the incident of being hit in the face over and over in her head until it began to make her physically ill. The recollection and the stress created by it brought on a state of nausea. She turned sideways. From deep within her she felt, then tasted, vomit as it left her stomach. A second later the surrounding terrain was covered by the semi-digested remains of her breakfast and lunch. The trauma caused by her upsurge caused her head to ache. She glanced down into her handbag and was reassured to see the bottle of pills in plain sight. Propping herself up against a tree, she closed her eyes and let the restful sound of flowing water calm her. A gust of autumn wind passed over the river and refreshed her. It was a beautiful afternoon for late October, she thought. Her mind drifted back to the house and the frantic state her disappearance would cause there. Quickly, she drove these thoughts from her head. She replaced them with thoughts of herself and the daily agony her life had become. The plan was set and already in motion: she would put off taking the bottle of pills until just before sundown and drift off under the cover of darkness.

It was about an hour before sundown when she decided to brave the water's current and to make her way out to the middle of the river. There, no more than twenty or twenty five feet away, sat five or six flat rocks. This stretch of the river widened, keeping the water's depth to no more than a couple of feet. Emma slipped off both shoes and cautiously stepped into the current. The water temperature sent a shiver through her body but she moved outward, all the time trying to avoid the surface of any slippery rocks. She had almost reached her destination when a sharp pain shot up from the bottom of her foot. She cried out and made a final leap for the nearest flat rock. Barely reaching the surface of the stone, she awkwardly took a seat on the makeshift island and examined the sole of her foot. A second later she watched as a trickle of blood made its way down her foot and onto the surface of the rock. Pain radiated from the sole of her foot. It appeared she had stepped on the sharp edge of one of the smaller stones resting on the river floor. She burst out into tears again, more from frustration than pain. Emma glanced back to the shoreline. She was alone. She was already questioning the sanity of her decision to wade to the middle of the river. She slipped on one shoe and re-examined her injured foot. A light stream of blood continued to flow from the wound. Relieved to see there was no evidence of any fragment lodged in the cut she took inventory of her situation. This was clearly not how she planned her last afternoon among the living.

Emma propped her injured foot atop her left knee and stared blankly at the river's current. When her eyes grew wet with tears, she touched her cheek and felt the swelling beneath her eye. It was a further reminder of what a pitiful joke her life was and reinforcement for the plan in place. Besides, the die was cast. There was no way she could face her parents in her present state, let alone face her tormentors at school, she thought. Now, her most difficult challenge was finding a way to get back to the bank of the river, given the condition of her foot. Cautiously, Emma raised her body up from the rock to a standing position, careful to put little or no weight on the injured foot. Gingerly, she allowed a modest amount of weight to come down on the sole of her right foot. A sharp pain jolted up her leg. She cried out and fell back onto the flat surface of the rock. It was becoming increasingly clear that this rock was destined to become her last resting place, above ground at least. She looked back through the trees at the descending sun. Sundown was still thirty to forty-five minutes away, she reasoned. Emma shifted her position atop the rock and inadvertently dropped one of her shoes into the moving current. She cried out and lunged for it but it was quickly out of reach and floating through the rapids. Frustrated and dejected, the sixteen-year-old burst into another crying fit.

"Are you okay over there?" called out a male voice from a distance away. Taken by surprise, Emma turned in the direction of the voice. Approximately twenty yards away on the far bank of the river stood a large man, his image camouflaged somewhat by the sunlight at his back. Her eyes focused on the intruder. "Do you need any help?" The voice barely carried over the sound of the rushing water, but the thick Down East accent and the slow cadence of his speech was unmistakable. The voice belonged to Finian Cromwell.

"I don't need anything from you," she shouted back to him. Her words had no outward effect on the Cromwell boy. He stood at the edge of the fast moving current, his eyes trained on his female classmate. "Stop standing there like an idiot and go away," she ordered. He did not heed her words but, instead, leaned against a nearby tree and folded his arms. His eyes never left her.

"Are you waiting for someone?" The towering youth raised the level of his voice to carry over the noise created by the moving water. She dropped her head in mock disgust. Following a brief interlude during which she simply stared down into the water, she raised her head and turned squarely in Cromwell's direction.

"If you must know, I'm stranded out here on this godforsaken rock," she called out to him. A moment later she was amazed to see the boy step down into the river and walk in her direction. He took one step after another through the current, never bothering to even glance down at the rock-strewn river bottom. Meanwhile, the moving water rushed against his legs and reached halfway up his calf. Cromwell seemed impervious to the cold river, moving swiftly through the current until he stepped up onto a large, dry stone close by Emma's position. It was rapidly becoming obvious that her plans to end her life were going up in smoke, at least at this time.

"You didn't have to join me here. I wasn't asking for your help." The youth ignored the girl's words. He stared into her face, his eyes lingering on the bruising under her left eye.

"How did that happen?" he asked, gesturing to the bruise on her cheek.

"That, along with everything else about me, is none of your business." Outwardly unperturbed, the young man continued to take Emma in, his eyes moving over her body in a curious manner.

"Where's your other shoe?"

"I cut my foot coming out here. My shoe floated away after I tried walking on my bad foot." Cromwell stepped from his rock and crouched down in front of the girl. Without asking, he took hold of her right ankle and lifted her foot. He examined the gash on her sole for two or three seconds before releasing the ankle.

"You might want to put some iodine on that tonight when you get home," he suggested.

"Oh, thank you, Doctor Kildare. I never would have thought of that on my own," she answered sarcastically. He stepped back onto the adjoining rock and returned to staring at the young woman. Emma grew uncomfortable. Glancing down at herself, she noticed a patch of wetness on the crotch of her jeans. A few silent, uncomfortable seconds passed.

"How do you plan on getting back to dry ground? Can you walk on your bad foot?"

"I don't know. I tried putting weight on it earlier, but it was too painful."

"I could go and get someone to help you," he offered.

"I don't want anyone else seeing me out in the middle of the river. Besides, the less people who see me with my face looking like this, the better."

"You can't stay out here," argued the boy. Emma placed her chin down on her knees and closed her eyes. There was both despair and desperation in her body language. "The other option is to have me carry you back to the river bank." His words hung in the air for the better part of a minute before she responded.

"Mr. Cromwell, you have to know that it is only out of complete desperation that I take you up on your offer to carry me back to the water's edge. The idea of a complete stranger holding me in their arms literally makes me ill." A pained expression broke onto the boy's face for a brief moment, then nothing. She was instantly sorry for her words but could not come up with a comfortable way to retract them. He gestured toward her purse and she tucked it under one arm. Stepping down from his rock, he quickly flanked Emma and pushed his right arm under her folded legs. A second later she was being hoisted up from the rock. It was done in a single motion and with almost comical ease. In a split second, she was face to face with the giant from homeroom. They stood in place with one of the boy's arms cradling her back, while the other supported her lower body from beneath both knees. After a brief hesitation, he plodded forward through the water toward the near bank. He looked past her to the river bottom, taking care to step only on flat, firm surfaces beneath the moving water. She took this brief opportunity to examine his facial characteristics. There was light stubble spread over his homely features, telling her he was already shaving a few times per week. His eyes were a pale blue and looked out from beneath a pair of thick eyebrows. His nose was flatter than most but showed no evidence of ever having been broken. Incredibly, Emma saw something she liked about his mouth. Cromwell had moderately thick lips in front of an imperfect line of white teeth. Reaching the river's bank, he stopped on a small patch of sandy terrain and carefully lowered her to the ground.

"You still haven't answered my question. Is anyone coming to get you and take you home?" Emma stared up at her six foot, eight inch classmate and hesitated before responding. Outwardly flustered, her reply to his question was feeble, at best.

"I can manage. You don't have to hang around. Thank you for what you've done, but I'm fine now," she answered timidly.

"So someone is coming to pick you up and you don't want them to see me here. Is that right?"

"No one is coming to pick me up. No one even knows I'm here."

"Then how can you be fine? There's no way you can walk on that foot, particularly with no shoe. Swallow your pride and ask for a little help. It won't kill you," he argued. She stared up at him, frustration beginning to show on her face. "I'll get you home."

"I'm not going home. The last place I want to go right now is home. Again, thank you for everything, but get lost." The boy ignored her words and took a seat on the nearby root of a tree. "Why don't you get it? I want to be alone!"

"The sun'll be going down in another half hour or so. I can't leave you alone out here. It's not safe," he reasoned.

"Oh, and I'm so safe here with a total stranger straight out of reform school!" Cromwell's head dropped. Reaching down, he snatched a half dozen small stones from the ground and lethargically tossed them, one at a time, into the moving water. "What do you care what I do? You don't even know me. A day ago you were helping them stuff me into my locker. Go away."

"When did I stuff you *in* a locker? I remember getting you *out* of a locker, but I don't remember putting you *in* one," he answered.

"You had to be there when they pushed me in. Otherwise, how would you have known to come back and let me out?"

"I just heard a bunch of those idiots laughing about pushing someone into a locker, so I went back into the school to let them out. I wasn't sure it was you, but I thought it might be." Cromwell spoke without raising his eyes from the ground, feigning to be in search of more stones. When Emma did not respond for a few seconds, he lifted his eyes and saw her staring at him.

"Please leave me," she begged.

"I'm not leaving you," he responded. She leaned forward, and then fell against him. This was followed by another outburst of tears as she released more of her frustration and despair. The boy did not dare embrace her, but allowed the young woman to grab hold of him and purge herself of her demons. The breakdown went on for another minute, with no words spoken by either teenager. Finally, Emma pushed herself away from her classmate and took a deep breath.

"So, Mr. Cromwell, what do you propose?" The boy broke eye contact with her, shifting his glance back to the river.

"I can carry you back to your house...like the way I took you back from the rock."

"I can't be seen with you in public. That I know. If we do that, it will have to be after the sun goes down."

"We can wait till it turns dark. I have no problem with that."

With the negotiations settled, the two sat back at the edge of the river and waited on sundown. Emma thought she sensed some withdrawal on her rescuer's part and decided to initiate a conversation.

"I have no idea where you live and what brought you down to the river today," she commented. The boy looked up at her.

"I don't live too far from here...on Friend Street. I was just out doing a little exploring when I came across you in the river," he stated.

"Friend Street. That's up behind Weeman's, right?"

"Yeah, the television store. I live in an apartment with my dad. He works at Kesslen Shoe."

"Wait a minute! You live with your father? He took you back after what you did to him?" A puzzled expression spread over the boy's face.

"Why? What did I do to him?" Emma grew uncomfortable.

"You know, you beat him up and sent him to the hospital." The boy gave her a peeved look.

"I didn't do that to my dad. I did that to my mom's boyfriend. It sounds like someone doesn't have their facts straight. I got sent down to Portland for protecting my mom from the animal she brought into our house. My mom and dad are divorced. I caught Mom's boyfriend slapping her around and kicked the shit out of him. He pressed charges." He spoke with intensity, which emphasized his Down East accent.

"But, given those circumstances, why did they send you away when you were just protecting your mother?" Cromwell did not answer her question at first, choosing to stare blankly into the Mousam instead. "Didn't they believe you or your mother?" Emma asked in astonishment.

"My mom puts a lot of stock in having a young guy's body in bed next to her at night. It was my word against theirs and a mother's word carries a lot of weight," he said despondently. Taken aback by this revelation, Emma decided to change the topic of conversation.

"So, how do you like Public Speaking class?" He rolled his eyes.

"I like Mrs. Bibber but I must've been out of my mind to take that. I'm gonna come off looking like a total idiot next week," he confessed.

"You did know that you get extra credit for picking someone to introduce from the opposite sex and with a background foreign to your own, right?" When her question was answered with a blank stare, she continued. "I already had all my research and notes done on Natalie Wood when I found out I could get extra credit for introducing Werner Von Braun. I'll give you my notes on Natalie Wood. You're halfway there, Mr. Cromwell." She watched the boy's face break out in a pained expression.

"When you call me, Mr. Cromwell, it makes me sound like some guy working at a bank. Call me Fin." Emma shook her head in the negative.

"It doesn't feel right," she insisted. He shook his head in mock disgust and tossed a rock out into the rapidly moving river.

Nearly an hour passed before the village was dark enough for Emma to venture away from the river bank and head home. Over this time the two teenagers sat six feet apart while the conversation moved between the trivial to the mundane. It was she who called the two to action. Cromwell rose to his feet and approached her. At that moment an unexpected quiver moved through her body. There was a curious and pleasant anticipation on her part of being lifted from the ground and cradled by this powerful young man. She disguised these feelings as much as possible, but found herself gazing into his blue eyes the moment she was lifted from the ground. Clearly more at ease in his grasp than only an hour earlier, she talked him in the direction of Water Street. She ran the route of their walk over in her mind. They would have to cross Main Street on the trek to her door. If they were to be spotted it would, in all likelihood, be at that point in the journey.

Emma directed the boy to the far side of Water Street where the shadows darkened the sidewalk as they made their way toward the village. Her foot had not stopped throbbing. She reached up to her face and touched her bruised cheek.

"How bad does it look?" she asked. He turned to her.

"The swelling has definitely gone down," he reported. When his eyes returned to where the two were headed she inspected him. He looked different in the shadows and artificial light.

"Why are you being so nice to me, Mr. Cromwell?" Her question came in a whisper.

"It's Fin. My name is Fin."

"But why are you being so nice to me?" He shook his head as if disgusted and continued to walk in the direction of Main Street. He glanced down and saw her staring up at him.

"I've always had a thing for girls I find trapped in lockers and smelling like egg salad," he said dryly.

"Oh please don't remind me of that," she blurted out. Her words were followed by a deep breath. Within ten minutes they were approaching Main Street and a steady flow of traffic.

"There's where my dad works, but I'm sure he's out of work by now," he announced. Before them was the Kesslen Shoe Company building, perched aside the Mousam River dam and facing the busy intersection at the foot of Kennebunk's upper village. The Cromwell boy paused in the shadow of an office building while Emma worked on a strategy.

"Why don't we duck down into Rotary Park? We can wait there until there's a major lull in the traffic and then run across Main Street," she suggested.

"Where's Rotary Park?"

"There, across the street," she answered, pointing across Water Street to a small sliver of land by the river.

"That's a park?" he asked in astonishment. The teenagers backtracked a short distance down Water Street before crossing the road and making their way into the park. Cromwell carried Emma to the base of the bridge, out of sight of passing traffic, and waited.

"You can put me down if I'm heavy," she instructed while the two waited for the traffic flow to subside.

"I'm fine," he answered, showing no outward sign of fatigue.

"How much do you weigh?" Emma asked.

"A little over two hundred and fifty pounds."

"That's probably just about the right weight for you. You're a tall guy. What do you think I weigh?" He hoisted her up a few additional inches as if weighing her on a scale.

"A hundred and five pounds," he guessed.

"Good guess. Actually, I'm one hundred and four pounds, soaking wet. Mr. Cromwell, why don't you put me down until it's time to cross Main Street," she suggested again. "It could be a while, with so many people getting out of work about now." He complied with her wishes and the two rested their backs against the base of the bridge. "Tell me something about where you grew up. You're from Jonesport, right?"

"Yeah, I'm from Jonesport. Jonesport's a pretty small town right on the ocean, where lobstering and fishing are real important. I grew up just up the road from the old sardine factory and..."

"You grew up near an old sardine factory?" Emma asked through a burst of laughter. The boy stopped and looked down at her. "An old sardine factory! God, it sounds so pitifully pathetic," she cried out. The uncontrolled laughter went on for half a minute before she began to regain her composure. However, it only took one look up into the boy's astonished face to prompt a new gale of laughter. She finally buried her face in his jacket, partly snuffing out her overblown reaction by depriving herself of oxygen.

"It's nice to hear my life is such a joke to you," he added. However, even he could not contain himself when their eyes met and Emma was forced to bite down on her lip to stifle more laughter. He glanced down at her. She was staring back in a more agreeable manner.

"That is probably the most laughing I've done in at least three months," she confessed. He responded to her words with a protective nod, his eyes trained on hers.

The two teenagers remained slumped in the shadow of the bridge for twenty minutes while vehicles passed by above them.

"If I am going home tonight then I can't let it get too late before I do so, or my parents will really have a bird," she announced. Emma gestured to him for assistance. "If you don't mind, Mr. Cromwell?"

"Trust me, Miss Corman, it's no bother." The teenagers rose to their feet in unison and the boy scooped her into his arms without any warning or preparation. He carried Emma up the sharp incline to the sidewalk lining the roadway and shot a glance in both directions. There were no cars at the intersection at that precise moment and no vehicles within sight traveling toward them from the north. The only vehicle in sight was a pickup truck over a hundred yards away, approaching from the south. The boy decided to make the crossing and stepped out onto Route 1 with Emma propped up in his arms. However, his advance into the road was interrupted by the sound of something falling to the pavement below him. She cried out in frustration as her purse hit the roadway by the double line and flew open. A roll of Life Savers and her bottle of pills spilled out onto the street. Cromwell froze in his tracks and looked down.

"Just hold on tight. I'll pick them up," he instructed her. Emma threw both arms around the young man's neck while he knelt in the roadway and snatched up the purse, pills and candies in one motion. Moving to recover his firm grip on the girl, he lost control of the Life Savers and they fell back to the ground. By now the headlights of the oncoming pickup had reached them and the teenagers found themselves illuminated in the middle of Route 1. The boy made a snap decision, kicked the candy to the side of the road, and made his way to the sidewalk and safety. Reaching the far side of Main Street, they looked back at the truck. Staring back at them from inside the beat up Dodge sat an older gentleman with white whiskers and a red face.

"Shit, it looks like Santa's turned to the bottle," muttered Finian in a low voice. Emma responded with another round of laughter, more from relief that their witness was a stranger than from any humorous content in the remark. Standing before them, illuminated in street lights, stood the Kesslen Shoe Company. The boy made haste to carry Emma around the corner and onto Storer Street for the last leg of her trip home.

"I was saving those Life Savers for a special occasion and now you've completely ruined my plans," lamented Emma. The boy shook his head and smiled, no doubt picking up on the growing connection between the two. "I don't know what I'm doing, clowning around. I'm going to get my head ripped off when I get home and my parents see me like this: my eye turning black and blue, a gouge in my foot and missing a shoe. What the hell are they going to think?"

"First of all, they'll probably just be glad you made it home in one piece," said Cromwell. "As far as the swelling on your face, why don't you just tell them the truth? It's not like you went out and asked for it."

"I'm ashamed. I can't confess what a loser I am to my mother and father. It's humiliating! I can't even believe I confessed it to you!" Emma buried her face back into the boy's jacket, but did not resume crying. It seemed she had shed her quota of tears for the evening. He walked up the street in silence, now aware of the girl's growing apprehension. The mood had turned downbeat. The roadway was nearly pitch black when the two teenagers crossed to the far side of the street and made their way toward her house. She looked up at him when he turned onto Mechanic Street. "How did you know I lived up this street?" she asked, appearing somewhat taken aback.

"You must have said something," he answered unconvincingly.

"I did no such thing," countered Emma. She stared back at him, her eyes scanning his face for a reaction. He appeared uncomfortable and stared straight ahead, avoiding her eyes at all cost. Finally, she softened her tone. "Do you like me?" she asked, her own voice burdened with insecurity. Her words caused his head to drop slightly. His eyes still had not returned to hers.

"I suppose I do," he answered shyly. She mustered no response to his admission.

"Stop right here!" Emma cried out while her body went rigid. "I can make it the rest of the way myself. I don't want my parents to see you," she hastily explained. Cromwell froze in his tracks, continuing to balance the weight of the girl in both arms. "Put me down right here," she commanded. The teenager hesitated before reluctantly lowering Emma to the ground.

She winced when her injured sole made contact with the pavement. Tucking her purse back under one arm, she half-turned toward her house. Staring apprehensively through the darkness at her family's home, her mind was focused on the pending confrontation with her mother and father. A few seconds passed and she turned back to Cromwell. He was moving away into the darkness down the road and barely still visible to her.

"Fin," she called to him. The sound of his boots striking the pavement stopped.

"Yep," he answered.

"Fin, would you walk me to school on Monday morning?"

"Sure, what time?" He responded with no hesitation.

"What if I met you down there at the corner at seven-thirty?"

"You're on. Good luck with your parents tonight, Emma. It is okay to call you Emma, right?"

"It's fine…and thank you. Thanks for getting me home and thank you for everything else," she called out.

"Take care of that eye and don't forget the iodine on the foot," he instructed. "I'll see you Monday morning." With that said, the young man of few words totally disappeared into the darkness.

Three sets of eyes in the kitchen turned in her direction when Emma limped awkwardly through the front door and presented herself to the family. Following a silent moment of shock, Harriet jumped to her feet and rushed toward the girl.

"What is all this?" Her mother gestured toward Emma's raised and barefooted right leg. "What's happened to your face?" she cried out while approaching the girl and examining the wound. "I thought you were going to be staying with a friend," she hollered at close range. Emma's eyes dropped to the floor as she hobbled toward the kitchen and her father. "What in the name of God is going on here?" bellowed her mother. All eyes were on Emma as she made her way to the kitchen table. Spotting the bruise on her face, her father rose from his chair and made his way across the room.

"I got hit in the face with a carton of juice while I was walking home from school," muttered Emma meekly. "Someone threw it out of a car and it accidentally hit me," she explained. She looked up and found her mother glaring into her face at close range, her eyes focused on the bruise adorning her left cheek.

"I don't believe that story. I don't believe it for a moment," she repeated. "There is something very wrong with you, Emma, and there has been for the past couple of months. Now are we going to get the truth or do we have to really punish you?"

"The truth is I was not planning to stay at a friend's house. I just needed some time to get away and think things through. I went down to the river out by Rogers Pond and that's where I cut my foot. I stepped on a sharp stone on the floor of the river while making my way out to one of the big rocks in the middle," she explained.

"Have you suddenly gone totally out of your mind?" barked Harriet at close range. This exchange brought Bertrand to his feet. He separated his wife from Emma and slowly eased the woman away from his daughter. A sense of relief came to Emma when the telephone rang and Harriet moved out into the hallway to answer it. The man turned back to his daughter and gestured her to take a seat.

"Let me take a look at that gouge on your foot. There's a chance we might have to take you to the hospital for a shot," he explained calmly. She propped her injured foot over her good leg and allowed her dad to examine it.

"I didn't cut it on a rusty nail or anything, Daddy. It probably only needs a little iodine or something to make sure it doesn't get infected," she added, parroting Fin Cromwell's advice from earlier. Following fifteen or twenty seconds of inspection, her father made his way to the downstairs bathroom and returned with a bottle of antiseptic. Passing by his teenage daughter, he tenderly kissed her on the top of the head in a show of reassurance. He had no way of knowing how much the gesture meant to her.

"Will this really hurt?" Emma asked apprehensively. He smiled and shook his head in the negative.

"It's not iodine. It shouldn't hurt too much at all." The soft-spoken man gently applied the medicinal liquid. Emma heard the phone conversation end in the hallway. Within seconds her mother was planted in the doorway, her eyes riveted back on her. A shock of apprehension passed through Emma's stomach.

"That was Gertie Harrison on the phone. She called to tell me that she was sitting in her car down on Main Street a half hour ago waiting on her husband and thought she saw Emma downtown in the arms of a boy," reported Harriet to her husband. "If that wasn't bad enough, the boy happened to be that piece of garbage the school just had to take in from reform school. Our daughter was out tonight gallivanting with that piece of white trash from Jonesport, the one who sent his father to the hospital. That certainly goes a long way towards explaining what happened to her face," snapped the woman. Bertrand, flabbergasted by the report, turned back to his daughter.

"Is this true, Emma?" The teenager's head dropped. She had been caught in a lie of omission and was not sure if even the truth could rescue her.

"Fin came upon me down at the river after I'd cut my foot. He offered to help," she explained.

"Oh, *Fin*, is it? She's on a first name basis with him," cried out Harriet to her husband and to anyone else who happened to be walking on Mechanic Street this night. Mr. Corman grew very serious and turned back to his daughter.

"Emma, I don't want any more tall tales. Did this boy hit you?" Emma stood up from the table and stared directly into her father's eyes.

"Daddy, someone threw a carton of orange juice out of a car window and hit me on the side of the face. I was not completely truthful with you and momma when I said it was an accident. In truth, I know it wasn't an accident, but I'm not sure exactly who it was who threw it. I know it was a boy."

"Who's to say it wasn't this Fin character?" injected Harriet from across the room.

"He's about the only one I know it wasn't," answered Emma. "He was walking a couple of hundred yards ahead of me at the time."

"What were you doing in this boy's arms?" asked the concerned father. Emma responded with a feeble laugh.

"He was carrying me back to the house from the river. It wasn't like I could have walked all that way," she explained. "As far as being in his arms, he was carrying me the way a man carries his bride over the threshold. How else was he supposed to do it?" The man scanned his daughter's face for truthfulness and glanced to his wife. The kitchen turned deathly quiet. Emma took this opportunity to limp over to her mother. "Momma, the story about him beating up his father and sending him to the hospital just isn't true. Fin lives with his dad. His dad took him in when he got out of reform school. It's true, he did beat someone up and send him to the hospital, but it was his mother's boyfriend, not his father. Fin caught the man slapping his mom around and put a stop to it. The man pressed charges and Fin's mom sided with her boyfriend." Mrs. Corman's demeanor softened, albeit slightly.

"Emma, he sounds very low rent and violent," she reasoned.

"He's become a friend in a very short period of time."

"I don't want you anywhere near this oversized goon. Do you understand?" Emma let out a frustrated whimper and turned back to her father.

"Daddy, I want and need this boy as a friend. I can't say too much more than that, but you have to trust me," she pleaded. Her father shook his head and studied his daughter's face for a moment. He reached a quick decision.

"You can spend some time around this boy, but never alone. That's the rule. Do you understand?" Emma quickly accepted her father's terms and extended him a hug.

"Bertrand, I want you to know that if they find our daughter dead in a ditch somewhere, then you'll have no one to blame but yourself." The man accepted his wife's determination with the nod of his head.

"Emma, for putting the entire family through this whole unseemly matter, I want you to consider yourself restricted to the house for the weekend," stated her father before making his way to the living room and an evening of television. Emma made haste to hobble toward the stairs and made her way up to her room, followed closely by her sister. She collapsed onto her bed and let out a long sigh. A few seconds passed before she became aware of Becky standing in the doorway.

"If you don't mind, I'd appreciate a little privacy," she stated in the condescending manner of an older sibling.

"Why would anyone want to be around someone that ugly?" asked the eighth grader. Emma's response was non-verbal. She leaned forward and closed the bedroom door in her sister's face.

Lying in bed later that evening, Emma played and replayed the events of the day in her head. It had truly been one of the most dreadful days of her short life. Only now did the realization that she had flirted with suicide and death register with her. The bruise on her face no longer hurt but the gouge on the bottom of her foot continued to radiate pain. Her mind flashed back to the river and the feeling of being swept up into the arms of Fin Cromwell. There was no denying there was something quite pleasurable attached to the sensation. She relived their conversation over the trek home to the house and the towering youth's temperament. He was nothing like the surly young man she had confronted a few days earlier at lunch in the darkened classroom. She remembered staring at his profiled face at close range as he lugged her along Water and Storer Streets and actually found something pleasing about it. She took inventory of herself and found that in spite of her injuries or the tongue-lashing she received from her mother, she was at peace. Then, incredibly, she became aware of another change that had come over her: the anxiety from the thought of returning to school following the weekend was no longer present inside her. Emma rolled sideways on the bed and smiled as the cause of her newfound sense of peace crystalized in her mind. She was no longer alone among her peers. She had a friend in Fin Cromwell and from this day on she would allow no one to prey upon her.

6

Monday morning and Emma's return to school was greeted with high, gusting winds and a driving rain. The weekend afforded her foot time to heal and by Sunday night, she was moving about the house with only a slight limp. Outside her windows the rain was stripping the trees on Mechanic Street of their brightly colored leaves, while rivulets of rainwater blew by the house toward Storer Street. Inside, the Corman family sat around the breakfast table and sluggishly spooned down their warm oatmeal. From the far corner of the room, the Biddeford radio personality commented at length on the terrible weather conditions on this morning and on how southern Maine was not likely to see the sun until the second half of the week. Mr. Corman advised his daughters that he would drop them off at school on this day and asked them to be ready to leave by seven-thirty. Meanwhile, Emma's mind was racing with thoughts of Fin standing at the end of the street waiting on her.

At quarter past seven o'clock, the Corman sisters retreated upstairs to their bedrooms and pulled raingear from their closets. During this time, Emma was plagued by the image of Fin Cromwell standing in the downpour at the end of her street waiting for her. She needed to make her father aware of Fin's presence but dared not bring it up in front of her mother. Emma and Becky were called downstairs a few minutes later and ushered by their father to the car. After giving their dad a few moments to start the vehicle, the two sisters made a mad dash for it at the back of the house. Emma made a point of surrendering the front seat to her younger sister and slid across the back seat to a position directly behind her father. With the windshield wipers swishing at full speed, her father slowly pulled the vehicle out onto the street.

"Daddy, could we possible go by way of Storer Street?" asked Emma in an angelic voice. Without a response, the man rotated the steering wheel in that direction. Emma strained her eyes, focusing them on the sidewalk and roadway one hundred yards in the distance. It was there she identified the hooded image of a lone figure standing in the blowing rain. Fin was draped in a bright yellow rain slicker and stood by the stop sign at the end of the street, his face hidden under a rain repellent hood.

"Oh, my God, that's him," called out Becky from the front seat. "Daddy, that's the boy Emma was with last Friday night." Emma reached forward and placed a hand on her father's shoulder.

"Daddy, please stop and give Fin a ride," she pleaded. Mr. Corman stared up and out through the windshield at the hulking figure standing in the rain at the side of the road. He rolled the vehicle to a stop and gestured to his daughter in the back seat. Emma slid sideways and pushed open the car door. Following a momentary hesitation, the towering young man moved forward and sandwiched himself into the back seat.

"Much obliged," the boy mumbled while tucking his long legs into the vehicle. Mr. Corman glanced back at his oversized passenger and smiled while Becky sat frozen in the passenger seat. Fin glanced over at Emma and appeared somewhat ill at ease.

"Daddy, this is Fin Cromwell. Fin, this is my father and the airhead sitting directly in front of you is my sister, Becky," wisecracked Emma.

"Very funny," whined Becky in response.

"I take it you and Emma share a few classes, Fin?" The boy nodded in the affirmative.

"We're in the same homeroom and we have Public Speaking class together. I've only been at Kennebunk High for a few days. For the most part though, Emma's in with the brains and I'm in with the dummies," he confessed. The college professor recognized there was more than a grain of truth in Fin Cromwell's admission and decided not to respond. It was less than a mile to the school and within a couple of minutes Mr. Corman had the teenagers at the door of Kennebunk High. Fin let out a groan as he unfolded his legs and awkwardly stepped out of the car.

"Thanks for the ride, Mr. Corman," he called out.

"It was good to put a face with the name," the man called back to the individual who had been the subject of more than one intense discussion at his dinner table. Fin then astonished the Cormans by circling the car and opening the back seat door for Emma. She quickly scooped up her school bag and stepped from the vehicle, her mouth open in surprise. Mr. Corman rolled his car window down and Emma leaned inside. She gave him a peck on the cheek and thanked him for the ride before he motored off with Becky. She turned back to Fin and together they made their way into the building. Fin advised Emma that he needed to speak with one of his teachers before class, but that he would join her in homeroom immediately afterward. She climbed the stairs and walked toward her locker. The bruising around her eye was still visible and she noticed that more than one of the students she passed in the hallway took note of it.

Emma swung open her locker door and gazed inside. It struck her that only four days had passed since she was locked within this tight space. She began to imagine how many laughs Whitney and her friends must have extracted from her humiliation. Incredibly, her new mindset allowed her to drive these thoughts from her head. She pulled a notebook from the back of the locker, peeled off her raincoat and hung it inside. Pausing in the hallway, she reminded herself of the change in circumstances that were now in place. She was no longer the friendless loner she had been a week ago. Everything had changed. She was not just allied with Fin Cromwell, perhaps the most intimidating boy at Kennebunk High School, but from all appearances she was also gaining a level of emotional control over him. There was no doubt in her mind that Fin was physically attracted to her. He had all but confessed he was. She was just as certain that he did absolutely nothing for her physically or romantically. She had spent much of the weekend thinking through her new relationship with Fin. He was the ally she had to cling to, no matter what. Her mental and physical well-being depended on it. After some consideration, she decided to show a measure of romantic interest in the boy. That was certainly the best way to assure a continuation of their friendship. It also helped that she was developing a platonic fondness for him. She rationalized away any feelings of guilt at the thought of using the boy. She could and would assist him academically in return for his contribution to her mental well-being. The bottom line, as she saw it, was that she needed Fin to survive her remaining two years at Kennebunk High School. He was the key to her survival. The sound of Whitney's laughter from within homeroom brought Emma out of her meditative state. She took a deep breath and closed her locker.

A number of heads turned when Emma entered homeroom on this Monday morning. Mr. Foster had not arrived yet, which contributed to an elevated noise level. There was a burst of laughter from a male at the back of the room on her entrance. Emma assumed it was in reaction to the bruising on her face but did not acknowledge it outwardly. The chatter of classmates dropped off as she approached her desk. Whitney turned her attention away from her friends and toward her. She snickered. She flashed Mandy a cruel smile.

"What happened, Dishrag? Did you have some rough sex over the weekend?" Whitney sniped. Outwardly unperturbed, Emma turned to her blonde tormentor.

"I have a strong suspicion you know who hit me with that orange juice carton last Friday," Emma stated calmly. A smug smile broke across the blonde's beautiful face.

"Don't get all high and mighty with me, Dishrag," she warned. "What he did was stupid. My guess is it will never happen again."

"You're right. It will never happen again. And it's only a matter of time until I find out who threw that at me," stated Emma coldly. Her words brought a spurt of laughter from Mandy Cowger.

"Listen to the tough talk from this little bag of shit," crowed the female jock.

"For every action there is a reaction," recited Emma coolly, staring directly into her tormentor's eyes. Mandy had heard enough and began reaching for Emma's hair. She halted her aggression abruptly when she caught sight of the towering man-child standing behind her would-be victim.

Fin's arrival in homeroom went largely unnoticed while everyone's attention was riveted on the brewing confrontation between Emma and the athletic Mandy. He had already crossed the front of the room before Whitney detected his advance. The blonde's eyes locked onto the lumbering giant as he approached Emma from the rear. Placing a hand on her shoulder, he crouched and half-whispered into his petite friend's ear.

"Where should we meet before going down to lunch?" he asked nonchalantly. Emma turned and glanced up at her newfound friend.

"How about out in the hall in front of the bust of Abraham Lincoln? You know where I'm talking about, right?" Mandy stood frozen in place and stared at the two in disbelief while Whitney looked on intently, processing what had happened in the last few moments. She gazed at Emma, her face exhibiting the same familiar contempt but, at least for the moment, tempered by a reluctant degree of respect. Emma Corman had played a powerful trump card in the person of Finian Cromwell and Whitney had not seen it coming. The classroom grew quiet. Whitney straightened the text books on the surface of her desk and pondered the change in circumstances. She stole a glance over at Cromwell. His hand continued to rest on Emma's shoulder while he quietly communicated directly into her ear. Every few seconds he discreetly directed his eyes in Mandy's direction, casting a threatening glare. A few seconds passed and Mr. Foster breezed into the room with a flourish, apologizing to the assembled for his near tardiness. The teacher's arrival was Fin's cue to return to his own desk; he shuffled to the front of the classroom and collapsed onto it with a thud.

"I'm not sure how many of those landings that desk can survive," muttered the teacher. Fin responded with a grin.

"Sorry, I'll be a little more careful next time," he answered, appearing to be somewhat embarrassed.

The clang from the bell calling the students to lunch period had barely evaporated from the school corridors when Emma glanced up the hallway and spotted Fin's head bobbing above the rush of juniors and seniors scurrying in the direction of the makeshift cafeteria. Her morning had gone well, but not in the conventional way. Instead, her usual dosage of abuse from Whitney and company was replaced with shunning. This was something she was happy to deal with in place of the physical and mental torment of the preceding two months. She shouldered her way out into the moving throng of teenagers and for the first time since the opening day of school, proceeded without fear of psychological or physical abuse. She scanned ahead and spotted Fin standing by the bust of the sixteenth president. Reaching him, Emma flashed him her best imitation of a seductive smile and playfully bumped her hip against his thigh.

"I hope you don't find talking to me too boring," he mumbled. She shook her head in the negative. "Where do you usually have lunch? I've been burying myself up in an empty classroom since I got here," he confessed. Emma stared up at him and laughed.

"Cromwell, I've got you so beaten in the world of pitiful losers. You see, for the past week I've been spending my lunch periods in back of the school beyond the tree line. It's just been me and the freaking squirrels," she admitted. Her confession brought a roar of laughter from the seventeen year old. They made their way downstairs to the back of the building to the makeshift area by the study hall where Kennebunk High School fed the young adults entrusted to them. Emma and Fin took their places in line. The cafeteria's special this day was macaroni and cheese. When Fin reached the server's station he amused Emma with his request.

"Slop it right on the plate there and don't be afraid of getting it on my bread," he instructed in his slow, methodical way. Emma burst into laughter.

"I don't think the cooks appreciate having the word *slop* used in conjunction with their food," she commented lightheartedly. Emma gestured her male friend in the direction of the gymnasium, where they had their choice of sitting at any one of a number of tables. They walked a distance across the gym floor and settled on an empty tabletop while a dozen classmates stared in bewilderment at the unlikely twosome. Fin seated himself directly across from Emma. He placed down his tray of food and stared into her eyes.

"How much time have you put into preparing the two minute introduction for Public Speaking class?" asked Emma. The boy's eyes widened. "You are doing Natalie Wood, right?"

"Doing Kennedy or Nixon would be easier," he answered without conviction.

"Half the morons in the class will be doing Kennedy or Nixon! Oh, and have you thought how it might be a little difficult introducing Kennedy when he's already dead?" Fin threw back his head and let out a sigh. "We'll work on it together after school. I told you...I'll give you all of my Natalie Wood notes."

"Where will we go to study?" he asked.

"Why don't we go to the library, the town library?" He nodded his head in acceptance of her plan and scooped up a fork full of macaroni. A momentary hush had fallen over the table when a female student approached the two. The young woman was Gloria Frey, a senior at Kennebunk High who, two years earlier, had been involved in a serious auto accident that left her partially crippled. The accident, suffered during a vacation with her family in Florida, mangled her left hip and knee, an injury that caused her to walk in an awkward, jerky manner. Gloria hovered over Emma and Fin and hesitated.

"Mind if I join you?" she finally blurted out.

"It'll cost you half your food," blurted out Fin before rising to his feet and pulling out the relieved girl's chair. Emma chuckled at Gloria from across the table before flashing a sweet smile.

"I actually thought you were serious for a second," admitted the girl while staring up at Fin. As it turned out, the handicapped girl contributed much to the conversation at the table on this day. Emma perceived reluctance by Fin to leave his safety zone of topics for discussion, perhaps out of a fear of appearing uninformed. However, the lunch period passed fleetingly with Emma and Gloria dominating the lighthearted repartee. Fin accompanied Emma toward her next class. He mentioned something about his coming Natalie Wood introduction and his great fear of looking like a jackass in front of the Public Speaking class. Emma was barely listening; her own mind concentrating on what a joy it was to walk the halls of Kennebunk High without fear of attack or humiliation. She glanced up at Fin. He was staring down the hallway at a cluster of sophomore girls. She threaded her arm inside his and rested her head against his shoulder.

"What was that for?" he asked.

"That's for making me comfortable...and for being my friend," she explained. He reciprocated by running his rough hand along her cheek. He stared down at her intently, his eyes focusing on hers before scanning down her face and stopping at her mouth. At this instant all doubt regarding her role in the life of Fin Cromwell was erased from her mind. Emma instinctively knew that this male, a total stranger to her less than a week before, was in love with her and would do almost anything to make her happy. Reaching her classroom door, she slipped her arm from under his, granted him a smile, and disappeared from sight.

The rain had subsided when Emma and Fin left school and methodically made their way in the general direction of the town library. Walking across the spacious front lawn of Kennebunk High, their voices were sometimes drowned out by the sound of car engines as a majority of the upper classmen left in their vehicles. On Emma's suggestion they decided to forego taking the direct route to the library and detoured onto

Storer Street. Along the way they witnessed the aftermath of that morning's wind and rain. The roadway was littered with an abundance of fallen leaves and branches in addition to the standing puddles of rainwater. When they passed the access to Mechanic Street, it seemed to prompt their conversation back to the events of Friday night.

"What did you think I was up to when you found me out in the river on Friday?" He shrugged his shoulders.

"I didn't know what to think. All I knew was it looked like a good time to try and break the ice between us." She smiled up at him.

"I don't think you have any idea what you did for me that night," she added seriously.

"I knew nothing good was going to come out of you sitting out there in the middle of the river." Emma hesitated, holding back her words for a moment.

"Do you remember when we were crossing Main Street that night and my purse and stuff fell onto the road?"

"Yeah, I do."

"Do you happen to remember what else fell onto the ground?" Fin continued to walk, his eyes focused on something in the far distance.

"I remember a bottle of sleeping pills," he answered.

"Well, that must have given you an idea about what I was up to," she suggested. He shook his head and looked down at her in disbelief.

"How could you, of all people, think about doing something as stupid as that? What the hell would that have solved?" Emma grew emotional.

"You cannot believe what those people were doing to me! I was literally getting sick every morning at the thought of going to school. Keep in mind, it was the same school I loved attending up until then. But then came September and I was without my good friend, Betty. I just couldn't deal with Whitney and Mandy and Benny Fadden." Emma took a deep breath, purging herself of the stress created just by reliving her experiences over the last two months. Fin placed his large hand down on her shoulder and held her in place.

"I don't want you thinking about doing anything that stupid again, okay?" There was something both reassuring, yet comical, in his words, delivered in his Down East accent. She leaned against him, her face coming up chest high.

"Fin, hear me out. I will never forget that you saved my life. Every day when I wake up in the morning I'll remember that you are responsible for giving me that day. I only wish I could tell my parents what you did so they could like you more. But, I can't do that because then they'll know they have a mental weakling for a daughter." She placed a soft kiss on his chest and then pretended to brush it off. Her words and actions set something off in him. He reached down to her, pulling her mouth to his. Surrendering for the moment, she returned the kiss before pushing him off.

"Fin, we're in public and I'm not a tramp," she scolded. He let his grip on her go. "If someone who knew my mother ever saw you doing that to me in broad daylight, you'd be banned from my list of friends," she reminded him.

"What list of friends?" Emma half laughed and stared back at him.

"Stop reminding me of how pitiful I am," she added, putting the incident behind them.

Emma and Fin reached Main Street and were greeted by the roar of water passing over the dam behind the Kesslen Shoe Company. She directed him across the street before he realized her immediate interest was in what was displayed in the window of Fashion Corner, a clothing boutique. She was merciful on this day, spending no more than a minute gazing through the window before ushering him northward up the street in the direction of the library.

"I don't think I've walked up this way in over three months," she confessed.

"How come?"

"Mostly because just up the street is Bowdoin's Drug Store where a lot of the kids from school hang out, including Whitney Crowninshield. The last thing I needed was to run into her or Mandy outside of school. They were nasty enough to me inside of school behind the teacher's backs. Imagine what they might have done to me away from the eyes of adults."

"Hey, I have a couple of dollars on me. Why don't we go in and have a coke or a frappe or something?"

"No, that's okay. It's just good being able to walk wherever I want and not worry about the teenagers from hell." They meandered up the street passing the Kennebunk Five and Dime, the Colonial Shoe Store and Western Auto, before coming up on Bowdoin's Gift Shop and Drug Store. On their approach the door to the drug store swung out and Benny Fadden emerged from the building. A look of surprise passed over Fadden's face when he spied Emma. Surprise was replaced by urgency when the fleshy teenager saw Fin standing next to her. Turning from them, Fadden made for the alleyway adjacent to the building in quick time.

"That's Benny Fadden, the boy who stuck the egg salad in my face," blurted out Emma. Her words launched Fin into another gear. He hustled around the corner in pursuit of the chubby teenager. A stunned Emma quickly looked around for witnesses before following Fin towards the back of the building. Turning the corner, she saw the boys about forty feet away. Fin had Fadden by the collar of his coat and was tossing him around like an oversized, pimple-faced rag doll. Even from a distance it was possible to hear Fadden's cries for mercy. Emma walked up on the boys just as Fin had lifted his victim from the ground and tightened the collar of his jacket around his neck. Fin glanced over his shoulder and saw Emma standing behind him. He turned Benny Fadden in her direction. She stared at the terrorized teenager with morbid curiosity, not knowing what sort of punishment her friend had doled out. She was surprised to see no bruising on the boy's face, only the redness brought on by near strangulation. On closer inspection, she saw that most of the damage had been inflicted on the lower body. There was blood showing through his pants at the knee where the fabric had been scraped away during one of Benny's trips to the pavement. Fin remained in a state of rage. He grabbed hold of Fadden with both hands and forced him down to the pavement in front of Emma.

"Now, fat boy, I want you to tell Emma that you're sorry," growled Fin. Fadden bowed his head and repeated the words from a nearly prostrate position. Emma could barely restrain herself from laughing. She looked up at Fin, extending him an appreciative smile.

"I accept your apology, Benny. But, be put on notice, if you ever say or do anything like what you pulled last week, I will see to it that Fin leaves your face unrecognizable. Do you understand?"

"Hey, I'm sorry. It was only a joke. But now that I know how you feel, you can be sure it won't happen again," blurted out Fadden. Fin hoisted the heavyset teenager to his feet and pushed him back toward Main Street. He had only traveled a few steps when Fin called out to him.

"And don't you go squealing on me. I have a witness that'll say I never laid a hand on you," he called out.

The entrance to the Kennebunk Free Library was on Main Street. Emma and Fin passed through the narrow front hallway toward the front desk. More than one set of eyes rose from their reading material when Fin made his appearance in the building. Emma directed him into a long room on the left furnished with four square tables where visitors availed themselves of the reference material and periodicals on hand. The impressive room caught Fin's attention immediately. From its white arched ceiling hung two brass chandeliers that illuminated the room on this overcast day. Additionally, natural light entered the room on two sides through a number of ornate windows. At the far end of the reference area was a fireplace trimmed in green marble, over which hung the uncompromising portrait of Mr. George Parsons, no doubt a town leader or community benefactor from an earlier time. The two teenagers shuffled across the room and claimed a corner of a table close by the fireplace. Emma combed through a notebook until she found the object of her search. She slid her notes across the table to her friend. He glanced down at her material with constrained interest.

"I'm handing you an 'A' on a silver platter, you idiot," she whispered into his ear. He frowned and began reading her outline.

"In Natalie you have an actress who was both a child star and an adult star. That's very rare. Plus, I don't think anyone has worked with so many giants of the movie industry. Think of it, she's worked with James Dean, Steve McQueen, Maureen O'Hara, Rosalind Russell, Robert Redford, Warren Beatty…"

"Yeah, I get it…lots of big stars," interrupted Fin.

"You can pad your introduction with these other stars' names and it also heightens your audience's interest because they start wondering who you are talking about," she explained. She glanced over and saw he was seriously focused on her notes. It was a few minutes later when he closed the notebook and conceded that the Natalie Wood introduction might be a good idea.

"I want you to practice giving the introduction in front of a mirror. Tomorrow you'll try it out on me and from there we'll polish it up for Friday." Fin turned toward Emma with a look of astonishment.

"You're expecting me to give the speech for you?"

"First of all, it's not a speech, it's an introduction. And secondly, yes I do. You're going to practice your intro over and over for me. Why? What was your plan? Did you plan on going into class on Friday and doing it cold?" she barked, albeit under her breath. He glanced down at her and shrugged his shoulders. She took that to mean that was exactly his plan. "This is what it takes to be really good at something…preparation." His eyes left Emma as he took in his surroundings.

"I really love this room. Someday I'd love to own a house with a living room this size, with chandeliers and a fireplace like this one in it," he declared. Emma removed her attention from the boy and glanced around the room.

"Yes, that would be nice. You're setting your sights quite high, you do know that?"

The two teenagers sat in the library reference room for the next thirty minutes in almost complete silence. Emma could not help thinking how curious it was that the other three tables in the room had people coming and going over the half hour that they were there, while Fin and she were left alone at their table. Finally, she closed her trigonometry textbook and stared intently at her new friend.

"I still can't believe what you made Benny do an hour ago," she whispered up to him. "I mean, you had him literally kneeling in front of me and apologizing," recounted Emma. She made no effort to hide her appreciation for his efforts.

"I should have made him kiss your feet and really humiliated him," stated Fin, a look of coldness taking possession of his features. "He would have, you know. I had him that scared." Emma found humor in his words and struggled to contain her laughter by burying her face in the sleeve of his jacket.

"Maybe next time," she blurted out from within blue denim. After taking a few seconds to compose herself, she straightened up and began gathering her study material.

"Where are we going to rehearse my Natalie Wood thing tomorrow? We can't do it in the library. Do you think your mom would let us do it over at your house?" She responded with a pained expression.

"I don't think my mom is ready to have a boy visiting me at the house just yet," she answered with no hesitation. If Fin found anything in her words to take personally he hid it well.

"We could go over to my dad's place. I'm sure he wouldn't have a problem with us being there." Emma hesitated for a moment before agreeing to join Fin at his house the following afternoon.

7

If Emma had any question regarding her new life at Kennebunk High School, these doubts were erased the following day. Her enemies at school were muted and all hostility was replaced by cold stares and shunning. She embraced her new circumstances and it was noticeable. On Tuesday morning, Mr. Foster commented on her brightened disposition and questioned her on it. She brushed off his inquiry with a reference to a newly adopted outlook on life. She caught word that her new relationship with Fin Cromwell was the talk of the school and it filled her with an unfamiliar exuberance. Upon dismissal from classes the two juniors walked together toward the village. Reaching the base of Mechanic Street they agreed to split up. This allowed Emma to return home and check in with her mother while Fin went home and prepared the apartment for their study session. Mrs. Corman was busy working on the family laundry when Emma stepped in through the front door and made for the stairs.

"Is that you, Emma?" called out her mother from the back of the house.

"Yes, Mom, I'm just home to drop off some books. I'm going right back out to do some studying with a friend," she answered in a loud voice. She scampered up the stairs and visited her bedroom just long enough to unload four or five pounds of textbooks onto her bed. Plucking a chemistry book from the pile, she made haste back down the stairs in the direction of the door. Her progress toward escape was blocked by her mother, who had taken position at the bottom of the stairs.

"It's good to see you getting out of the house, but I'd appreciate knowing who you'll be studying with," asked the woman with a hint of suspicion. Emma knew she could not act flustered by the inquiry. She calmly looked her mother in the eyes and responded with the first name that came to mind.

"Gloria Frey, she's a senior."

"Is that the unfortunate little cripple who was in the car accident?" Emma nodded yes. The lie brought on a fresh wave of criticism. "You do know that who you chum around with goes a long way toward establishing who you are, don't you? Now I have nothing against the girl, but you can be labeled as socially inferior if you're seen in the company of unfortunates and misfits. You'll be applying very soon to some top notch colleges and universities and it wouldn't hurt to get involved with people and organizations a little higher in society," lectured the woman. Emma nodded her head in acceptance and moved past her.

"In time, Mother, in time," she answered and hurriedly exited the house.

The day was overcast and this made the walk down Storer Street seem longer than it was. Reaching Main Street she crossed the bridge above the Mousam River and continued up the road toward Friend Street. It was not until now, the final leg of her walk, that she considered her actions. She would be alone with Fin in his dad's apartment. She was sure he had told her that his dad worked days and that meant he would probably not arrive home until after five o'clock. She grew apprehensive; reminding herself she had known this boy less than a week. There was so little to judge his character on, she thought. She was about to turn around when the overriding argument in his favor came to mind; he had not only saved her life, but now had made her life bearable at school. Emma turned the corner onto Friend Street and spied what had to be Fin's house a short way up the quiet roadway. The outside of the residence cried out for a fresh coat of paint, while weeds sprouted from the small amount of yard surrounding the house. There were two apartments in the building and Emma was careful to press the doorbell that corresponded to Fin's address. Within a few seconds, the door swung open and he was before her, his head almost touching the top of the doorway. She flashed him a smile and tentatively made her way into the hall. He smiled back and hand gestured her in the direction of the kitchen. Entering the room she was surprised by two things; the age of the appliances and furniture and the total cleanliness of the floor and counter tops.

"My grandmother has a porcelain table just like that in her kitchen," she pointed out while Fin pulled out a chair for her to rest in. He appeared both happy to see her and nervous. He walked toward the refrigerator.

"My dad bought some cream soda for us in case we got thirsty," he announced.

"There's a lot of sugar in cream soda," she replied, more to keep the conversation going than as a dietary objection.

"Are you saying you don't want any cream soda cause it's too sweet? Is that what you're saying, Miss Boney Maroney?" Emma laughed at his sophomoric humor and asked him to open a bottle for her. Fin made haste to pull two glasses from the cupboard and poured out their soft drinks. In the meantime, Emma allowed her eyes to drift around the room in search of anything that looked even remotely feminine. She observed nothing to indicate there was any maternal influence within the apartment. Fin crossed the kitchen with two glasses of soda in hand and took a chair beside her.

"My dad is hoping you're still here when he gets home from work. I told him a little about you and he's anxious to meet you."

"I hope you didn't tell him how we met."

"Do you mean out in the middle of the river or inside your locker when you threw egg salad at me?"

"Either." Fin grinned.

"For all he knows, we met at the library," he acknowledged.

"Oh, before you ask, I have no desire to get a tour of the house because I would rather not know what your bedroom looks like," she declared.

"I kind of feel bad about my bedroom. Dad was using the room as a hobby room and a place to store some of his sentimental belongings before I wound up at his door. I'm hoping to find a part-time job in a while to help him with expenses," explained Fin before taking a swig from his cream soda. Emma cast a glance at the sheet of notes from public speaking class.

"So, are you ready for a dry run?" she asked lightheartedly. He nodded yes. "Why don't you stand at the other end of the kitchen table and treat me like your audience of one," she suggested. He rose to his feet and ambled across the room. "You're going to be at a disadvantage when you give your introduction on Friday. Mrs. Bibber's lectern is not real high. You might be better off practicing standing behind nothing and keeping your notes in your hand." Fin shook his head in a gesture of frustration and took a deep breath.

"Our guest tonight was born on July 20th in 1938—"

"Oh, my God, are you insane?" Emma hollered out while jumping to her feet. No grown woman wants her age blurted out to a room full of strangers." Flustered, Fin peered down at his notes and then back at his friend. "You can't use that opening line. Mrs. Bibber will jump right on that and mark you down for it."

"Well, what do you suggest?" She thought for a moment.

"Few people in Hollywood would not agree that our guest tonight is one of the most beautiful women in the entertainment industry," she responded. Fin stared at her for a moment then scribbled something on his notes. "Remember, you want to keep the identity of your guest a secret until the last moment," she cautioned. "Okay, you can continue now," she prodded, demonstrating she had taken complete control of the study session.

"Our guest is one of the few actresses to make the transition from a child star to an adult star, and has worked with many of the giants in the industry. A partial list of these motion picture legends includes Orson Welles, Maureen O'Hara, James Dean, John Wayne, Gene Kelly, Steve McQueen, Warren Beatty and Robert Redford." He glanced down at her for encouragement or critique and received neither. She gestured him to continue. "Her first appearance in a movie came at the age of four in 1943."

"Take out the year of the picture. That gives away her age again," called out Emma. Fin leaned down and scratched out something from his notes. He continued shortly after, listing Miracle on 34th Street, Rebel Without a Cause, Gypsy and West Side Story among other films as achievements of her career. He also mentioned the role that Bob & Carol & Ted & Alice played in reestablishing her in Hollywood as a force at the box office. Through the rehearsed introduction Emma was surprised by Fin's focus for, in spite of his thick accent and some garbled words, he still managed to stay on message. Glancing up at his kitchen clock, he seemingly recognized that the two minutes allotted to him were almost up.

"And so, ladies and gentlemen, it is my honor to present our guest speaker this evening. To her family and closest of friends she is Natasha... but for us here in this room she will forever be Miss Natalie Wood." Fin focused his eyes on Emma and waited for her verdict.

"I love, love, love, love, love your ending! That Natasha thing really works. You came in twelve seconds short of two minutes. Remember what Mrs. Bibber said, you must come in within ten seconds either way of two minutes or get a deduction.

Emma had Fin repeat his introduction over and over until he was barely glancing down at his notes. At some point the repetitive nature of the exercise gave way to clowning, with Fin inserting some mildly off-color remarks during his rehearsed introduction. They were sharing a laugh involving the fictitious role Benny Fadden would play in Natalie's next film when a sound came from the front door.

"That must be my dad," he announced and sprang to his feet. He met his father in the front hallway and escorted the man into the kitchen to meet Emma. Eli Cromwell looked nothing like she anticipated. He was of average size, standing a couple of inches under six feet and weighing no more than one hundred and seventy pounds. His looks were also average, with not even a hint of his son's simian facial characteristics. Emma's mind conjured up the image of his mother, while Mr. Cromwell extended her a boisterous greeting in a dialect closely akin to Fin's. The man invited his son's guest to stay for supper, but she refused the invitation. It was only a few minutes before Emma was excusing herself and discreetly making her way toward the door. Fin threw on a jacket and insisted that he escort her home.

They had just begun the walk back to Mechanic Street when Emma thought she might try shedding some light on Fin's mother. Approaching the bridge and with the sound of the crashing water overflowing the dam, she discreetly moved their conversation in a new direction.

"What's your mother like?" she asked nonchalantly. Fin looked to the heavens and gave an awkward grin.

"My mom is tall and physically strong for a woman. She's an inch or two taller than my dad. She's a number of years younger than my father, too. They met up in Machias at a festival about twenty years ago. She was from a family that lived out away from town, way out in the boonies. They had electricity, but it came from a generator and not power lines. They were very poor and my grandfather was a brute. I remember meeting him just once and he was scary as hell looking. Anyway, he started courting my mother right off. He told me how he took her for a ride back to Jonesport and showed her where he lived."

"Did he show her the sardine factory?" quipped Emma. Fin laughed.

"No doubt he did. My mom has a different sort of look. She's quite pretty but in a different way. A lot of people have said how pretty she is. It's hard for a son to see that kind of thing in his mother. She has a space between her two front teeth that stands out."

"Like Lauren Hutton?"

"Who?"

"Never mind, go ahead," insisted Emma.

"Some people say that comes from people intermarrying. I have no idea. Ma also had a real wild look in her eyes. Even I could see that. I'm sure it had something to do with growing up way out in the middle of nowhere in the Maine woods. Anyway, from what I've been able to piece together, my mom and dad did some necking and making out over the festival weekend but nothing too, too serious. She went back to the woods with her family when it was over, but Dad never quite got over her. Later that year, my grandfather went on a drunken tear, slapping the boys around and screaming at the girls. My grandmother used to wear her hair in a bun and my grandfather got a hold of it one night and started tossing her all over the kitchen. All of the kids just stood back and watched, they were that afraid of the bastard. But something went off in my mother. While my grandfather's back was turned, she pulled a frying pan out of a drawer and hit him on the back of the head. Her brothers pulled her back after the old bastard had taken three off the skull. He was out cold and she made for the door. She ran away from home that night. It was fall and the nights were already getting cold. She walked to Route 1 and began hitchhiking her way south. She got picked up by an eighteen wheeler and began her escape. When they passed through Machias, she remembered my father. When they got to Route 187, she asked the truck driver to let her out because she wanted to go to Jonesport. All he did was reach over and put his hand between her legs."

"Oh, my God! What did she do?"

"Well, as you can imagine, my mom didn't trust men too much at this point and she was ready for anything. She'd picked up a rock the size of a small grapefruit on the side of the road waiting for a ride. She hit the driver right over his eye and he struggled to keep his rig on the road. When he smashed her in the face with his fist, she hit him again with the rock. This time she did some real damage. By the time she jumped out of the truck, he was gushing blood and hollering in pain. That night she walked the ten miles from Route 1 to Jonesport and finally to my dad's house. He's told me how he couldn't believe his eyes when he opened the door and saw her standing there. Dad told me once how he put her in the shower and got her cleaned up before they spent the rest of the night together. It was only in the morning that he found out she wasn't yet fifteen years old." Fin let out a sigh and glanced down at Emma. She appeared mesmerized by her friend's story. Emma walked ahead through the lengthening shadows extending over the sidewalk along Storer Street.

"If I may ask, how old was your mother when you were born?"

"Sixteen and a half," he answered. There was something in his response that told her he had been asked the question before.

Emma grew noticeably tense when they turned the corner onto Mechanic Street. Fifty feet from her house she turned to Fin, staring into his chest and not making eye contact. He leaned forward and kissed her on the top of the head.

"I didn't say you could do that," she snapped. He planted a second kiss on the same spot.

"I was wondering if you would go out somewhere with me on Friday? My dad will let me borrow his car, I'm sure." Emma's body language gave him no reason for encouragement.

"Fin, I told you on day one that we were only friends," she reminded him.

"Is someone else taking you out?" His question and the insecurity trapped in his voice caused her to chuckle.

"Pray tell, who in our school would ever see fit to ask me out?" Fin shrugged his shoulders.

"If they wouldn't, then they're blind." Emma looked up at him and saw the pain her indifference was causing him. She kissed the tips of her fingers and brought them up to his lips. He responded by first kissing, then running the tip of his tongue over her finger tips. She sighed.

"You don't know where those fingers have been," she chided.

"It doesn't matter…they're yours." Her eyes dropped to the ground.

"I'll ask my mother. If she has no problem with it, then we'll do something. If she says no…then it's no. I can't risk any more battle royals with her."

"That's fair enough," he answered, before kissing the crown of her head a final time.

8

It was Friday morning and Emma knew she could not delay the question of her date with Fin any longer. She decided to ask her parents' permission over the breakfast table. Descending the stairs, she picked up on her sister's voice in the next room. She hoped her father might put in a good word for Fin after meeting him earlier in the week. There was little or no conversation on this morning, which somehow made her task seem even more difficult.

"Momma, Daddy, I need to ask your permission about something," she said meekly. Her parents both tilted their eyes up from their plates. "I've been asked out on a date tonight and I'd like to get your okay on it," she stated tentatively.

"Who'd ask you out?" blurted her sister. Harriet Corman stared across the table at Emma.

"Who, pray tell, asked you?" asked the woman.

"Fin Cromwell," Emma answered.

"Absolutely not," spat out her mother. "I'd be worried sick from the moment you left until the moment you got home…if you got home at all." Becky burst into a gale of laughter.

"Why would anyone want to go out with him? He's ugly and a greaser," called out the thirteen year old. Harriet continued to shake her head in the negative.

"We had this conversation the other day. The people you associate with are very important in molding what kind of young adult you become." Emma threw back her head in frustration.

"Daddy, please help me here," she implored. The man put down his fork and locked eyes with his daughter. It was clear to Emma that he was internally debating the question at hand.

"Harriet, we were just talking last night about the improvement in Emma's temperament over the last few days. I don't think it is mere coincidence that this change has come since she began her friendship with this boy. I've met and spoken to him and, while he is intimidating to the eye, he seems to have a genuine fondness for her. For this reason, I don't think we should stand in her way."

"Thank you, Daddy." Harriet let out a groan to express her disproval.

"All right, Bertrand, have it your way. Just don't expect me to go down to the county morgue with you to identify the body," she warned.

Emma sent a steady stream of smiles across the room to her father on this morning. Leaving the kitchen she made a point of planting a kiss on his cheek before scurrying up the stairs to her bedroom. She was in the final stages of pinning up her hair when Becky's face materialized in her doorway.

"Is that really the best you can do? My God, Fin Cromwell is a freak. How can you even stand being seen out with him?" questioned Becky. Emma turned slowly toward her sister.

"So help me, if you call Fin a freak one more time, I'll put your face through the wall." Becky responded with a pouty smile.

"You're so pathetic," her sister replied before disappearing down the hall.

When Emma entered Public Speaking class that morning she was quick to see Fin at his desk hunched over his notes. After shooting her a brief glance, his eyes returned to his five by seven inch note cards. He appeared on edge. Passing by his desk, she placed a hand on his shoulder and squeezed.

"Relax, you're going to do fine," she whispered down to him. Mrs. Bibber brought the class to order by announcing that they would hear the final two students' introductions this morning before heading into the next class assignment. She then called Joanne Taggart to the front of the class to speak. The Taggart girl's hands shook noticeably as she began her introduction in a lifeless, monotone fashion, her eyes never leaving her note cards. After plodding through a seemingly endless list of awards and accomplishments she announced her guest speaker. It was Peggy Fleming. The second syllable of the skater's last name was barely out of her mouth when Miss Taggart sped by Emma and rushed to the relative protection of her desk at the back of the room. Always sensitive to the feelings of her students, Mrs. Bibber proceeded to diplomatically point out the flaws in the introduction. Among the problems was the lack of sufficient eye contact, the need for more personal information and the need to lengthen the address. It had only covered one and a half minutes.

"It's always good to follow a train wreck. It makes you look better than you really are," Emma whispered to Fin. He continued to look quite nervous. "Pretend that you're only talking to me," she encouraged. Fin's name was called and he made his way up to the lectern. Emma could not help thinking that he looked somewhat ridiculous as he towered over the prop. He looked up from his notes and out to the class.

"Few people in Hollywood would not agree that our guest tonight is one of the most beautiful women in the entertainment industry," stated Fin to his classmates. Emma sat back and watched as her friend parroted her words. For the next ninety seconds Fin managed to keep his delivery smooth and tight as he threw out the names of movie icons and blockbuster motion pictures. A deathly quiet had fallen over the classroom as many there, Mrs. Bibber included, could not believe their eyes and ears. He gained confidence as he moved deeper and deeper into the introduction. Emma held her breath as Fin moved toward his close. She glanced up at the clock and saw he was going to run a few seconds short. Fin, too, glanced up at the time and saw he could run just short.

"To her family and closest friends…she is Natasha. By the way, I am proud to be able to call myself one of Natasha's close friends," he added. Emma's eyes widened as she recognized one of the lines they used while clowning around at Fin's house. She realized he was padding his speech in order not to come up short on time. But for the rest of you, ladies and gentlemen, she will forever be…Miss Natalie Wood," concluded Fin. Mrs. Bibber pressed down on her stop watch and smiled.

"Very good use of dramatic pause," observed the teacher. Fin nodded his head in acceptance of the compliment and walked back to his desk. He glanced over at Emma. She silently mouthed the words, "You were great".

Ten minutes before the end of class, Mrs. Bibber called each of the students up to her desk and confidentially gave them their grades. After learning of her 'A' Emma carefully scrutinized Fin's expression as he leaned over their teacher's shoulder and eyed his grade. Poker faced, he nodded his head and returned to his desk. Upon dismissal she cornered him just outside the classroom door and demanded to know what mark he had received.

"I got an 'A-'," he answered with a shrug of the shoulders.

"That's good," came back Emma, stunned at the lack of emotion from her friend. His homely face broke into a wide grin.

"No, that's damn good!" he quickly replied.

9

It was shortly before seven o'clock when the bell rang at the Corman house, sending Emma racing to the front door. Forever understated, she wore a purple, pleated dress and a white blouse. Outside on the porch stood Fin, dressed in a clean pair of slacks, dress shirt and a heavy Aran sweater. He ducked his head through the doorway and followed his friend into the kitchen. The rest of the Corman family were seated in the living room in front of the television. Mr. Corman rose to his feet and joined Emma and Fin. He shook the seventeen year old's hand and remarked how it was good to see him dry and not dripping wet. Through the exchange of pleasantries, Harriet remained in her living room chair, her eyes glued on the tall stranger.

"I want Emma home by eleven," she ordered from the next room. Fin nodded that he understood and smiled back at her. "What do you plan on doing on this so-called date?" Harriet asked. Fin stepped around Mr. Corman and walked to the edge of the living room. The opening theme to *The Lawrence Welk Show* was sounding from the television.

"My dad gave me an advance on some work I'll be doing for him next week. I'm going to take Emma out to a restaurant and then we're going down to Nubble Light. I think I'm the only guy in the world who has never seen Nubble Light."

"Maybe not the world, but certainly North America," joked Mr. Corman, stepping forward to rescue his daughter's date from the interrogation. He nudged Fin away from the living room and back into the kitchen.

"Your reputation precedes you, Mr. Cromwell," called out Harriet from her chair. "And whatever you do, don't take that as a compliment." Fin placed his massive hand on Emma's shoulder and guided her toward the door. Mr. Corman escorted the couple out to the car, a Chevrolet Biscayne. Reaching the vehicle, he slipped a five dollar bill into his daughter's hand and warned the teenagers of the importance of honoring his wife's curfew. They agreed to comply with Harriet's mandate and immediately motored their way away from the house.

When the couple reached Main Street, Emma asked Fin to pull over. He brought the car to a stop in front of the Littlefield Agency, a real estate office, and turned off the Biscayne's engine.

"I don't want you dragging me to some restaurant until I've given my approval. Besides, I know the area a heck of a lot better than you," she reasoned. He nodded in agreement. In truth, Emma was determined to dictate where the two would appear in public. She was not proud of the fact that she was reluctant to be seen in certain public places with Fin. She could not bear the idea of running into people from school in his company in any formal or even semi-formal setting. It was the thought of people laughing at her behind her back that brought out these feelings.

"My dad suggested going to the Glen Mor Restaurant up at Shopper's Village," he suggested.

"No," she answered immediately. It was not even a question of whether they would run into people from Kennebunk High there, just how many?

"The Kennebunk Inn?"

"No."

"Howard Johnson's?"

"Which one?"

"The one by the turnpike."

"No."

"How about the one down in Wells?" Emma pondered his suggestion for a moment. That was probably far enough away to not have any familiar faces, she thought.

"Okay, I'm in favor of that," she relented. Fin breathed a sigh of relief and turned the ignition key. He eased the Chevy out from the curb and headed it southward toward Wells.

The Howard Johnson's Restaurant was only half full when they arrived. The flow of tourists in southern Maine had slowed to a trickle and this resulted in a return to normalcy for local residents. Emma and Fin were ushered to a large table at the back wall of the building, which afforded them a distant view of the Atlantic Ocean. Emma glanced around the dining room and was relieved to see no familiar faces.

"How far away from the ocean would you guess we are?" Fin asked. His question caught Emma sipping on her water.

"Well, seeing that we're a stone's throw from the top of Mile Road and it ends at the ocean then my guess would be one mile," she answered. He shook his head knowingly.

"Now that's why you're the class genius and I'm the class dope."

"You're no dope. Dope's do not get an A- in Public Speaking class." He shrugged his shoulders and accepted her compliment.

"A lot had to do with Kennebunk High's girl genius who studied with me and made me practice," he admitted.

"Whitney Crowninshield is Kennebunk High's girl genius.

Intellectually, I'm sloppy seconds."

"Don't run yourself down. You're sloppy seconds to no one in any department. Oh, and by the way, you look beautiful tonight," he added. She peered across the table and thought how wonderful these words would sound if they came from Keith Gorman. She briefly closed her eyes and pretended they did come from Keith. "Has Whitney and her butch friend that sits behind you backed off from all that shit they were pulling on you?"

"Yes, totally," replied Emma. "Oh, I'm still getting the evil eye from Whitney. I'll catch her staring over at me sometimes and I know she's trying to come up with some nasty plot to do me in. But thankfully, I have this wonderful guy in my life now."

"I'm glad you know that. No one's going to pull any of that crap on you anymore as long as I'm around," vowed Fin. Emma was about to respond, but was interrupted by their waitress. She handed them menus and took orders for their beverages. While perusing the menu, Emma tossed Fin a question. Her tone was serious.

"You wouldn't ever turn your back on me and let things go back to what they were before, would you?" He looked up from his menu. There was a certain needy quality to her tone of voice.

"Emma, all I ask in return is your friendship and times like this, when I don't have to share you with anyone else."

"What if Whitney came on to you and told you how great you were? I've seen her turn guys into pathetic clowns and that was right in public with other people watching. God knows what she could do to a boy if she got him alone when his pride wasn't at stake."

"I would never turn my back on you. That's a promise."

"So you're admitting that she could wrap you around her little finger. Is that right?" He shook his head in frustration and glanced out the window toward the ocean. The sky was dark, but the house lights illuminating the oceanfront homes were quite visible. "She's much prettier than me."

"She's prettier only because she makes herself up every morning like she was a movie star and probably pays a fortune to have her hair done every week. She also dresses to kill with her short skirts and everything. You're pretty with barely any makeup at all and normal clothes. I've seen you with your hair down and you looked great," he confessed.

"You saw my hair down the night you saved my life." Emma whispered. He shook his head in amazement.

"I still can't believe you were going to do that and I stopped you. It really makes me feel like I'm worth something," he admitted.

The dinner portion of their date went smoothly. They both had the clam strips dinner. Fin opted for a dish of coffee ice cream for dessert while Emma asked for a hot fudge sundae. When the dessert dishes were cleared they ordered two cups of coffee to prolong the meal. The conversation flowed effortlessly throughout their time at the restaurant. It was shortly after nine o'clock when they left Howard Johnson's and agreed they had time for a quick visit to Nubble Light. Emma directed Fin to take the shore road from Ogunquit to York and they slowly snaked their way along the winding, undulating roadway toward their destination. Arriving in the village at Short Sands, she guided Fin through a few darkened neighborhoods until they arrived at the neck of land overlooking the lighthouse. The tide was high and it roared around the small island just off shore that was home to the single family residence and lighthouse. The sound of the sea thundering just twenty feet away lured the teenagers from the car. The beacon from the tower partly illuminated the foaming sea and drew Fin closer to the ocean's edge. When Emma became hesitant to follow he returned to her side, scooped her up in his arms, and carried her closer to the action of the waves. There was a fresh breeze by the water that blew Fin's hair wildly about his face. She half expected him to carry her down to the edge of the rocks and dangle her over the pounding sea water. He did not. He had many shortcomings, but immaturity was not one of them, she thought. Following five minutes on the rocks he carried her back up to the parking lot. He pressed his lips to her hair and attempted to bring them down to her mouth. In response, she struggled in his arms and he placed her down.

Bertrand and Harriet Corman sat across the room from their television set as *The Dean Martin Show* wound down toward its conclusion. From upstairs in Becky's room, the sound of the Rolling Stones made its way through her walls and door and provided unwelcome background music. Harriet glanced up at a wall clock and dramatically threw her head back against the cushion of her chair.

"I knew this was going to happen," she muttered. "I won't say I told you so...but I told you so," she moaned. Looking anxious, her husband rose from the couch and made his way to the front of the house. He split open the Venetian blinds and gazed outside. He turned back to his wife.

"They're saying goodnight out on the porch," he reported back to her. She frowned and turned her attention back to the television.

Out on the porch, Emma attempted to bring what had been an enjoyable night out of the house to its awkward conclusion. She had been honest with Fin from the beginning and now she sensed he wanted her to kiss him goodnight. She took a seat on one of the porch chairs and pretended to search for a key. He responded by dropping to his knees. The hem of her skirt reached down just above the knee. This prompted him to begin kissing the surface of her knees, one and then the other. This went on for ten seconds before he spoke.

"I love you, Emmy," he whispered up to her. She became flustered.

"The people living across the street can see you," she advised him.

"I don't care. I love you."

"Fin, you mustn't. I told you on day one that you were my friend, not my boyfriend. You mustn't do this to yourself," she cautioned him.

"I have no control over this. It's what I feel," he confessed. She ran her fingers over his hair and scrambled up from the chair. He remained kneeling while she inserted her key in the door.

"Thank you, Fin. Thank you for a wonderful evening. Thank you for everything," she said hurriedly before vanishing into the house.

Emma was peppered with questions about her date by her father while she peeled off her coat. When she revealed the restaurant they had visited, her mother commented on the distance they had travelled just to dine out. Emma opted to withhold the real reason for choosing the Howard Johnson's in Wells and instead reminded her parents it was directly en route to Nubble Light. She retired to her room after the eleven o'clock news and was lying under her blankets well before midnight. Staring up at the plastered ceiling, she considered the drama playing out in her life: in just over a week she had taken possession of the most feared boy in the school. She had witnessed the conquest of the opposite sex in movies, on television, in books and most certainly in real life over and over again. However, she had never envisioned herself taking possession of a male to the degree she most certainly had taken Fin Cromwell. She rolled onto her side. It was troubling that she would have to balance an on-going friendship with Fin against his desire to grow closer to her. She would have to hold him at bay romantically while giving him just enough incentive to continue his pursuit. She knew her mental and even physical well-being depended on this delicate balance. The image of Fin kneeling in front of her on the porch flashed into her head and she felt sorry for him. For nearly two months Whitney had held her hostage and had driven her to the brink. Now she was free of Whitney's wrath and she held Fin hostage. Emma felt a small measure of guilt come over her but she dismissed it. It was nothing compared to the fear and anxiety before the arrival of Fin Cromwell into her life.

10

Emma entered homeroom on Monday morning to the sound of talk of the annual egg fight. It was tradition on Halloween night to have teenagers from Kennebunk and Kennebunkport line up on opposite sides of the lower village bridge separating the townships and fling eggs at each other. With Halloween only two days away, preparation on both sides was underway. Emma had not spoken to Fin since Friday night and she hoped to have a word with him before class. Unfortunately, he arrived in homeroom with the bell and went directly to his desk. Following the morning Pledge of Allegiance and a list of announcements, the bell sounded for first class and she scooted up to her friend's desk.

"Same time, same place for lunch?" she asked.

"Yeah, same place," he answered listlessly. She pinched his cheek and waited for a reaction. He barely raised his eyes from the desk. Fin's unresponsiveness was not lost on her and she found herself pushing it to the back of her mind throughout her morning classes. At the close of English class, she was asked to stay behind and clarify two issues in a short story she had submitted. It caused her to reach the cafeteria line late. She was disappointed to see that Fin had not waited for her. She slowly plodded forward until she finally reached the cash register. With tray in hand she hurried into the gym and spotted Fin seated at their familiar table in the company of Gloria Frey, Barbara Yager and two other girls she did not know by name. Emma pulled out a chair two seats away from Fin and started on her lunch. When Barbara finished a story concerning her parent's tradition of decorating for Halloween, Fin looked down the table at Emma and raised his eyebrows. This minute gesture brought her a small measure of relief. For the remainder of the lunch period, the girls at the table chattered and Fin listened. About halfway through her meal Emma's eyes locked onto the beautiful face of Whitney Crowninshield. It appeared that her attention was not focused on her own table but at what was unfolding at Emma and Fin's. She felt a sudden knot of anxiety form in her stomach. It was not until the bell sounded for the next period that those seated at the table rose and moved off. Again, the girls from the table continued to mill around Fin, affording Emma no opportunity to speak with him privately.

Fin shuffled back into homeroom only seconds before Mr. Foster called it to order. He made no eye contact with Emma and carried no books with him. Meanwhile, ever observant, Whitney's blue eyes scanned back and forth between Emma and her male protector. Fin was on his feet at the sound of the dismissal bell and walking toward the door. Emma grabbed her armful of books and started up the aisle in pursuit. However, at the front of the row she was headed off by Whitney.

"Emma, is there any chance you could spare a minute or two of your time to help me with something from chemistry?" asked Whitney behind a fabricated smile. Flustered, Emma tried to elbow her way past the girl.

"I promise to help you tomorrow," she answered impatiently. The blonde stepped sideways and blocked her path.

"But, I have this creepy feeling we're going to get quizzed on it tomorrow, so tomorrow will be too late," she argued. Frustrated, Emma froze in her tracks and grew misty eyed.

"Miss Crowninshield, it appears Miss Corman is not in a position to help you at the moment. Please step aside," ordered Mr. Foster. Whitney hesitated for a brief moment before making way for her enemy to pass. With five text books cradled in her arms, Emma hustled from homeroom and dashed down the hall towards the stairwell. Her exodus from the building was further delayed by a swarm of freshmen loitering by the doorway. Exiting the front door she caught sight of Fin at the far end of the front lawn. She called out to him but the sound of vehicular traffic on the road drowned out her voice. Laboring under the weight of five books, she struggled to close the distance between her and her friend. She was already breathing heavily when she reached the street. She looked up the road and saw that Fin was further away from her now than when she left the building. At the moment, the street was free of traffic.

"Fin, please," she hollered at the top of her lungs. The boy stopped in his tracks and turned around. She waved one hand in the air and clumsily ran in his direction. He responded by walking back toward her. When they finally reached one another, Emma found the need to lean her head on his chest to grab her breath. "I needed to speak to you and we never had a chance back at school. I have this terrible feeling you're mad at me and I needed to patch things up," she muttered, still out of breath.

"Please don't feel that way. We're good," he replied. He turned from her and attempted to continue on his way.

"Walk with me, Fin, so we can talk," she pleaded. He stared up the road and nodded yes. "It's important to me to be your friend. You mean a lot to me," she explained.

"Emmy, I know our friendship means a lot to you and you don't have to worry. I won't let anyone bother you at school or anywhere else. That's a promise." Struggling to keep up with the boy's long strides she started to lose control of her books. "Here, let me carry some of those," he insisted. He snatched up four of the text books from her and cradled them in one hand. He was not making eye contact with her as they moved up Fletcher Street. A full thirty seconds passed in silence before he decided to unburden himself. "I made a perfect fool of myself last Friday out on your porch. I'm embarrassed and ashamed."

"Fin, you're not a fool and you have nothing to be embarrassed about," consoled Emma. He stopped and looked down at her.

"It's just that I've never felt anything like the way I feel towards you. You're in my head all the time and when you push me away and don't want me even touching you, it hurts wicked," he confessed. "No girl's ever done this to me before and I'm having a hard time dealing with it," he continued. Emma closed the distance between them and rested her head on his arm. She was unsure of how to console him. "My God, I knelt down in front of you like a perfect idiot. It's just that all these feelings going through me are stronger than my own willpower." Still lost for words, Emma remained quiet while her friend further unmasked his affection for her. His soul stripped and exposed, they continued up the road toward her neighborhood. "I got a part-time job last weekend. I start on Friday night."

"Where?"

"At the Glen Mor Restaurant. I'm just going to be washing dishes and it's only on Friday and Saturday nights," he explained.

"You didn't get it just to pay your father back for our date, did you?"

"No, I told you I was going to go out looking for a job even before we went out," he reminded her.

"I guess that means we won't be going out on any more dates?" Fin dropped his eyes to the ground and shrugged his shoulders. They reached Mechanic Street and the conversation was replaced by an uncomfortable quiet. Fin handed Emma her text books and lowered his head. She plucked them from his hands and placed them on the ground. An instant later she pushed Fin toward a small crop of trees by the corner. "Kneel down, you're too tall," she commanded as they disappeared from the view of passers by and traffic. Surprised, confused and a little overwhelmed, he dropped to his knees. Emma proceeded to cup his face with her hands and kiss him on the mouth. He returned the kiss and threw his arms around her slender waist. "I won't have us drifting apart. You're mine, Fin Cromwell. I have your number and I'm not going to let you walk away from me. Do you understand?" He nodded his head yes and tried to return his mouth to her lips. She pushed him back. "Let's not try to get too much of a good thing," she insisted. He laughed and rose to his feet. "Can we study at your house or would you rather go back to the library?"

"We can use my house. I'm sure my dad wouldn't mind."

11

Emma and Fin remained a couple through the last months of 1973. She managed to keep their relationship mostly platonic, limiting romantic activity to kissing and light making-out sessions. About a week and a half before Christmas, Emma was invited to the Cromwell house for dinner. In addition to Emma, the Cromwell men invited Eli's girlfriend, Yvonne LaVallee, for the Sunday night get-together. In the weeks leading up to the Christmas holiday, Emma had learned of Eli's cooking talents. On one occasion, she had brought home a dozen homemade blueberry muffins to her mother that drew raves from the rest of the family. Little did she realize that this chance meeting with Yvonne LaVallee would transform her physicality for the rest of her life.

On this night, Eli served his guests roast duck. This was a treat for Emma, who had never eaten this particular delicacy. Mr. Cromwell had spent part of Saturday and all of Sunday slowly roasting the meat and potatoes and continued to field compliments well after the table had been cleared. Emma had noticed Yvonne staring intently at her from across the table on more than one occasion but did not question her on it. For most of the late afternoon and evening, the older couple dominated the conversation. Finally, Yvonne peered across the kitchen table at Emma and shed some light on her fixation with the sixteen year old.

"Do you have any idea what I could do with that face if you gave me the opportunity?" remarked the redheaded woman. Emma reacted with a confused look. "Darling, I throw house parties and sell cosmetics for a living. I'm just thinking how amazing you would look with some foundation and some work to accentuate those eyes," she added. Emma blushed. "I have a box of samples out in the car. Would you let me try a few things on you? If you don't like what you see then you can just wash it off," the woman explained. Emma turned to Fin and he encouraged her to take Yvonne up on her offer. The females disappeared from the kitchen, first out to the woman's car and then into Eli's bedroom. For the next thirty minutes the sound of female voices and laughter bled through the walls until Yvonne appeared in the kitchen doorway and announced Emma's return. Fin was seated at the table, his huge hand encircling a bottle of Royal Crown Cola, when his eyes focused on his friend as she slowly entered the room. Her long hair cascaded down over her shoulders and framed a face that was familiar to but vaguely different from the one he had grown to know over the last two months. He stared at Emma for the next few seconds in something akin to a trance. The girl's transformation was most noticeable in her eyes and mouth. Yvonne's use of liner, shadow and mascara illuminated the teenager's brown eyes as she shifted her glance between Fin and his father. She separated her lips, outlined in a subdued shade of red that made them shapelier and accentuated her white teeth.

"My word, it's like having Sophia Loren in the house," exclaimed Eli, while vaulting from his chair and crossing the room for a closer look at the sixteen year old. For the next half an hour, the topic of conversation went back and forth between Yvonne's talent as a beautician and the beautiful swan that had come to life on this evening. During this discussion, Emma found her eyes returning to the kitchen cabinet mirror across the room. It was almost as if a lovely stranger had taken possession of her body, she thought. When the evening grew late and the neighborhood deathly quiet, the teenagers excused themselves from the get-together. Following a round of hugs, during which Fin and Emma waived off a ride back to Mechanic Street, they set off across town on foot. A small storm had blown through southern Maine two days earlier and the sides of Friend Street and Route 1 were lined with plowed snow.

The banks of the Mousam River were encrusted with ice on this night as the frigid water meandered past and snaked its way toward the Atlantic. Halfway across the bridge, Emma glanced up and eyed Fin staring down at her.

"Stop staring at me," she commanded while pushing him away. He laughed and pulled her back into a playful embrace.

"I can't help it. You're such a fox with your hair down like that and your big eyes just looking back at me. I always thought you were really pretty and special but now it's almost like you're this angel sent down from heaven to be with me. I'm just blown away," he conceded.

"I'm nothing special," she answered with a measure of false modesty.

"Emmy, you've always been special to me. Maybe to other people you were nothing special, but to me there was never a second you weren't special. I mean, that's going to change now when people at school and in town see you. You're going to blow people away." Fin's words and flattery set Emma's thoughts into an upward spiral as she imagined the looks on people's faces when she returned to Kennebunk High the next morning. She knew the new Emma Corman would not surpass her nemesis, Whitney, but was sure she could begin walking with confidence in her company. Her mind continued to race as she envisioned the reactions from other students and teachers. She found herself eager to return home and stare long and hard at herself in the bedroom mirror. She glanced down at the small bag of cosmetics she carried home, compliments of Yvonne LaVallee. She loved her life at this moment in time. Then, to add even more to the moment, her thoughts went to Keith Gorman, the boy she had fantasized over since junior high. She was confident that he too would notice the new girl in school in the person of Emma Corman. She imagined herself approaching him from the opposite end of the school hallway with no one else within sight. She would throw her long hair back over her shoulders and lock her piercing, brown eyes on him. She would and could render him helpless, she thought. Fin raised his voice and she was torn from her thoughts.

"Are you even listening to a word I'm saying?" he asked with a degree of frustration. She refocused her eyes and attention back on him.

"Oh, I'm sorry, what did you say?"

"I asked you if your family had anything special planned for Christmas Eve?" She assembled her thoughts and pushed Keith Gorman back to a secret compartment in her mind.

"Not that I'm aware of. We aren't a religious family, so it's just the exchanging of presents and the like. Why do you ask?" Fin shrugged his shoulders.

"My dad and Yvonne might have plans. There's a gathering of her family and friends somewhere and he's only going to go if I won't be alone," he explained. "If you guys don't have anything special planned then I thought you and me could find something to do together. I don't want my dad to stay home just because he doesn't want me to be alone on Christmas Eve." Emma paused for a moment before speaking.

"I don't think my parents would be too keen on not having me home the night before Christmas. What if I ask them if it's all right if you come to dinner that night?" Fin's eyes grew wider and he appeared apprehensive.

"Wow! Are you sure?" She shrugged her shoulders.

"I can't have my sardine factory boy sitting by himself on Christmas Eve," she explained whimsically.

Emma and Fin reached the front door of her house and there came a brief, uneasy pause in the conversation. Before she could open her mouth Fin dropped to his knees and pulled her body against his own. She went to speak but stopped when he lifted her gloved hands to his face and showered them with kisses. If there had ever been any doubts in her mind concerning this young man's feelings for her, they were now completely obliterated. Fin Cromwell adored her. She was sure of this. The boy that had waded out into the river and saved her from herself, the boy who had let it be known that no one was to torment her now or in the future, was now completely under her control. It occurred to her that as a young female, she had arrived in time with the great women in literature she had read about. She would and could be Fitzgerald's Daisy Buchanan, Phillip Roth's Brenda Patimpkin or Jack Kerouac's Maggie Cassidy. The alpha male kneeling at her feet was irrefutable evidence of this. Glancing down at Fin, she knew there was nothing he would not do for her. In his present state of mind, a state born of his desire to please her, he would jump off the highest bridge or battle the fiercest foe if asked to do so by her.

"Stand up, Fin, and say good-night," she said in a soft voice. He continued to stare straight ahead into her torso. Separating her hands and leaning forward he kissed the fabric of her coat, not at breast or waist level but at vaginal level. The light pressure exerted by his lips against her coat sent a wave of erotic reaction through her. Emma reached down and lifted his head from under the chin. She kissed him on the mouth and backed away.

"Emmy, I love you more than anyone or anything I've ever known," he confessed quietly.

"I know you do," she answered before vanishing behind the door.

Emma moved quickly toward the stairs in an attempt to retire for the night before detection, but was confronted by her mother halfway to the second floor.

"What have you done to yourself?" exploded Harriet Corman from the doorway to the kitchen. Emma froze in her tracks. From the living room came the sound of footsteps headed in their direction. "You're painted up like some Biddeford trollop and why is your hair all over your shoulders like you've been sharing some man's bed?" Emma whirled around and confronted her mother.

"You know where I was. I was having dinner with Fin and his father and his father's girlfriend. She's a beautician and she sells cosmetics. She gave me a makeover."

"Makeover for what, an evening with the Seventh Fleet?" bellowed the woman. The remainder of the family made their way into the hallway and got their first glimpse of the new Emma. Her father stepped forward, placing a hand on his wife's shoulder in an attempt to quiet her. Becky moved up to the bannister to afford herself a better look at her older sister.

"You look idiotic and cheap," spat out Becky.

"I think the title of family idiot is already taken," countered Emma.

"I want you to wash that garbage off of your face before you come downstairs to watch television," ordered her mother.

"If I wash it off it's just going back on tomorrow morning," she shot back. "And by the way, I won't be coming down tonight," she added before climbing the stairs and barricading herself in her room.

Emma was seated in front of her bedroom mirror when a series of gentle raps came on the door. She paused for a few seconds before responding to the interruption.

"What is it?" she asked.

"May I come in?" It was her father.

"Yes, Daddy, you can come in." The door swung in slowly and Bertrand Corman appeared in the doorway holding two bottles of soda. He extended one to his daughter and sat down on the edge of her bed. The caps had already been removed. "If you're up here to talk me out of wearing makeup, then you're wasting your time," she informed him. He shook his head no and took a swig from his bottle of Moxie.

"I'm up here to tell you how good you look," he answered in his typical soft-spoken manner. "I've spoken to your mother. She's had time to calm down. Emma, you have to remember that, to her, you're just a little girl and not the budding young woman the rest of the world sees. Her kids are everything to her and, unfortunately, she sees them getting closer and closer to flying from the nest." Her father's words softened her mood and she joined her dad seated at the edge of her bed.

"So you think I look good?" The man raised his eyebrows and nodded his head in an agreeable manner.

"I think back to the apprehension we all had when you first began associating with Fin and realize how wrong we were. I also remember the funk you were in before he showed up and how you have come full circle since. Your mother and I were really worried about you not that long ago, the moodiness and the isolation, but now we see all this improvement. It can't be a total coincidence; part of the credit has to go to Fin. Even your mother has had to concede that, albeit begrudgingly." Emma leaned her head sideways onto her father's shoulder.

"This might be a good time to bring up something," she said. Her father nodded her to continue. "When Fin walked me home tonight he mentioned the fact that he would probably be alone on Christmas Eve. Daddy, is there any chance we could invite him over to have supper with us?" Her father answered with a quizzical expression.

"If nothing else, your timing is impeccable. I'll speak to your mother. I'm sure it will be okay."

It was ten-thirty before Emma finally slid under her bed covers and attempted to go to sleep. Relaxation did not come easy. Instead, her head was alive with the thoughts of boys and the reaction she expected the following Monday at school. Her thoughts wandered to the image of Fin humbling himself on the porch. His actions further reinforced her growing self confidence and feelings of self worth but were accompanied by a sense of sadness. It was not long before her mind moved to more pleasant things like Keith Gorman. She was incredibly curious to see how he would react to the new Emma. So on this Sunday night, with the image of Keith Gorman plastered across her thoughts, she pleasured herself under the covers of the bed and almost breathlessly anticipated the following morning.

Emma's arrival and morning at Kennebunk High School the following day was triumphant. Escorted by Fin from home to the doorway of the school, her entrance into homeroom caused a chorus of gasps and murmurs. No reaction was more satisfying than the scowl that formed on Whitney's face when she first set eyes on Emma. Mr. Foster stopped her by his desk at the front of the room and inquired into her transformation. At lunch she was treated like a rock star with the half dozen girls who now frequented Emma and Fin's table showering her with questions, compliments and adulation. None of this went unnoticed by Whitney Crowninshield and her circle of friends. If there was any letdown on this day, it came with the compliments of Keith Gorman. Emma and Keith's paths did not cross until late morning just before lunch. Just as in her earlier daydream, they passed in the hallway. However, unlike in the dream, there were distractions in the form of classmates moving about them. Nevertheless, they did walk by each other on the second floor and Keith's eyes were captured taking in the image of the new Emma. On locking eyes with the handsome junior, she morphed her glance into a seductive gaze. It proved all for naught. The look that would have literally prostrated Fin Cromwell merely held Keith's eyes for the briefest of moments before he glanced away and moved on.

12

Harriet Corman scurried around the kitchen, flitting from stove to counter top, as the family prepared for their dinner guest. In the nearby living room, the Christmas tree was illuminated and stood above a pile of beautifully wrapped presents. It was Monday night, Christmas landing on a Tuesday in 1973. Outside it was lightly snowing. The forecast from Channel 8 in Poland Spring called for anywhere from three to six inches in the next twelve hours, assuring southern Maine of a white Christmas. It was a few minutes short of six o'clock when Bertrand meandered out of the living room and offered to help his wife with the preparation.

"Just go back to what you were doing. I'm fine," she assured him. "I just hope our guest isn't late and the chicken dries up," she added. He wandered over to the stove and gazed down into a pot of potatoes. "I'm sure he'll go home and tell his father how mistreated he was…having to settle for chicken instead of roast duck."

"I sincerely doubt it," replied the man before returning to the living room. A few seconds later, a knock came on the front door, and there came the sound of feet scurrying down the stairs.

"I'll get it," called out Emma as she made her way to the front of the house. Unlocking the door, she swung it in to see Fin towering above her, snow blanketing his hair and the shoulders of his coat. She stepped back and ushered him into the warm house. Reaching down, he plucked a large, canvas bag from the porch floor and shuffled inside. Harriet looked up from a bowl of green beans.

"You didn't walk here, I hope?"

"I'm afraid it's worse than that. I walked to the Glon Mor Restaurant and then I walked here," he informed the room. Mr. Corman rose to his feet and started toward their guest. "I hope those aren't all presents for us because we didn't get you anything," Mrs. Corman announced. Fin recoiled slightly from the woman's frankness.

"Actually, there's something in here for Emmy, but no one else. Most everything else is for my dad. I had to hide it at work because he has a bad habit of looking all over the house until he finds his presents. He must think I got him nothing," he explained. Emma sidled up to Fin and took his arm.

"I got you something," she whispered. He affectionately brought his finger down on the tip of her nose and looked at her oddly.

"Oh, Mrs. Corman, I brought the family a bottle of white wine. It's white because I'm hoping you made chicken for supper. It's my favorite." He presented her with the bottle of wine. Surprised by the gesture, Harriet had no reply. Mr. Corman walked up to Fin and shook his hand.

"You'll have to forgive my wife, Fin. She's making us a chicken supper tonight and then she's stuck making a turkey dinner tomorrow. It's left her in a fowl mood," he jested. Emma responded with a polite laugh but the pun was lost on Fin and Harriet. Fin reached down into the canvas bag and presented Emma with her gift. It was neatly wrapped.

"No opening your present until Christmas...when I'm not here to see the disappointment on your face," declared Fin. Emma skipped to the tree and snatched a present from the back wall. She approached her friend wearing a childish grin and extended the gift to him.

"Ignore the ticking and try to be far from the people you love at midnight when you open it," she instructed him. He was about to respond to her instructions when Becky made her entrance downstairs. Her eyes went straight to Fin and she let out an audible sigh.

"That will be enough of that, young lady," warned her father.

The meal went smoothly with compliments to Mrs. Corman for the perfectly mashed potatoes and the moistness of the chicken. The question of whether to allow Becky to share in the wine went to a vote. It was Fin who broke the tie to allow the thirteen year old to sample the wine. Halfway through the meal Mr. Corman asked their guest, in a very serious voice, how things were going with the family sardine business up in Jonesport. It took only a few seconds of reflection for the teenager to see he was the object of a family joke, leading him to glare across the table at Emma in mock anger. By the time the egg nog and a plate of assorted cookies was served, Fin was quite at ease with the family. All the while, Becky, who had brought a copy of Teen Beat Magazine to the table, was ignoring the banter going on around her. Noticing this, Fin subtly began removing the fancy cookies from the edge of Becky's plate and replacing them with plain, shortbread ones. After five minutes of this, the girl began to visibly question her sanity, her eyes darting around the table in confusion, while Fin and the Cormans were hard-pressed to restrain themselves from laughing out loud.

"Hey, what's going on? Why do I only have the crappy cookies?" Becky finally cried out, unleashing a chorus of laughter.

Mr. Corman insisted on driving Fin home to Friend Street on this night. Outside, the snow continued to fall softly, while the temperature edged down toward twenty degrees. Fin was inside saying his good-byes and wishing everyone a Merry Christmas when his host marched dejectedly back into the house.

"It won't start," he called out in exasperation. "It was running fine just this morning and now it won't start," he repeated. Mrs. Corman rushed toward him at the door.

"It has to start. We have to go down and visit my sister tomorrow night. I'm not going without seeing my family on Christmas!" she barked. "Call someone!" she demanded.

"Who am I supposed to call? It's Christmas, for God's sake." He removed his hat and tossed it down on the kitchen counter. Fin looked at Emma and stepped forward.

"First of all, don't worry about me and my getting home. It's no big deal. Second, would you mind if I took a look to see if I can spot something?" Mr. Corman accepted Fin's offer and retrieved his hat from the kitchen. Both men headed outside while Harriet began a fresh rant about her need to visit with her brothers and sisters on Christmas. Five minutes later, Fin reappeared at the front door and went in search of his canvas bag. Emma, Becky and Mrs. Corman stared up at him. "The battery seems to be turning over all right. Every year my dad has to put one or two containers of dry gas in his tank or the gas line freezes. That could be all that is wrong here. I happen to have a couple of containers on me. He'd asked me to pick them up for him. We might as well give it a shot," he declared, racing back outside. It was only a couple of minutes later when Fin came back to the front door and announced the car was running fine. Stepping inside, he scooped up his bag of presents and flashed Emma a smile. Walking to the front door, he cautioned Becky to keep her eyes on her cookies and thanked Mrs. Corman for having him over. Finally, he turned to Emma and stared long and hard at her. She pulled her winter coat down from its hook in the hall and followed him out onto the porch.

"No kneeling down in the snow for me," she cautioned as snow began to collect in her hair. He closed his eyes and threw his head back.

"It almost hurts thinking about everything I would do for you," he confessed.

"On second thought, go ahead and kneel," she said, remembering their height differential. He dropped slowly to his knees, making an impression in the snow accumulated on the porch. She cupped his face with her cold hands and kissed him intensely, her tongue breaking though his lips for the first time and feeling the moistness inside his mouth. "You are so incredibly wonderful," she declared while pulling away from him. He remained on his knees, seemingly content to stay with her under any conditions. "My father's waiting for you," she reminded him as she ducked back into the house.

Bertrand and Harriet sat in the living room after a rather hectic Christmas Eve. The house had grown quiet and the two were taking advantage of the peacefulness. It was during a lull in their conversation that they heard the muted sound of bare feet descending the stairs. A few seconds later Emma appeared in front of the refrigerator and pulled a half gallon bottle of milk out. Both parents beckoned the teenager into the living room. She sat back into a chair a few feet from them and took a sip from her glass of milk.

"I'm glad you prodded us to have Fin over for supper. It was quite enjoyable, in spite of all the drama with the car," confessed her father. Emma smiled over at them sweetly. "Your mother and I were discussing you and Fin just before you came down. "Emma's eyes opened widely at this revelation. "Emma, you do realize how deeply, deeply in love with you this boy is, don't you?" Her face saddened before nodding yes. "Emma, you're a smart girl, a very smart girl. You do know that this cannot end well, right?"

"He is a good friend and I need him in my life right now," she insisted.

"Darling, be real. That boy is as homely as sin and as dumb as a bag of rocks. Now, you know how I hate to admit it when I'm wrong, but I was wrong about Fin. He is a decent boy and he's got a good heart. But leading him on and treating him like a boyfriend will not end well for either of you. It will be a lot easier on him if you end it now and not six months or a year from now."

"He knows he's not my boyfriend."

"Not in his heart, he doesn't," responded her father calmly. "Please, just think about it."

"Fin knows that someday I'll have to walk away from him and he accepts it," reaffirmed Emma before easing out of her chair and making her way from the room.

On Christmas morning, Fin rose before his father and put on the coffee. He waited to open all of his presents but one. He wanted to open Emma's Christmas gift in private. Ripping away the wrapping paper he tore open the flimsy, cardboard box to find a paperweight. He looked down at it and laughed. The words, "Maine Sardines," were inscribed on the side of an ungodly looking, lead sardine paperweight.

Emma was still smarting from her parent's lecture the night before when she descended the stairs, poured herself a cup of coffee and joined her family in the living room. It was a family tradition to open all presents on Christmas morning and 1973 was no exception. She carefully avoided opening Fin's gift for as long as possible but was finally faced with no other options. She felt her parent's peering eyes as she peeled off the brightly colored paper. Her best guess was a large box of chocolates, but the package seemed too heavy. With all of the paper removed, she was staring down at a beautiful pink and white box. She slipped off the cover to find an extensive assortment of exotic soaps from around the world. Each bar of soap was packaged in a unique color and artistic design. It was clear that her gift was expensive and well thought out. Emma smiled weakly back at her parents as they lauded her present. She guiltily remembered finding Fin's gift in an antique shop, discounted and gathering dust on the bargain table.

13

Daylight hours were in short supply and the icy fingers of winter took hold of the southern Maine coast, driving any and all tourists back to their warm inland homes and leaving the frigid Atlantic to massage the abandoned beaches in complete privacy. This is the time of year in Maine when human beings, deprived of the distraction of warm sunlight and endurable water temperatures, turned inward in search of all things unexplored.

A short time after Christmas and at the start of a cold winter, Emma made an interesting discovery in the back pantry of the house. While passing through the small unheated room, her eye spotted something worth investigating. What she picked up on was the corner of the front cover of *Playgirl Magazine.* Apparently, the issue that had set off the Corman household a few months earlier was just the first of a yearly subscription. It seems Mrs. Corman had not called and cancelled the service, but instead elected to merely toss each one out upon delivery. It was on a bitingly cold evening that Emma first smuggled a copy of the magazine under her coat from the pantry and up to her bedroom. Over the next couple of weeks she stole time in her room to read the issue from cover to cover and ogle the photographs of naked men. Over this period, she took to locking her door much of the time and was vigilant to hide the steamy magazine when she was not home. The winter rolled on and it was not long before she snatched up a second Playgirl from the pantry. Whether from the influence of the magazine or from her ongoing invasion into adulthood, she found herself more and more preoccupied with sexual thoughts. On a blustery, March afternoon she specifically asked Fin if it would be all right to study at his house. It was a Wednesday afternoon and the two friends braved a northerly wind and trekked from Kennebunk High School to Friend Street, a distance of over a mile. On arrival, he offered to make Emma some hot chocolate and she accepted.

Fin turned around from the stove and noticed that Emma had made her way out of the kitchen. After pouring them each a cup of the hot beverage, he found her curled up on the living room couch. After handing off the drinks, he collapsed down on the sofa beside her and let out a contented sigh.

"Do you ever read *Playboy Magazine?*" she asked before taking her first sip from the hot chocolate. Fin responded with a surprised smile.

"I look at the pictures when I get to see one. I can't say I read much of it, to be honest."

"I've been looking at *Playgirl Magazines* up in my room for a couple of months now. I told you how Whitney had them delivered to my house a few months ago, just to screw me over. Well, they're still coming and I happen to know where my mother puts them when she's throwing them out. So, I've been sneaking them up to my room when my parents aren't looking," she confessed. Fin laughed and shook his head.

"Now I know who I can go to when I'm confused about something involving sex, which is most of the damn time," he added jokingly.

"I'm hesitant about bringing up anything too heavy about sex in front of the kids at school. You never know who will wind up hearing it. But I trust you, Fin." He reached over and played with her hair.

"Do you masturbate a lot?" she asked. Fin grimaced and shook his head in disbelief. "No, I want you to be very adult about this. I want to talk about sex. The garbage that is our homework can wait."

"I masturbate," he stated firmly.

"Do you masturbate a lot?"

"All guys masturbate a lot. Teenage guys would go totally insane if they didn't do it a lot. Trust me, Emmy, trust me." Emma stared deeply into his eyes, her mind trying to decide on where to proceed with the questioning. "Do you masturbate?" Fin asked, following up on his friend's inquiry.

"Yes, but probably not as much as you guys do." Her mind flashed to the fantasies employed while pleasuring herself and the image of Keith Gorman materialized in her head. This was something she could not share with Fin. "If what they say is true, some of the girls in our class have already had sex," she added matter-of-factly. "Mandy, the bitch who sits behind me in homeroom, she talks like she's had sex. I don't know if Whitney has. If I had to guess I would say she hasn't," she added. Fin continued to play with her hair and just listened. She focused her eyes on him intently. "What do you think about when you masturbate?" she asked with an almost clinical detachment. The question unsettled him and he rocked back against the couch.

"Come on, Emmy, that's real personal," he contended. She reached up and ran her fingers through his hair, mimicking his efforts. She watched as his eyes lost focus and he began entering a trancelike state. Emma never ceased to be surprised at the effect her most simple actions had on her friend. His eyes closed and his breathing grew heavy.

"Tell me, Fin," she coaxed, her voice softened.

"I think about the woman from the *Summer of 42,* Jennifer O'Neill, and I think about you. I think about holding you in my arms. I relive that night when I carried you back home from the river and what you felt like. I think about your arm over my shoulder and talking to you with your face only inches from mine. But, there are other things I think about and they're really, really sexual. I think if you knew what I did in some of those fantasies you'd jump up and run right out the door." Emma interrupted him with a burst of coquettish laughter. He let his head drop down in a show of resignation. "I've told you how much I love you. What and who do you think I think of?"

"Do you do the same things to me that you do to Jennifer O'Neill?" Her question forced a burst of laughter from the boy. "Do you have your way with her at that beach cottage in the movie?" she asked. He rolled his eyes and shook his head in disbelief.

"Actually, I make out with her in the loft," he answered, causing Emma to chuckle.

"You say some of the things are really, really sexual. Try to be more specific," she insisted. He let out a prolonged sigh and shook his head no.

"I'm embarrassed now. You have to understand that when you're in love with someone, there seems to be no limits or boundaries. Whatever your wildest thoughts are, then that's what I'm thinking…and then some." He leaned forward in an attempt to place his lips on hers, but she avoided his advance. Following a momentary lull in the conversation, Emma rose to her feet and seated herself in Fin's lap. He knew she had taken to playing with his head, but was powerless to order her off.

"Fin, you've been honest with me and now I'll be honest with you. I've probably been spending too much time reading about the sexuality of women, but it's too late now. If you're waiting for me to tell you that I'm ready to have intercourse with a young male, and therefore you, then you're in for a disappointment. The last thing I can let happen is for me to get pregnant. No amount of protection is foolproof and I will not tempt fate, at least not until I'm out of college. I also will not, under any circumstances, have an abortion. That, too, is etched in stone. However, I will lend you one of my magazines. There's an article in there on female gratification that I would like you to read. After you've read it I want you to let me know if you're interested in sharing this experience with me."

"You know I will," he shot back. She started to laugh.

"Read it before you commit to anything," she insisted. "A lot of people would think I was being totally selfish if they knew. Naturally, this is our secret," she reminded him. He nodded, indicating he understood. She made a subtle move atop his lap, knowing it would raise the temperature of his blood. She was sure he enjoyed being the hapless victim of her sensual torture as much as she enjoyed being the perpetrator. Lastly, she pressed her lips to his and fulfilled her promise from minutes earlier. Before leaving the house for the frigid walk home, Emma pulled the bookmarked copy of *Playgirl Magazine* from her book satchel and handed it over to Fin with orders to read it before school the next day.

The walk back to Mechanic Street was more playful than usual on this day. With Fin lugging all of her books, Emma's hands were free and she repeatedly slipped them under his coat and shirt, her cold hands making contact with his bare skin and causing him to cry out in agony.

Owing to a wet, slushy morning, Emma and Becky were driven to school on Thursday morning by their father. This meant she was in the building well ahead of Fin, who sloshed the nearly mile and a half from his house to Kennebunk High through the wet, foggy air alone. Emma sat quietly at her desk in homeroom while the air around her hummed with teenage voices. She looked up from her trigonometry notes each time someone entered the room. Finally, with less than five minutes before the opening bell, Fin materialized in the doorway and plodded toward his desk. She followed his movement with her eyes until he finally lifted his gaze from the floor and met her glance. Staring at her blankly for a moment, his face finally broke out in an adoring smile. He mouthed the word, 'yes,' before rotating his body and onto his seat. She felt a pleasurable jolt of energy move through her torso. Although his decision had come as no surprise, his positive gesture set her mind racing with anticipation.

Emma was delayed at dismissal answering a question about the family from Mr. Foster. When she finally made her way out into the hallway she found Fin standing patiently by the bust of Abraham Lincoln. They had barely talked all day, even during lunch. Approaching her towering friend, she handed him her three text books and the two walked toward the stairwell. On the front grounds, the accumulated snow from the long winter wore a glaze of slush. They walked to the main road by way of the driveway and headed in the direction of Fin's house. They were both unusually quiet.

"Fin, if you're having second thoughts, I'll understand. I'll be disappointed but I'll understand," she reassured him. He waived her off immediately.

"Emmy, you know how I feel about you. How could I have second thoughts? I just hope that it's everything you're expecting and I don't screw anything up," he explained. "I'm not exactly Joe Experience." She turned and buried her face into the fabric of his coat.

"I don't deserve you. You are so good to me," she exclaimed. "Here I am doing nothing for you and receiving everything and you're still worried I might be disappointed. I can't believe it."

Emma had only time to remove her coat when Fin reached down and scooped her up into his arms, cradling her much the way he had on the October night at the river. He moved through the house until they reached his bedroom. Just as she had observed from passing his doorway during prior visits, his bed was full sized and appeared extra long.

"The bed has all clean sheets and pillow cases. My dad just put clean covers on both beds last weekend," he assured her. Leaning forward, he placed her gently on the bed. She threw her head back on one pillow and closed her eyes. He sat at the very edge of the mattress and deliberately began the process of removing Emma's clothing. She offered neither assistance nor resistance. Emma found herself becoming more and more relaxed as her clothing was removed garment by garment. For a brief moment she considered the vulnerable position she was in, literally at the mercy of this hulking, young man, only six months out of reform school. Her momentary anxiety was replaced by a sense of calmness. She trusted Fin Cromwell with every fiber of her being, she thought. Fin had just shimmied off her skirt, leaving her lying on the bed in her bra and panties.

"Please leave my bra on. I don't want you to see how flat I am," she asked. He answered her request by kissing one, then the other of the cups. She felt herself grow wet with anticipation. A few seconds passed and she felt his lips make contact with the soft flesh surrounding her pubic area. She was breathing more quickly and deeply now. She completely relaxed her body while he removed her underwear. A second or two later an incredible wave of pleasure came over her and took possession of her body. She moaned involuntarily and seized this moment in time. The author of the magazine piece had not exaggerated or embellished the experience, she thought. It was then that time stood still. She brought her hands down, curling her fingers through and around Fin's hair in a nonverbal expression of her approval.

In the end, Emma needed to kick Fin away as her ecstatic experience became unbearable. She had purged her body of magnificent demons twice in under fifteen minutes. Fin slowly slid down the bed and away from her, his mouth tasting the flesh of her slender legs until he eased himself down onto the floor.

"Do you have any idea how wonderful you are, Fin Cromwell?" she asked as she slowly withdrew from her erotic trance.

"Now you can go to school and tell everybody how cheap and easy I am," he answered. She laughed and scrambled to the bottom of the bed. She craned her neck and brought her lips to his. Fin's mouth tasted of her and this somehow ignited a new and more primal feeling of arousal within her. This new instinct raised a caution flag in her head and she pushed herself away from the boy.

"We have to make sure we're not here when your father gets home from work. Please, Fin, hand me my clothes." He collected her panties, skirt and blouse and handed them to her. His eyes remained largely trained on her practically naked body. Emma dressed hurriedly, a little unnerved by the unconcealed attention her body was receiving from her male friend.

It was shortly before four-thirty when Emma and Fin slipped into their winter jackets and prepared to leave. Passing by his bedroom doorway, Fin stopped in his tracks.

"Wait a minute," he instructed her and headed toward the bathroom. He returned with a can of air freshener and sprayed into the room.

"My room smells of sex," he explained.

"You mean it smells of me," answered Emma. He stared down at her, placing his massive hands on her shoulder.

"I can't have my dad come home and notice that. He's not stupid." She shrugged her shoulders and acted hurt. "Emmy, if it were just me living here, I'd seal the door and windows shut in my room and never come out," he confessed. "That's how much I care for you." Emma blushed and let out a nervous laugh.

"Poor, poor Fin, you really have it bad for me," she sang out while making her way to the front door.

There was still another hour of daylight left as Emma and Fin walked in the direction of the Mousam River. Halfway across the bridge they stopped and watched the water cascade over the dam and churn its way under the Kesslen Shoe Company building. They had just turned up Storer Street when Emma looked up at her friend.

"You must think I am quite the selfish, little brat," she stated. He looked down at her and gave the impression he did not know what she was referring to. "Come on, Fin, don't be coy. You know perfectly well what I'm talking about. You sacrificed yourself to pleasure me and I just stand around thanking you. I promise it will come in time, but right now I'm just not ready for anything that intense," she explained. "God, I can't believe how relaxed I feel!" she added.

"God, I wish I felt relaxed at about this time," he lamented. She shook off her friend's sarcasm and raised a finger to argue a point.

"If the roles had been reversed, then I would have left your house a slut or, as my mother would say, a trollop. You, on the other hand, would have left some kind of stud. As it turned out, I left your house a beloved princess, worshipped by her subjects and you left as one of my adoring serfs." He reached down and harnessed his right hand around her delicate neck.

"Emmy, half the time I don't know what you're talking about, but it sounds so damn cute I just can't get mad at you," he confided. She laughed and tickled him through his winter coat.

Emma and Fin arrived at her house on Mechanic Street just as Becky made her way onto the porch from the opposite direction. The eighth grader tossed Fin a half-hearted wave and disappeared into the house. Emma climbed up onto the porch and spun around to face him. They were at eye level. She leaned forward and gave him an innocent peck on the lips. A smile appeared on her pretty face and she whispered into his ear.

"Your mouth smells of me," she informed him through a coquettish giggle.

"Yes, and it will keep smelling of you until I wash it off…tomorrow morning before school." His response brought a new round of guilty laughter from the girl.

"That is both sweet and gross. Poor Fin, you have it so, so bad for me," she cooed. A moment later she turned and rushed into the house.

14

Emma and Fin's relationship survived the winter of 1973-74 and continued forward into the spring. By springtime Emma had grown accustomed to the admiring glances and flirtatious comments from young males. Understandably, most all of this attention came when she was not in the company of Fin Cromwell. It was April and the first warm day of spring when she was approached by Keith Gorman during study hall and asked if she had been asked by anyone to the junior prom. The question, dropped in after twenty minutes of meaningless chit-chat, appeared to come out of nowhere and left her borderline speechless. At this point she had come to the conclusion that no one outside of Fin would ask her to the prom and, therefore, he would be her escort. This was not to say that he was the only one interested in escorting her. It was more to do with the reluctance of any of the boys to face Fin for the honor. In finally mustering an intelligible reply, Emma informed Keith that she had not been asked to date and was leaving her options open for the right boy. Keith's response to her answer was the word, 'Really...' repeated over and over until she had to insist that he stop. He concluded the conversation by asking her not to commit herself to anyone else until he had the opportunity to ask her to the event. As best she could piece together, he was unable to positively commit himself to attending the prom until the scheduling of a family matter was finalized. He assured her that the chance of him being out of town on the night of the prom was marginal, but Murphy's Law was Murphy's Law.

On the day after Keith Gorman's overture, Emma and Fin were studying together at the library under the portrait of the venerable George Parsons. Fin was busy solving a series of math problems when Emma leaned into him, breaking his concentration.

"I've been meaning to talk to you about the prom," she whispered into his ear. He put down his pencil and looked into her eyes. "I've been giving it a lot of thought and I think we should broaden our horizons a little and maybe make ourselves available to other people...for the prom, that is," she suggested. Her words caught him by surprise and it reflected on his face. "Nothing else between us will change, of course," she added.

"What other people are you talking about?"

"No one in particular...just someone different. We're beginning to act like an old, married couple and we're just too young for that," she explained. Fin shifted his weight on the chair and looked down at her suspiciously.

"Emmy, for me things are simple. If I'm not with you at the prom, then I'm not interested in being there at all." Emma folded her arms impatiently and stared across the room. Her body language spoke volumes. A minute passed and Fin returned to his math problems.

"Everything has to be your way or not at all," she spat out, albeit under her breath. "There's only going to be one junior prom in my life but apparently it's going to have to be carried out under Fin Cromwell's rules and that's final," she added bitterly. He lifted his eyes from the table and threw his pencil in anger, hitting the far wall. More than one head rose to take in the drama unfolding at the far end of the room.

"Go ahead, do what you goddamn please," he declared before rising from the table and storming from the library. Embarrassed by the altercation she returned her attention to her science notes and waited for the tension level in the room to subside. She walked home alone, comforted in the knowledge that the cord tying her to Fin Cromwell had been loosened, if not severed. She was now free to accept Keith Gorman's invitation to attend the prom with him. Her mind wandered at the dinner table as she marveled at how easy her severance from Fin had proven to be. There was no phone call from Fin on this evening, providing further proof that their relationship had changed dramatically.

The cafeteria table was crowded with the usual suspects at lunchtime on the day after Emma and Fin's squabble. Fin was one of the first persons served on this day and this allowed him to lay claim to the chair at the far end of the table. Soon after he was joined by Barbara Yager, Mary Montminy and Gloria Frey. Through an established understanding, the chair next to Fin's was left open for Emma. Arriving at the table late, she at first hesitated then laid claim to the chair on Fin's left. Barbara Yager was recounting one or two experiences on her uncle's lobster boat, a topic that had captured Fin's complete attention. At the conclusion of the girl's firsthand account of trapping for lobsters, Fin peppered her with a handful of questions about her experiences. Nothing at the table on this day seemed out of the ordinary, until Fin stood up and excused himself from the gathering, extending Emma no extra attention or eye contact. His actions spread a blanket of sadness over her. It was Gloria who finally leaned across the table and asked Emma if something was wrong. She explained to the girls that, through a mutual agreement, they had decided to see less of each other.

For the next week, Emma's exposure to Fin was limited to homeroom and in the cafeteria. Public Speaking class had ended at mid year. Emma's cafeteria group had continued to grow over the course of the spring and now included a dozen regulars, Fin included. He was one of only three males in the grouping. Fin was one of the least talkative of the table regulars, but still managed to toss in a pearl of Jonesport wisdom every now and again. As lunch period wound down on a Friday afternoon, Gloria Frey asked Fin if he could stay behind for a moment. He indicated yes with a nod and waited on the girl. It was not until the table had cleared of people that the partially crippled girl awkwardly scrambled into the chair next to him.

"I needed to ask you something but I didn't want to do it in front of anyone and put you in an uncomfortable position," she explained. Fin widened his eyes in a comical gesture. "My parents are on my case about the prom. I didn't go my junior year and my folks keep hounding me about how this is my last chance to attend a prom. To make a long story short, I told them I'd ask a boy to take me even though I didn't expect finding anyone pathetic enough to do it. So, Fin, that's what I'm doing. Would you come with me to my senior prom? I'll understand if you say no. The junior and senior proms take place together, so I'm sure Emma will be there with someone. I'll understand if you say no. You wouldn't have to dance with me much...maybe one or two dances and no more. We could even leave early. I wouldn't mind," she continued nervously, her sentences fused together in an anxious ramble. It was impossible to not pick up on the girl's total lack of self-confidence and desperation.

"Yeah," he answered, hoping to put her out of her misery.

"Yeah, you'll go?" repeated Gloria.

"Yeah, I'll go." The pretty teenager's face lit up and she began drawing in deep breaths.

"Oh, God, I'm going to cry," she blurted out. "This is going to make my parents so incredibly happy," she exclaimed.

"Your parent's happiness is all I live for," he added drily. "There's only a few weeks to go. I'll have to get right on renting my tux."

Emma arrived early at study hall and was pleased to see Keith seated in the back corner of the room. She hustled to the far aisle and claimed the vacant desk on his right. Barely looking up from his text book, he scarcely acknowledged her arrival. Nonetheless, she rewarded him with a sweet smile and let her books spill across the desk. A few seconds passed before she leaned playfully across the aisle and whispered in the boy's ear.

"We have less than two weeks before the prom and we still have a million details to sort through," she advised him. She watched as a painful expression took hold of his face. "What's the matter, Keith?" He looked back at her indifferently and shook his head side to side.

"It just seems like this whole thing is turning into a big hassle. My old man still hasn't ruled out that family weekend away and then there's this whole bullshit with Fin Cromwell."

"Fin and I are no more," she argued back.

"No, I think it's best if I just back away from this whole thing and you should go out and find someone else to take you," stated Gorman with no emotion. Stunned, Emma sat motionless at her desk and stared at the handsome junior.

"You're asking me to find someone for the prom when it's only two weeks away? And what about all the time and preparation I've put into this?" Gorman shrugged his shoulders and trained his eyes back onto his books. Emma briefly considered pleading her case further, but instinctively knew it was hopeless. There was no link or attachment between her and this coldhearted stranger. The bright-eyed young man with the whimsical personality that had approached her a month earlier was dead to her. Holding back a tearful outburst, she collected her books and rushed out of the room.

15

It was nearing three thirty on Thursday afternoon when Fin pried open a can of metallic green paint and sized up the four bathroom walls of his father's apartment. After spreading newspaper across the linoleum floor he covered the bathtub, sink and toilet bowl with plastic tarps and tried to estimate how long a job he was facing. It was a small room, no more than eight by twelve feet. He paused, remembered something his father had cautioned him about, and went in search of masking tape. A half hour earlier he had contemplated visiting the library in the hope of running into Emma. The contemplation was short lived. It was painful enough seeing her at school. He did not need the added heartache of trying to steal a glimpse of her from across the room in a setting like the town library. In addition, there was always the chance she would be there with another guy from school. He did not need to indulge himself in that sort of torture, he thought. His return to the bathroom with the needed masking tape was interrupted by the sound of the front door buzzer. He whirled his large frame around in mid stride and made for the front hall. Reaching the front door he swung it in and saw Emma Corman standing on the front step. She looked up at him with sad eyes and said nothing. The sight of her hauntingly lovely face and petite frame rattled him.

"Emmy," he murmured, unable to put together a full sentence.

"I miss you," she answered. "Will you ever be able to forgive me?" He threw his head back and gestured her to enter. She walked past him and made her way to the kitchen. There, he pulled her out a chair. "I smell paint," she added and looked around the room for evidence.

"I was about to paint the bathroom...shiny green."

"Could you put that on hold so we can talk?" she asked. He scurried into the bathroom and placed the masking tape down on the top of the clothes hamper. Returning to the kitchen, he found Emma gone. He raced toward the front door and was surprised to find her seated on the couch. She gestured him to join her there. He complied. "The kitchen is too rigid and formal. We've both had to be too rigid and formal for the last couple of weeks," she added. She rested her head on his shoulder. "Have you missed me?" She glanced up to see Fin's eyes close as he attempted to contain the emotional turbulence within him.

"Emmy, I've been a wreck. My father can tell you how I haven't been sleeping well and my appetite has dropped way off," he confessed.

"Because of me?"

"Who else?" She slipped her body up onto his lap and ran her hand along the side of his face, as if feeling it for the first time. He went silent and his breathing grew deeper. She fidgeted her body and felt her male friend react to her movement.

"I take full responsibility for all of this craziness between you and me. Women are so much more emotional than men and I let my crazy emotions just run away with me," she admitted. "Fin, I won't beat around the bush here. You've probably written off going to the prom this year because of my stupidity, but I wonder if I could change your mind at this late date. The flower shops and tuxedo rental places are accustomed to last minute changes, so I think we still have time," she theorized. She turned her brown eyes on him and waited for his capitulation. Instead, he let out a sigh of frustration.

"What's the matter?" she asked.

"I already have a date for the prom. After you blew me off, I planned not to go at all. Then Gloria Frey asked me if I'd take her to her senior prom and I accepted. She's a real nice kid and she seemed so down about not going. She's a sweet girl, Emmy." Emma's facial expression tightened on learning of this development in Fin's social life.

"You accepted Gloria's invitation before you learned of our reconciliation," she reasoned. "You'll just have to tell Gloria that you've had a change of heart," insisted Emma. Fin shook his head and grew more serious.

"I can't do that, Emmy. It means too much to her." Emma jumped to her feet in anger.

"You've known me a lot longer than you've known Gloria Frey. You can't be serious, Fin," she exploded. "With everything we've been through together, are you really going to do this to me?" Fin dropped his head into his hands, giving the appearance of a man in search of an answer. Seconds passed and he glanced back up at her.

"What if the three of us went together? I'll pick up Gloria first and then come around for you. Officially she'll be my date for the prom, but we'll all go in together. No one will know who's with who," he contended.

"Stop being a moron, Fin. Tell you what…I'll lay this all out for you in real simple terms. You can go to the prom with Gloria Frey and look like a complete idiot out on the dance floor, or you can go with the girl that you claim you're in love with. It's just that simple," concluded Emma. She did not have to wait long for his final decision.

"Emmy, I have to go with Gloria," he announced despondently. She rushed from the room and out into the hallway.

"I don't want you calling me, or talking to me, or even looking at me from this day on," she hollered back to him. He knew it would prove futile to chase after her. A second later the front door slammed shut and the apartment grew quiet around him. Curiously, his mind flashed back to the two occasions when Emma had come to the apartment and shared her body with him. This only served to intensify his sense of loss.

Emma asked her father for a ride to school the following morning. She did not want to run into Fin Cromwell and this assured her that she would not. Arriving at the school a full thirty minutes before the opening bell, she loitered in the halls and at her locker for as long as possible before making her way to homeroom. Her spirits dropped upon entering the room when she caught sight of Whitney and Mandy out of the corner of her eye. Emma walked to her desk and was quickly joined by her two arch enemies. She spilled open an English Literature book and set out to ignore them. Whitney started in on a seemingly rehearsed and stilted conversation involving the prom. Emma attempted to disregard their words, but the mere proximity of the two young women made this impossible.

"For God's sake, Whit, have you come to a decision and accepted anyone's invitation to the prom?" Mandy asked.

"Are you serious, Mandy? I made that decision weeks ago. I just didn't tell him until last week. I'm going with Keith. I feel a little guilty keeping him hanging for so long. He played it safe. From what I hear he kept some hog dangling on a string for weeks until he knew he had me," gushed Whitney. Emma sat in silence while the girl's words tore through her emotionally. Her morbid curiosity caused her to steal a glance over at the gorgeous blonde. She was not surprised to find Whitney's eyes trained on her. Her longtime nemesis wore a smug, self-satisfied look on her face that communicated the utter pleasure she received from tormenting Emma. She buried her face back in her study material and longed for first period. There was a vacant chair beside Fin later that morning, as Emma did not make an appearance at the lunch table with her friends on this Friday.

16

Emma had grown accustomed to staying home on Saturday nights with Fin working at the Glen Mor Restaurant. However, this particular night proved to be particularly disheartening. It was the night of Kennebunk High School's junior and senior proms and she had decided to forego attending the event. It was a decision that prompted a barrage of questions from her mother. Emma had kept the deterioration of her relationship with Fin from her parents and so it was understandable that her mother would question Fin's absence on an evening as important as this one. Unknown to most everyone at school, Emma did receive a last minute offer to accompany her. Jake McSweeney, a short, muscular junior who shared a number of classes with Fin approached her a few days earlier and sheepishly asked her if she was interested in attending the prom with him. Jake was a fairly good-looking young man with a cheery personality who lived in Arundel. However, he was also ill bred and lacking in social graces. In some ways Fin was the same way, but he always seemed to have the good sense to hold his tongue at the appropriate time. Jake did not have this gift. For this reason, Emma had politely turned down the boy's invitation.

Emma spent much of the evening perched in front of the television beside her parents. Her mother attempted to satisfy her curiosity by tossing out questions regarding Fin's whereabouts these days. Harriet followed this up with a direct question for Emma on whether Fin was able to get the night off from the Glen Mor. She answered the latter by indicating that he had but refused to answer the former, explaining that it was too complicated to expound upon. At eleven Emma bid her parents a good night and climbed the stairs to her bedroom. Light was escaping from under her sister's door while the faint sound of a Partridge Family song wafted out into the hallway. She moaned and sought refuge behind the door to her bedroom. She sat on the edge of her bed and stared at herself in the bureau mirror. Incredibly, the magic passed on to her by Yvonne LaVallee at Fin's house had not faded. She still loved looking at herself in the mirror. The music from her sister's bedroom died away and was replaced by the sound of bare feet making contact with linoleum in the hallway. Her bedroom door swung open and revealed her sister standing before her. It struck her that her baby sister had grown even prettier in the last few months, an observation she would never share with Becky.

"In three years when I'm a junior, I'm not coming home on prom night. I'm going to go down to Parsons Beach and watch the sun rise the next morning," declared Becky. "Emma, you are such a loser," she added behind a sardonic smile. Emma sprang from the bed and slammed the door in her sister's face.

"Go back to your bubblegum music and your dreams of David Cassidy, you idiot," she snapped back.

Emma retired to bed a few minutes after the brief confrontation with her sister. She had not slept well over the course of the week and nodded off quickly. Her bedroom was as black as pitch when she slowly regained consciousness to the sound of a series of stones making contact with glass. She looked in the direction of her bedroom window and listened more closely. The sound of rock striking glass continued every five or six seconds and seemed to be coming from her near window. She rolled herself out of bed and made her way across the room. She raised the Venetian blinds and peered down on her darkened back yard. There she could make out the figure of a man.

"Emmy, it's me, Fin," he called up in a projected whisper. "I couldn't stay away from you any longer," he added. She lifted the window in order to hear him more distinctly.

"What time is it? Are you crazy?"

"It's about two-thirty. I got home from the prom at about midnight and couldn't sleep. I just kept thinking about you. At some point I decided to walk over here and hang out in your back yard. I just needed to be near you," he explained.

"Fin, you're insane," she called down to him. He shrugged his shoulders but it was lost on her in the darkness. "You probably think you're like Romeo and I'm Juliet up on my terrace."

"Actually, I hadn't thought of that," he confessed. "I'm here because I want you to know that from this moment in time I will be there for you in all things. The whole thing with the prom and Gloria was something I had to do. I wouldn't have ever forgiven myself and I don't think God would have forgiven me if I had backed out on her. That's behind me now. Emmy, you have my word. I will never turn my back on you again. Please take me back into your life," he pleaded. She knelt at the window, peering down on her friend. Seemingly deep in thought, she remained silent for ten seconds. To Fin, it felt like an eternity. "Emmy, the bugs are having a field day with me down here," he exclaimed.

"Meet me on the porch at the front of the house," she instructed him.

Fin was already seated on the porch when Emma slipped out the front door dressed in a robe and joined him. He rose from his chair on her approach. She stood before him and waited on his response. The towering teenager enveloped the girl in his arms and pulled her close to him. After kissing her on the top of her head repeatedly he pushed her to arm's length.

"You must really think I've totally lost my mind by coming here in the middle of the night. I've gone nuts in the head for you, it's that simple," he confessed.

"You're crazy for coming here and no sane person would do it. But I'm glad you did," she said. He dropped to his knees, where their bodies aligned more closely, and embraced her body again.

"What is this magic hold you have on me? Why does the girl that makes me so happy also have to tear me apart and kill my appetite and keep me awake at night?"

"Read Gibran and you'll understand," she suggested.

"I have no idea what you're talking about…Emmy, just say things are right with us," he begged.

"Fin, I wouldn't be downstairs with you if things weren't all right with us. Please believe me when I say I've missed having you around. I never should have stormed out of the house on you over the prom. I was being selfish and a real brat," conceded Emma. Fin chuckled.

"Emmy, you're a fox now and that's how foxes are. They can be more demanding than average girls because they know that guys will put up with the grief just to be around them." Emma pulled Fin closer.

"You're saying exactly what I need to hear right now. I need you more than you know and more than I can get out in words." He brought his mouth up to hers. She returned his kiss and reveled in the feel of his masculine body pulled against her. They talked for a few minutes more before Emma began to shiver from the night air. Fin finally broke away from her and jumped down from the porch.

"I'm going to sleep a hell of a lot better tonight," he called back to her as he slowly began the walk home down Mechanic Street. Emma waved to him from the front door. "Emmy, I love you so much it hurts," he called back to her from the darkness.

17

In May, Bertrand Corman received news that was to change his and his family's lives. After years of applying and interviewing to fill academic openings across New England, he was offered a lucrative position at the University of Massachusetts and accepted. The professorship carried with it a substantial increase in salary and status. Word came on a night when Emma was to join Fin for an evening at the Kennebunk Drive-In Theatre. This came about after Emma prodded Fin into taking her to the Jerry Lewis Cinema in Sanford to see *The Way We Were,* with Barbra Streisand and Robert Redford. In exchange he made her commit to an evening at the drive-in theater with him. She made a point of waiting for Fin out on the porch and away from the family. Inside her parents were attempting to calm down a nearly hysterical Becky who saw herself being torn away from her friends at Kennebunk Junior High and dropped into a school of unfamiliar faces in faraway Massachusetts. The car rolled up to the front door and Emma quickly laid claim to the passenger seat beside Fin. The automobile pulled away while Emma's mind searched for the most delicate way to break the news to her friend.

The Kennebunk Drive-In Theater was situated on the west side of Route 1 and north of the upper village. Fin pulled his father's car onto the driveway by the theater sign that spelled out the motion pictures playing that evening. Emma was relieved to see that *Paper Moon,* a film receiving some critical acclaim, was the main feature, along with something called *Bang the Drum Slowly,* a low budget motion picture she knew nothing about. Fin found a spot in the middle of the grounds, checked to make sure the sound worked on the speaker box and turned off the vehicle.

"What size popcorn can I get you? Do you want large, jumbo, super jumbo or mega jumbo?" he clowned. She was taken with his high spirits on this evening and wondered if they would hold up after she broke the news of her father's new job.

Between films, Fin quizzed Emma on her plans for the summer and asked her if they included a job at the beach or in town. He informed her that the restaurant would be expanding his hours to forty a week and how this might allow him to buy a car by the end of August. He was particularly animated this night and even questioned her on whether she thought President Nixon would survive the Watergate Hearings. It was nearly midnight when the car motored out onto Route 1 and southward toward Mechanic Street. It was at that moment that she knew she could no longer delay the task she absolutely dreaded.

"Fin, I received some news today that I know you're not going to like. It has me pretty shaken up, too," she said softly from the passenger seat. They were parked in front of the house. He turned to her, Emma's tone of voice telling him that he should be concerned. He stared into her eyes and waited for the details of her news. "My father has accepted a job at a university down in Massachusetts. It means moving out of Kennebunk. I'll be living and going to school down there in the fall," she explained. Fin sat stunned for a few seconds while Emma watched the vitality drain from his body. "They want him on the job by August first," she added. He remained frozen behind the wheel, his eyes glazed over. She slid sideways and kissed him on the cheek. The emotional pain registered on his face was difficult for her to bear. "There's still two months before we have to go. Why don't we try to make the most of every day of it?" She pulled back and reached for the door handle.

"I'll call you tomorrow. Right now I want to be alone," he stated in a voice void of energy. He stared intently across the front seat as if trying to memorize every detail of her face.

"Goodnight, Fin," she murmured and rushed from the car toward the front door of the house.

News of the Corman's move out-of-state spread through the school the following week. It was the primary topic of conversation at the lunch table the following Monday. Emma fielded questions from her friends while Fin remained noticeably quiet. Over the remainder of the school year, she went out of her way to walk close to Fin in the hallways whenever possible, often hooking her arm around his in a show of innocent affection. On the final day of classes in June, Emma and Fin packed a picnic lunch and drove to Parsons Beach, where they sat by the mouth of the Mousam River and recounted the experiences they had shared together. However, nothing could change the fact that they marched together toward the inevitable: the time when the threading of their lives would be severed.

In July, the 'For Sale' sign in front of the Corman house also carried an 'Under Contract' sticker across its front. The family's time as residents of the state of Maine was growing short. Emma rose early on this morning and joined her parents in the kitchen downstairs. After pouring herself a cup of coffee, she took a chair at the table next to her father. She plucked a piece of toast from his plate and put it in her mouth before he could raise an objection. Emma broke the silence in the room.

"I wonder if I could share something with you and ask for your advice?" Her father looked up from his newspaper and prompted her to speak. "I saw Fin last night and he started going on about coming down to visit me in Massachusetts once he has his car. He's working his rear end off this summer and expects to buy a car before Labor Day. I don't think he quite sees the finality of everything once we're gone from here," she explained.

"Have you taken the time to tell him that this will mean a totally new life for you and your sister?" queried her mother briskly, while watching over a pair of three-minute eggs.

"He's my friend. I don't want to hurt him," moaned Emma.

"Oh, for Christ's sake, Emma, grow up! Women have been dismissing unsuitable men since the beginning of time. There's no good way to do it. You'll be doing him a favor if you bluntly let him know that the friendship is over. Is he really that stupid, to think that there could be some long-term possibility for your relationship?"

"Mother, he has been very good to me…more than you'll ever know," countered Emma.

"We all go through life using and being used by others. Some people prove to be stepping stones for others. If you used Fin from time to time, it wasn't out of malice. Your problem was having that boy fall head over heals for you. Your father and I warned you about that way back at Christmas time. We could see it then. We warned you that it would come to no good end. Unfortunately for you, missy, we were right," Harriet concluded. Emma turned to her father.

"I'm sure he would grow very tired of driving all the way to Amherst every week to see you. His car might not hold up to it for very long either. It's the easy way out and sometime the easy way is the best way," he theorized.

"Ending it now or ending it later, Fin is not in your long-term future. Emma, the kind thing to do is to make it short and sweet and let him begin the healing process as soon as possible," added her mother. Emma gulped down the remainder of her coffee and climbed the stairs to her room where she would mull over her options for the rest of the morning.

Emma called the Cromwell house and learned that Fin had the day off. She asked him to meet her down at Rogers Pond later in the afternoon and he agreed. It was a hot and humid July day with a cloud cover that partially neutralized the rays of the sun. Emma made her way to Water Street and turned right onto the driveway that led to the small pond and Mousam River. Reaching the parking lot, she noticed her friend leaning against a tree close by. She was nearly upon him before he became aware of her. Twenty feet beyond Fin, the Mousam meandered listlessly by in the direction of the sea. She cleared a space next to Fin at the base of the tree and eased herself down beside him. He was deadly quiet and serious.

"My father is sending the rest of the family to Massachusetts ahead of him. We're leaving tomorrow," she stated almost apologetically. He had no outward reaction to the news. He inhaled deeply and glanced down at her. His eyes appeared troubled. "I thought this might be a fitting place to say good-bye. It's as good as anywhere else," she explained. "I've been thinking about something you said and I needed to make my feelings known on the matter. Fin, I would prefer that you did not drive down to see me in Massachusetts when you get your car." Her words hung in the still, humid air around them. Again, there was no reaction from him. He appeared content to stare straight ahead in the direction of the pond. "I won't even try to thank you for everything you have done for me. I don't think I would even still be in this world right now if it weren't for you." Fin's silence was beginning to unnerve her, sending her into a rambling dissertation on their relationship. "My mother said that you were simply a stepping stone on my life's journey, but she has no idea of everything that has gone down between us. Fin, you are and will always be the first boy I could ever relate to. At times I may have used you, but I never stopped caring deeply for you," she confessed. Emma began to weep. "This is really hard. I guess what I'm here to do is to say a final good-bye," she concluded, choking on the final word out of her mouth. He turned to her with a pained expression and held his tongue. Emma kissed Fin on the cheek and rose to her feet. She burst into tears and turned from her friend of nine months. She scrambled away from him and walked quickly toward Water Street. She turned and looked back once, only to see Fin's eyes trained on her. She ached inside. Emma was sure this would be the last time she would ever set eyes on Fin Cromwell. She was wrong.

Part 2

18

September 7, 2005

"If people's lives were played out in chapters then this, most certainly, was the dawn of a new one," thought Emma Lipton as her vehicle passed over the bridge spanning the Piscataqua River and joined the Maine Turnpike. She was more than aware that her comfortable life built on a foundation of academic friends and associates was about to be replaced with a solitary existence at the edge of the Atlantic Ocean in a state she had barely visited since her teenage years. She ran the math in her head and realized it had been thirty-one years since she was a resident of the Pine Tree State. She flicked on her wipers as an ocean mist began to accumulate on her windshield. Something prompted her to think of Frederick and she was reminded of their real estate trip to Wells Beach the previous February. They thought they had been blessed that day, stumbling upon the beachfront cottage at Wells Beach. It had only been on the market for two days when they wandered into the real estate office and were whisked down for a showing. The agent told them it was one of the 'Four Sisters,' a group of once identical cottages constructed side by side on the ocean's edge in the late nineteenth century. A tour of the inside of the cottage revealed only minor modifications over the past one hundred years, which greatly appealed to both of them. They had hardly been able to hide their enthusiasm. The following day they made an offer twenty thousand under the listed price. The slightly insulted seller reduced the price by five thousand dollars and drew a line in the sand. Frederick and Emma gleefully accepted his hard ball price and a month later they were seated in a lawyer's office in Wells signing the papers. They had only made use of the house on two occasions that spring before the morning when Frederick complained of an abnormal pain shooting through him. They feared for the worst and hoped for the best. It was only days before the diagnosis came down: it was pancreatic cancer. Frederick's downward spiral came on quickly. His battle with the killer only went on for three months. Now, at the tail end of summer, Emma motored northward to the oceanfront Victorian accompanied only by her loneliness and guilt. She had already sold the house on the edge of the campus. The white colonial came with too many painful memories. She saw the sign for the last exit before the toll road and steered onto the ramp. It had been twenty-five years since she last needed to pinch her pennies but she did nonetheless. It was the Yankee in her and she made no apologies for it. Turning onto Route 1 in York she headed into a patch of heavier rain. The colorless sky and rhythmic movement of the windshield wipers put her into a semi-trance that she would only briefly emerge from by spotting familiar landmarks like Flo's Hot Dogs or the Ogunquit Theater. Emma finally returned to the here and now when the traffic lights at the Mile Road intersection came into view a hundred yards ahead of her. Easing her Volvo into the right lane, she turned her vehicle in the direction of the Atlantic Ocean and her new life.

Emma was still unaccustomed to her life as a widow. It was not unusual for her to see or hear something of particular interest and make a mental note to share it with Frederick later, only to come to the realization that this was just one of the many deprivations doled out to widows by the loving god she never believed in. She glanced into the rear view mirror and caught sight of her salt and pepper hair. Her mind flashed back to discussions with Frederick and how he had encouraged her to color it. *It makes you look ten years older,* he would argue. Emma's rehearsed response was always the same: she did not fear growing older like most women, but this was not completely factual. The truth was that Scott loved her black hair naturally feathered with white and had on more than one occasion pleaded with her to keep it that way. Her hair was now one more thing on which to conjure up feelings of guilt. She motored eastward through the heavy, wet air. In the distance the sea was cloaked in fog. The car approached Billy's Chowder House and she considered stopping for a bite. It was one o'clock and the parking lot was somewhat crowded. She was not terribly hungry. She decided to come back in a couple of hours, but before any dinner time rush. She reasoned there would be less people at that time, to see and feel sorry for the pathetic woman sitting by herself at the corner table.

Emma proceeded up Webhannet Drive and turned onto the gravel driveway while a fog bank moved slowly over and around the brooding nineteenth century house. The cottage's pale white exterior was muted even more on this gloomy afternoon as the rainfall fluctuated between mist and light. Slowly proceeding up the driveway she stared up at the cottage as if seeing it for the first time. She lingered behind the wheel and conjured up thoughts of Scott. This was not unusual. Even before she lost Frederick, she would often pause and focus on the man who introduced her to the meaning of drop dead, physical love. Over years past she would often summon up recollections of how they first met, isolated in a corner of a dreary university gathering, two intellectual wallflowers cast off by their spouses. It was Scott who initially garnered the attention of Emma, dazzling her with his knowledge of politics, current events and motion pictures, both new and from the past. Before long they were meeting for an innocent rendezvous over coffee, always two or three towns from the university and away from prying eyes. It was Emma who pushed the relationship beyond the boundaries of friendship. At first afraid to admit her deep feelings for him, she proceeded ahead in the affair under the guise of a sexual adventure. A month into the carnal life of their liaison she stumbled upon his erotic weaknesses and pounced on them. Fate was kind to her. She was extremely petite and Scott was a leg man. Had his deepest desires run toward the female breast then his mastery over her would have continued, she often thought. However, on a spring afternoon she had experimented with her lover, overexposing him to the soft skin of her legs and the seductive lines of her lower body. The product of a fifteen minute routine of repetitive movement over and around his upper body was a male thoroughly stripped of his free will and inhibitions. Emma made note of her technique that day and perfected the ritual in the weeks and months that followed. By summer, Scott Harrington was little more than a piece of clay in her hands and she had wrested total control of the relationship from him. The balance of power became so obvious that, in private moments, he would comment on his state of helplessness behind closed doors in her company. Emma had never had this sort of power over Frederick, a fact she found somewhat curious.

The house was larger than she had remembered it. She thanked herself for timing her arrival during daylight hours. She was not sure she could have confronted her new home alone in the dark. Stepping out of the Volvo, Emma slipped on a raincoat and climbed the porch stairs to the main floor of the building. She fiddled with a set of keys while approaching the doorway leading into the kitchen. She found the correct key on the second try and pushed in the door. The phrase, 'the silence was deafening,' had to have been written at the dining room table of this house, she thought. Emma flicked on a kitchen light and moved into the dining room where she did the same. She became aware of the cold and dampness while moving about the first floor and remembered the instructions regarding the furnace. On went two more lamps and then she set out to bring some physical warmth into the building.

There was an informal dining area between the living room and a downstairs bedroom and Emma gravitated to this area of the house. There was nothing extraordinary about her surroundings except for its unobstructed ocean view. She switched on the furnace and loitered in the living room and kitchen until she felt a rush of warmth penetrate the front of the house. She spent most of this time staring hypnotically out over the listless ocean. Hopping up from the table, she entered the kitchen in search of food and supplies. She was not surprised when she found none. She grabbed her purse and scrambled down to the car. Moments later her Volvo was weaving its way back toward Route 1. From the top of Mile Road it was only a two minute drive to the Wells IGA, where she filled a carriage to the brim with food, cleaning detergents and a variety of beverages. In the back of her mind was the hope of running into a familiar face from Kennebunk High. She did not, but did manage to return to the house with five bags of much needed groceries and supplies. Unpacking her groceries and the car kept her busy for part of the grey afternoon. By four o'clock she was relaxing at a table in the lounge area of Billy's Chowder House. To her surprise, she did not feel uncomfortable seated alone with her meal of baked haddock and the novel, *Atlas Shrugged,* for company. On more than one occasion she lifted her eyes from the book and saw she was on the receiving end of an admiring glance from a male seated at the bar. This attention lifted her spirits, albeit only slightly.

Back at the house, Emma discovered that she was without any television reception. Apparently, Frederick had never activated the cable service and she had never noticed the absence of a bill. She made a mental note to take care of this in the morning. It was beginning to grow dark outside when she slipped off her shoes and made her way out the front door and over the sand to the water line. The air was still damp and the lights in the distance from the main parking area of Wells Beach were shrouded in fog. Reaching the almost nonexistent wave action at the water's edge, she let the cold Atlantic wash over her feet. She retreated from the chilly water following ten seconds of invigoration. Turning back to the northernmost of the 'Four Sisters' she noticed it had taken on a foreboding air, the lighted rooms on the main floor crowned by a second story in absolute darkness. The sight of the house at dusk made her apprehensive about sleeping there. She had spent her forty-eight years scoffing at people who went on about ghosts and haunted buildings but now, at this moment of truth, she lacked the courage of her own words. She walked back toward the charcoal trimmed house and scoffed at herself for these groundless fears. In the end Emma was able to gather up a set of linens and one blanket from a first floor closet. She slept in the downstairs bedroom on her first night, content to put off venturing upstairs until the following day.

19

The beach communities of southern Maine entertain two suitors in the course of a year. The first come only in July and August and can be likened to a college boy in pursuit of a sexual adventure on spring break. Visitors at that time are drawn primarily by warm sunlight, beautiful waters and the allure of the natural surroundings at their pinnacle. They appreciate the region at its time of maximum pleasure and lose interest when the days grow shorter and the air temperature cools, just as passion-driven males lose interest in familiar women when more favorable opportunities arise.

The region's second and more dedicated suitor is the visitor who comes in the spring and fall when the bloom is off the petal and the ocean air turns a cold shoulder to callers. His or her attraction to the beaches and expanse of ocean water is both spiritual and physical and is not tempered by the change in seasons. It is this more faithful suitor that Emma Lipton chose to join in Maine for the next chapter of her life.

Emma rolled onto her side while light bled through her closed eyelids. She opened her eyes to a modest bedroom illuminated by sunlight that poured in through an eastward facing window. Beyond the panes of glass, the Atlantic Ocean surged against the three foot thick seawall that bordered her grassy back yard. She took a deep breath of fresh sea air and was reminded of the euphoria she and Frederick shared the previous winter when they came upon the house. She had slept soundly her first night alone at the cottage. A gust of wind blew, confronting the building and rattling a number of windows. Emma took stock of herself. She was warm within the sheets and single woolen blanket, with the exception of her hands and feet. She sat up and peeked out at the blue Atlantic. The continuity of the ocean was broken by a solitary lobster boat that motored past about two hundred yards out. Although still drowsy, her desire to remain nestled within her sheets and blanket was overridden by her yearning for a cup of coffee. She rolled off the bed and plucked her robe from atop a nearby chair. Making her way to the kitchen she opened the can of Chock Full of Nuts coffee and spooned out grounds for four cups. Within seconds the dated Mister Coffee appliance was dripping her hot beverage into its pot.

Emma was seated outside on the terrace a short time after eight o'clock when her cell phone rang. She placed down her coffee and lifted the phone to her ear.

"It's going to be very difficult getting accustomed to you being two states away," said a male voice. It was Scott.

"I'll send you a New England road map. Maine shouldn't be all that hard to find," she answered. "You told me how much you wanted to see the house in person."

"Trust me, Emma, I'm working on it. Barry is taking a week off in October to hike up in New Hampshire and Maine. I've already told Bev that I'm seriously considering joining him. I'm sure he'll cover for me, given the number of times I've covered his ass."

"It would be wonderful having you here for a week or even for just a few days," she added wistfully, her tone softened from just moments earlier. They talked for another twenty minutes on matters known only to them, of stolen weekends and afternoons of bliss away from the eyes of a judgmental world. These were their only commonly held possessions. Frederick's illness had kept them apart since the spring and Emma found herself yearning for her lover's touch. "Scott, you will love it here and I'm beginning to wither away from loneliness," she confessed. The conversation ended the way so many had ended in the past, with a mutual profession of love. Emma brought her coffee to her lips and looked over her 'to do' list. At the top of the list was the cable company.

In the course of running errands on this day, she was reminded of the plan she and Frederick laid out concerning their investment in the cottage. They decided to restore their Victorian jewel to its glory days back at the turn of the last century. In addition, their plan was to rent the house for five or six of the prime summer weeks and roll all of the rent money back into the restoration process. Their rental scheme, along with much else, was ruined by Frederick's cancer. It was mid day and she was searching out late season bargains when the inspiration hit her: she would restore the cottage in his memory. She added a copy of the *York County Coast Star* to an armful of bargain items and wrapped up her shopping. It was less than a mile back to Webhannet Drive from Route 1 where she ascended the stairs to the house and brought her newspaper and bag of beach clothing into the living room. She plucked out the classified section and began perusing it for local builders, contractors and restoration experts. Primarily focused on the larger ads initially, her eyes finally fell upon a small advertisement buried at the bottom of the page: *Building & restoration projects, big and small. Call for a quote. Fin's Building Specialists.* Emma stared down at the tiny advertisement while her mind sped back to her days at Kennebunk High. She read and reread the ad to assure herself this was not some figment of her imagination. She went to the kitchen in search of a telephone book and found one in a cabinet drawer. She checked the book's date. It was two years old. Within thirty seconds her finger was pointed at a name and number. The name read: Cromwell, Finian, Kennebunk. She opened the refrigerator and grabbed the bottle of pink wine chilling inside.

Armed with a half-filled wine glass, she stepped outside and walked the nearly two hundred and seventy degrees of porch rimming the house. On examination she could see that the salt laden, ocean air had taken its toll on this exterior section of the Victorian. There were floorboards that could use replacing and window trim in need of restoration, she thought to herself. She continued around the outer limit of the house and grew more and more overwhelmed by the project she faced, until she reached the eastern face of the cottage and took in the sparkling waters of the Atlantic Ocean. The sight of four foot waves crashing forty feet from her dining room window invigorated Emma and pumped a fresh sense of enthusiasm into her.

By three-thirty her wine bottle was empty and Emma climbed the narrow stairwell up to the second floor. Reaching the landing, she gazed into a full bathroom and checked the hooks and towel bars. She stepped inside and spotted Frederick's bathrobe hanging from a hook on the back of the door. She burst into tears and walked briskly from the room, leaving tangible evidence of happier times to stand guard over plans unfulfilled. She made her way down the narrow hallway, glanced into both bedrooms and remembered her and Frederick's initial tour of the cottage and the restrained euphoria it prompted eight months earlier. There were two bedrooms on the second floor of the house and she had all but settled on the cozy, comfortable one on her left when she pushed in the door to the other. Her eyes widened at the sight of a queen-sized bed resting beneath a yellow, chenille spread and illuminated by sunlight pouring in through the room's south facing window. On her left was an easterly window with an unobstructed view of the whitecaps dancing atop the blue Atlantic Ocean. This is where she would sleep on this night, she thought. She sat on the edge of the bed and remembered buying the bedspread the night before finding the house the previous winter. The cottage also had a third floor, with an additional two bedrooms. These rooms had sloped ceilings that followed the line of the roof. The rooms were quite small and were probably occupied by maids or nannies a hundred years earlier. Emma scurried downstairs and lugged two suitcases of clothing upstairs to the second floor and, eventually, into her closet. Her next order of business was to open both windows and let in the divine air.

Emma retreated upstairs to her bedroom early on her second night at the house and the last day before the cable service was to be turned on. Her retirement to bed only came after an exhaustive assessment of each and every door and window on the first floor. With the passing of Frederick, security took on an elevated importance. A lamp above the bed provided muted light as she simultaneously read Ayn Rand and attempted to put together a working restoration plan. She decided to speak with two or three local contractors before committing to anyone. She had already ruled out Fin Cromwell based on his undersized newspaper ad, in addition to the potential discomfort that any reunion might bring about. She dropped off to sleep with *Atlas Shrugged* draped across her chest and the lamp on.

Emma opened her eyes to a sliver of pink on the horizon. She gazed hypnotically out over the ocean and waited on the appearance of the great, yellow orb. While waiting on the sunrise, she had to concentrate to come up with the day of the week. It was Friday. She remained stretched out in bed for a good hour, breathing in the crisp, sea air, before finally making her way downstairs to the kitchen. It dawned on her that she was growing comfortable with the house in a short period of time. She had just started the coffee brewing when a thought struck her: why not pick up donuts from Congdon's instead of preparing something herself? Her internal debate was short-lived. Congdon's donuts were one of the best, if not the best, in the state of Maine and they were approximately a mile up the road. She threw on a pair of jeans and a sweatshirt and hopped in the Volvo for an early morning errand.

In spite of the early hour just before seven o'clock, Emma found herself in a short line to buy pastries. Her mind shot back thirty-five years to a memory of accompanying her father down to Wells to this very shop. It saddened her and she pushed it to the back of her mind. She stared ahead to the front of the line and thought there was something vaguely familiar about the woman calling out her donuts of choice to the girl behind the counter. The woman paid for her order and turned for the door. This brought her to within two feet of Emma.

"Barbara Yager, is that you?" Emma asked while extending her hand. The middle-aged woman stopped and focused her eyes on Emma.

"Yes, but it's Barbara Cornish now," she explained. A moment later the woman's face brightened and she stepped forward.

"Emma Corman, is that you?" Emma nodded in the affirmative and the two broke out into laughter. The former lunch mates moved to the side of the growing line. "Oh, my God, how long has it been?" Emma raised her eyebrows and informed her friend that over thirty years had passed since she lived in York County. The two women slid into a booth and caught each other up on the respective paths of their lives. Barbara extended her former classmate a hug when the subject of Frederick's death came up. Emma learned, among other things, that Whitney Crowninshield was an attorney married to another lawyer and that she still resided in Kennebunkport. The two women exchanged phone numbers, promised to get together in the near future and were about to go their separate ways when Emma remembered the small advertisement in the paper.

"Barbara, I saw an ad in the paper for a building contractor. It was for a company called Fin's Building Specialists. Is that our Fin from Kennebunk High by any chance?" The question caused her old friend to burst into restrained laughter.

"You mean your Fin, don't you? How many Fins do you suppose there are in the area? If I remember correctly, that poor boy had a horrible crush on you back then," added the woman.

"It's just that I'm going to have to find someone to do some work at the house and I saw his name in the Coast Star," injected Emma. "I briefly thought of calling him, but some of the work will be very delicate and intricate and I want to find someone competent," she explained. Her friend reached out and stopped her immediately.

"Fin's very, very good. I state that without hesitation. He ran into a run of bad luck some years back and hasn't made it all the way back yet. Now, I've never had any work done by him on my house but everyone I know who has had work swears by him." Emma nodded thoughtfully as she deliberated on the woman's statements. They were just about to part when Barbara turned back to her. "If you're really interested, there's a better than a fifty-fifty chance that Fin's having his breakfast out in the second dining room. He's here every day, as far as I can tell, and usually sits in the same corner booth every morning. No one's brave enough to ask him to sit at the counter. He's almost always alone." Barbara pointed in the direction of the dining rooms. Emma stood frozen in place. "It can't hurt to check," she suggested. Emma gave the woman a farewell hug and rejoined the donut line.

Emma headed toward Congdon's parking lot with a half dozen donuts and the words of her friend from Kennebunk High School lodged in her head. Reaching the door she did an about face and marched toward the dining rooms. She followed Barbara's suggestion and walked to the second room. In an instant, she noticed one head towering above the others. His back was turned from the other patrons and he was alone. She proceeded forward. She observed that her old friend still had a full head of hair, at least in the back. Reaching Fin's booth, she stopped and looked down at him. His face was tanned and mildly wrinkled.

"So, stranger…rescued any skinny girls from the middle of the river lately?" Emma asked, causing the man's attention to rise from the table. His eyes widened and he briefly stopped chewing his food. He appeared stunned, as if doubting his senses. "Barbara Yager told me that you hang out here in the morning, so I took a shot at finding you." Fin just stared up at his old friend for the next few seconds, seemingly unable to respond to her. Then, following a deep breath, he did.

"Emma," he said in almost a moan. It had the woeful sound of the last word from a dying man. She gestured toward the adjacent side of the booth for an invitation and he extended her one. She slid into the booth opposite her old friend and smiled warmly at him.

"Fin, I've just moved back into the area. I own a house, a Victorian, down on Wells Beach and I'm going to be in need of some help fixing it up. It needs some repair and restoration work outside and in. I'll be talking to a few people, getting some estimates, and making a decision soon. We only have a couple of weeks left of summer." Fin took a sip from his coffee and finally responded in sentence form.

"Now who will be making the final decision, you or your husband?" he asked and made a gesture in the direction of her wedding ring.

"I lost my husband to cancer nearly two months ago. It's just me," she explained for what seemed like the thousandth time in the last sixty days. "I want to get moving on this as quickly as possible. Now, I want to be totally frank with you. You will not be the only person I will speak to. How soon can we talk in earnest?" There was an affirmative, no-nonsense quality to her voice. Fin responded with the faintest of smiles.

"How about two o'clock this afternoon?"

"That works for me," she answered. "My house is a white Victorian with charcoal trim down on Webhannet Drive. It's one of the 'Four Sisters.' Do you know the cottages I'm talking about?" He nodded that he did.

"Aren't you going to write it down or something?" He took a lazy bite out of his toast and lethargically brought his eyes back to her. "Oh, my God, I just noticed that you've lost your Jonesport accent," she exclaimed. He nodded his head sheepishly.

"I know the house, Emma...and I lost the accent a long, long time ago," he answered. She rose to her feet and extended her hand. She noticed he was not wearing a wedding band. "How are your folks...and little Becky?"

"Little Becky is forty-five years old and still a royal pain in the ass. My mom and dad have both passed away. Becky and her brats are about the only kin I have left in the world." He shrugged his shoulders sadly. Emma stood over Fin for a prolonged moment, half expecting him to tell her how good she looked or how fit and trim she had remained. He did neither but opted instead to return to his breakfast. She turned from him and started for the door.

"Take it easy on those donuts or you'll lose that high school girl's figure of yours," he called out to her, prompting more than one of the surrounding customers to chuckle.

Emma was seated on her sun drenched porch when a pickup truck came to a stop in the driveway at the back of the house and a door slammed. She glanced down at her watch. Fin was early. Pushing her newspaper aside, she got to her feet and walked to meet him on the other side of the cottage. She glanced ahead and saw her old friend critically assessing the floor, walls and ceiling on the far side of the porch. She approached Fin and guided him to the other side of the house. Directing him toward a wicker chair she instructed him to sit down. She was taking charge of the meeting. He casually glanced out to sea then took a seat. It was clear the ocean view had little effect on him. She explained again her plan to interview a number of contractors and then led Fin on a tour of the property, pointing out the various projects she wanted done in each room. Outside, it was Fin who made suggestions on what work he saw as critical. The review of the house took just over half an hour. They returned to the dining room table and Emma made them iced tea.

"Here's how I see things being done. I want my worker or workers here Monday through Friday from eight until five with an hour off for lunch. I want this ongoing so I can monitor the progress."

"I don't see anyone agreeing to those conditions," interrupted Fin matter-of-factly. Emma made no effort to mask her displeasure.

"May I continue?" she asked. He indicated yes with a light-handed gesture. "As I said, I want the work ongoing and I will cover the cost of materials and specialized labor. In addition, I will pay my worker or workers two thousand dollars a week in total on Friday afternoon at the end of the workday." Her final statement caused him to raise his eyes from the table. It seems Emma had garnered his complete attention.

"So, what you're saying is, if I decide to do all the work myself then I will take home two thousand dollars every week," he stated emphatically.

"That's right. There will be no long-term contract. I'll monitor the work and as long as I'm satisfied that I'm getting a one hundred percent effort then it will go on," she affirmed. He leaned back in his chair and took a long sip from his iced tea.

"What about my other customers? What if I get a call and something needs to be done in a couple of weeks?"

"That's why we have weekends," she snapped back at him. He nodded his understanding and took another gulp of tea. "Fin, as you may have surmised by now, I'm worth a few dollars, thanks to my husband's years of investing and multiple life insurance policies. I want this house totally restored and I want it done right." Her words were followed by a short period of silence interrupted by the ringing of her cell phone. She raced to the kitchen to answer it. A conversation ensued and Fin overheard Emma agree to meet a woman named Barbara for a drink the following week. She returned to the table and apologized for the interruption. Seconds later she was flabbergasted as her friend from Kennebunk High School played his trump card.

"Emmy, I'm going to be completely honest with you. I want this job," Fin stated. Her eyes widened at the sound of her pet name from their youth. "I know you'll be speaking to a few more outfits before you're done but, I assure you, I can do as good a job, if not a better job, on anything we looked at today. I really want this job and, what's more, I need this job," he said with an unmistakable ring of sincerity. Emma stared across the table at her high school comrade. It occurred to her that Fin Cromwell was not soliciting Emma Lipton for the financial opportunity ingrained in this project, he was asking Emmy Corman, the girl he had rescued from the middle of the Mousam River; the girl he had saved from the small band of teenage predators at Kennebunk High so many years earlier and the girl he had professed his love to on the family's porch in 1974. Stunned, she said nothing and averted her eyes. Slightly embarrassed by his own honesty, he rose from his chair and walked toward the door. There was something in his body language that told her he already regretted being so forthright with her. "You have my number. Let me know one way or the other," he added.

"Fin, be here on Monday at eight o'clock," she called out to his back. The towering man froze in the doorway.

"Thanks, Emmy," he said softly, without turning around, and left the house.

Emma looked out onto the Atlantic Ocean and marveled at what she had accomplished in just a few hours. The restoration of her beach cottage was no longer some vague scheme in her distant future. Thanks to her bold decision, work would begin on the house the following week. Her thoughts traveled back to her years at Kennebunk High and the circumstances that brought Fin Cromwell into her life. The young man who had spread apprehension and fear throughout her graduating class would report and answer to her on Monday morning. The frail, little girl who lived in fear the first six weeks of her junior year of high school now held her former protector under her thumb, at least financially. Throughout their marriage, the Lipton's personal wealth was something she had always taken for granted. Most all matters of finance were handled by her husband. Now, with Frederick gone, the wealth with the respect and power it commanded, were hers.

20

Fin arrived at the house early on Monday morning. The sky was overcast but the weather report expected little in the way of precipitation. He spent the first half hour of his workday unloading his truck. He asked Emma for permission to store his major tools and supplies downstairs in the cellar. Thirty minutes passed and she was called outside. Fin took her around the open porch and pointed out the floorboards he thought were in need of replacement. The remainder of the morning was spent measuring, planning and ordering the material needed at the outset of this exterior work. He combined a trip to the wholesale building supplier with lunch seated at the bar at Billy's Chowder House. Emma glanced out the back window in the middle of the afternoon and watched as a shipment of lumber was dropped off in the back yard under Fin's direction. He spent a good portion of the afternoon ripping up distressed planks from the floor of the porch. She wandered outside a short time before four o'clock and casually reviewed the progress. Fin was dressed in denim jeans and a light blue tee shirt that showcased his biceps and general fitness. She approached him with a glass of lemonade in hand. There was perspiration bleeding through his shirt, which Emma found strangely appealing. Fin took a step back from his work and placed his crowbar against the wall of the house.

"I came out to make sure you were working and not sitting in the shade writing poetry," she joked, handing him his beverage. He laughed and shook his head.

"I got my poetry done while you were out this morning running errands," he answered in the same light vein. She stepped over planks scattered on the ground and observed the growing pile of distressed wood at the far end of the yard. If Fin's progress on the first day was any indication of his work ethic and efficiency, then he was the right man for the job, she thought. She meandered back in his direction.

"Do you have any definitive plans after work tonight?" she asked. He looked, long and hard, up at the sky as if consulting a detailed social calendar etched on the far side of a cloud.

"No."

"I bought way too much haddock for my dinner tonight. If you wanted to save yourself a few dollars and you didn't mind listening to the musings of a crazy old woman, then you're welcome to join me," she suggested. "Please do not feel obligated." She suddenly feared she might be coming off as seeming needy. He climbed to his feet and handed her back the empty glass of lemonade.

"There's nothing crazy or old about you, Emmy. Yeah, I'll hang around for supper."

It was almost five-thirty before Emma heard the sound of activity in the cellar below the kitchen. In the dining area, the table was set for her and Fin. Outside there was a parade of couples walking in both directions at the edge of the crashing surf. Fin entered the house without knocking and made his way to the bathroom to wash up. Emma instructed him on where to find a clean towel and opened the oven door to check on the fish. His face and hands washed clean of the day's accumulated grime, he circumvented his hostess and made his way out to the dining room table. She called out and advised him that their meal was about five minutes away. He answered there was no rush and stood at an easterly facing window and looked out to sea. When Emma finally joined him with the food, he apologized for his perspiration drenched shirt. She waved him off but did not admit that she found the scent from his work anything but objectionable. They spent the next hour at the dinner table talking about the progress made on the house and a possible time line for completing all of the exterior work. Fin was quick to remind her that they were at the mercy of the weather and that an inside project should be ready to commence whenever the elements turned against them. On two or three occasions Fin grew too technical in explaining what needed to be overcome to complete the work outside and her mind wandered. Emma had just risen from her chair and begun clearing the table when she asked Fin if he would join her and share a bottle of wine in the living room. He appeared ready to beg off her invitation but then accepted. The sun was casting long shadows from the oceanfront homes across the beach when she filled two wine glasses to just under the brim and collapsed onto the couch beside him.

"You know, Fin, I don't know a thing about you from the time I moved away to the present. I don't know if you ever got married or if you have any children. Why don't you catch me up on your life? When you're done, I'll do the same. First a warning: my life has been very, very boring," she confessed. The tall man fidgeted in his chair and stared long and hard at his old friend. Finally, he shrugged his shoulders and began to speak.

"I'll try to just go over the highlights and not every tiny hill and valley in between," he answered.

"Broad strokes, Fin. Give it to me in broad strokes."

"I had my heart broken my junior year in high school. There was this skinny, little girl who broke my heart and went away," he recounted in a half-serious manner. Emma listened intently and found her mind jettisoned back to Kennebunk, 1974. The image of Fin kneeling before her on her front porch, kissing one knee and then the other, came to mind and was followed by the sight of him standing down in the yard below her bedroom on prom night and begging her to forgive him for doing the right thing and honoring a promise. She had controlled him over that nine month period, but never more than when she convinced him to help her satisfy her sexual curiosity. She wondered if he remembered that whole incident. Images from that time went speeding through her mind: Whitney Crowninshield; Mechanic Street; Mrs. Bibber's class; Benny Fadden; Gilbert O'Sullivan; her father reading his *York County Coast Star;* Beaudoin's Drug Store; the Kennebunk Drive-in; *Becky has the looks, Emma has the brains;* homeroom and Mr. Foster; *In a little while from now, if I'm not feeling any less sour.* Emma took a deep breath and brought herself out of the semi-trance. "I got a job with a construction company out of Lyman a short time after I graduated," said Fin. "I liked my boss, he was the owner, and I learned a hell of a lot from him. I sort of became the son he never had. He had three daughters. One of his girls, the oldest, was named Phyllis and she took a shining to me. This was something I was not used to. Well, over time we started going out together. Phyllis was not a great beauty. She wasn't ugly. She was sort of in between. But she was sweet and, in time, I grew very fond of her. This made her father very happy and, I can honestly say, I was happy at this time. A few years passed and Phyllis and me were on the verge of getting engaged. I was making good money in construction and was now handling projects all by myself. One night, me and my buddies went out visiting bars in Sanford and we ran into a pack of wild girls. In this pack of Sanford girls was one I just couldn't take my eyes off. Her name was Audra and she had these sleepy, bedroom eyes that blew me away. The old-timers said she kind of looked like Lauren Bacall. Anyway, over the course of the evening, the girls had latched on to us by now, Audra noticed who had most of the cash in the group of guys. That, of course, was me. She gravitated to me and unleashed those eyes and her killer body on this poor, unfortunate kid from Jonesport. I started taking her out, behind Phyllis' back, of course. She lived in this glorified shack out in the boonies. I was dating white trash and I knew it, but I couldn't walk away from her. Her eyes and her way about her were hypnotizing. Eventually, Phyllis found out about Audra and confronted me. I had to decide between the two of them," explained Fin, his voice trailing off.

"I think I know where this is going, but go ahead," coached Emma.

"I turned my back on Phyllis and took up full-time with Audra. She had her hooks in me so deep, there was no breaking away. I lost my job with Phyllis's dad, but got hired right away by someone else. I was damn good at my job and I could control people under me because of my size. In the back of my mind I saw myself getting away from Audra. Then came the one-two punch: she got pregnant and I found out she wasn't even seventeen yet. I was screwed and I knew it. The family gave me the option of marrying Audra or going to jail. I took consolation on how beautiful she was. That was before I had to live with her. Actually, the first few years weren't too bad. My new employer took me in as a partner and I started taking home very good money. This made Audra happy and pretty soon we were living the American dream with the new house and two cars. Then came the recession and that's when a lot of stress was put on the marriage. By then, we had two kids and all of the expenses that came with it. After less than a year of scraping by and trying to keep ahead of the bill collectors, I found myself locked out of the house and dealing directly with lawyers and no longer with Audra. There was an ugly divorce and I got clobbered. Audra got the kids and the house and some nasty child support payments from me. I found out a couple of years later that there was another man all along, which she had kept quiet. Everything crashed in on me and I eventually had to file for bankruptcy. It's been a rugged thirteen or fourteen years, but I'm out from under the child support payments and I'm in the home stretch paying off my old debts."

"I thought you said you filed for bankruptcy?" asked Emma.

"I did. But I didn't feel right about stiffing all those people, so I've been paying them back a little at a time ever since. Now, if I can keep the fine lady I'm working for right now real happy, then by Halloween everyone will be paid and I can go back to looking people in the eye again," he added.

"What are your children's names?"

"Trevor's the oldest and Victoria is my baby. Don't worry, Vicky doesn't look too much like me."

"And where's your ex-wife?"

"She's living with her attorney husband in a mansion near Higgins Beach," he answered with little or no bitterness in his voice. Emma leaned forward and refilled Fin's wine glass. She half expected him to wave her off, but he did not. She was tempted to ask him about his relationship with his son and daughter but decided to save that for another time.

It was Emma's turn to fill in the blank pages of her life for Fin. He looked at her from the opposite end of the couch as she recounted her introduction to Professor Frederick Lipton. He was a man only a few years her father's junior when they met. The attraction was not immediate, at least not for her. She earned a bachelor's degree, then her masters before entering the teaching profession. It was not long before she realized that she enjoyed intellectual debate with her father's associates more than teaching.

Teaching, she learned, had too many of the elements of hard work if done properly. It was at this junction in her life that she gained control over the emotional well-being of Frederick Lipton. This pleased her and it was not long before she turned his affection into a full blown obsession. Professor Lipton courted his colleague's daughter with the vigor and intensity of a man twenty-five years his junior which, coincidentally, was the age difference between them. Following a courtship of nearly eighteen months, they were married on campus. Unlike Fin, Emma had no accounts of children entering her life or divorce proceedings altering it. She finished up the abridged version of her adult life with a brief description of her last months caring for Frederick. Purposely, she omitted any mention of Scott Harrington, the married man she had loved for the last eight years. She reasoned that Fin might not be open-minded, given his own life story.

The beach was practically invisible to the eye when Emma escorted Fin to the door. It was nearly ten o'clock. They had talked for over three hours. Part of the time was spent with Emma tossing out the names of classmates from Kennebunk High School and Fin filling her in on their whereabouts and circumstances. Many of the accounts had brought a wave of laughter from her. He paused at the door for no clear reason. She pulled on his shirt sleeve and coaxed his head down closer to hers. She planted the most innocent of kisses on his cheek and wished him a safe journey home. He responded with a surprised expression short of a blush, displaying that he was taken by surprise.

21

By Thursday, the work on the house was moving along efficiently, with the sound of the electric saw and driving nails filling the oceanfront neighborhood. In mid afternoon, Emma approached Fin and asked him for a ride back from a nearby garage. Her Volvo needed a two day repair and she would be leaving it on Route 1 for that period. Fin followed her to the garage and taxied her home in his pickup. He needled her by apologizing for the lack of a back seat, making a reference about losing out on a *Driving Miss Daisy* experience. He finished work on the porch just after five o'clock and set off to Biddeford to join friends. Emma retired to bed early this night and fell into a deep sleep.

Emma's eyes blinked open to a darkened room and she looked over at the alarm clock by the bed. It was nearly one-thirty. Something had jolted her from a sound sleep and she listened for any unusual sounds from outside. The ocean waves were audible, but certainly nothing out of the ordinary. Lying still in bed, she let a few seconds pass before assuring herself there was nothing wrong. That is when she distinctly heard the sound of glass breaking. It came from downstairs and seemingly from the far side of the house. Rolling onto her side, she reached for the night table and her cell phone. She came up empty. She heard a second series of sounds. These were male voices. She jolted up to a sitting position and frantically scoured the darkened room for her phone. It was nowhere to be seen. She thought back to earlier that evening and a conversation with Scott while lying in a hot tub. It occurred to her that the phone could be on the first floor and there was no land line upstairs. There was audible movement in the rooms on the floor below. She heard footsteps move across the house and stop directly below her in the area of the living room. Fear took hold of her but she forced herself to climb out of bed and creep to the bedroom door. There were voices again from below and they sounded like young males. Driven by unbridled fear, she made an on-the-spot decision and went with it. She slowly pulled open her bedroom door and stepped out into the hallway.

"Bubba! Bubba! There's someone in the house. Get your gun from the closet and for God's sake, be careful!" she cried out in a hysterical voice. Her words set off an immediate scramble of footsteps from the first floor below and a volley of profanity. Within seconds came the sound of more breaking glass followed by the thud of feet making contact with the ground outside. Emma burst into tears and raced downstairs in search of a phone. She settled for the land line in the kitchen and called the Wells Police Department. Following a frantic account of what had transpired, a cruiser pulled up behind the house in less than five minutes. Emma sat with an officer and recounted what had taken place and indicated that she did not think anything had been taken. The cop jotted down a few details and examined the window where entry was made. The policeman asked her if there was someone who could come over and stay with her. He also offered to refer someone to help with fixing the damage to the window. She thanked the young patrolman and stated emphatically that she would be calling in a friend as soon as he was done.

Emma dialed the phone and waited on her friend to answer. After four rings, a male voice mumbled hello.

"Fin, I need you to come over to the house. I've had a break-in and there are three missing panes of glass in one of my windows. I'm still a little shaken up," she confessed. She could practically hear Fin trying to collect his thoughts at the other end of the line.

"Emmy, are you all right?" She answered yes and pleaded with him to hurry over. He indicated he would throw on some clothes and be there as soon as possible.

There was an interlude of about a half hour between Emma's call and Fin's arrival at the house. He appeared at the door disheveled and looking tired but was more than a welcome sight for her eyes. She whisked him through the dining room to the place of entry. He examined the broken panes of glass and window frame through half-opened eyes and gave her an immediate report.

"I'll have the window fixed before noon tomorrow," he promised. Emma closed her eyes in frustration and nervously shook her head.

"That's not as important to me right now as knowing I'm not going to wake up later tonight with a man's sweaty hand over my mouth," she argued.

"First, let me go down to the cellar and get some plywood to put over the window," he stated as he made his way past her. She stepped back and watched him disappear out the front door.

"Fin, you can't leave me alone in this house, not tonight."

"Don't worry, I'll stay," he called back to her.

Emma put on a pot of tea while Fin put a temporary fix to the window. Fin's tea was resting on the dining room table when he ambled back into the room.

"It won't keep out a stampede of longhorns, but it should keep any raccoons or skunks out," he reported.

"It's not the skunks I'm worried about," she mumbled into her cup of tea. He glanced out to the clock in the kitchen. It was one of the black cat clocks whose eyes and tail move in unison while counting off the seconds. It was nearly three o'clock.

"You said you wanted me to stay and not leave you alone. Where exactly do you want me to crash?" She threw her head back and searched the ceiling for an answer, or so it appeared to him.

"Why don't you stay in the downstairs bedroom where they tried to come in? Just don't get any ideas about slipping upstairs," she warned.

"I would have to find you halfway attractive to do that," he wisecracked back.

"What? You don't find me attractive?" Emma asked, sounding insulted.

"Emmy, it was a joke," he answered before erupting into laughter.

Emma scurried to a hallway closet and put a fresh set of linens on Fin's bed before he settled into the downstairs bedroom for another three or four hours of sleep. She was standing in the dining room when he settled in and shut the door, staring at him oddly but saying nothing.

"I want you to fall off to sleep right away and don't let this whole business keep you awake. I won't let anything happen to you," he reassured her from within the room.

"I know you won't, Fin. I know you won't," she responded and quietly made her way back upstairs. Reaching the second floor hallway, she felt her anxiety dissipate. Fin was here, she told herself. He promised to have the broken window fixed by noontime. She slid back into bed and pushed the break-in to the back of her mind. No one could get by Fin, she told herself, and promptly drifted off to sleep.

Fin spent a restless night in Emma's makeshift guest bedroom. Much had to do with the size of the bed compared to his six foot, eight inch frame. He tried both sleeping at a fifteen degree angle and in a modified fetal position, but neither worked. Following two to three hours of shifting back and forth, he finally dropped off to sleep. Unfortunately, his rest was short lived. The cawing of sea gulls just after sunrise awakened him from his newfound sleep. He remained in bed for some time, staring up at the ceiling and listening for activity from Emma. It was after seven o'clock when he lifted himself off the mattress and went into the kitchen to make coffee. He eyed a pot of Chock Full of Nuts brewing there when he heard a cell phone ring upstairs. He meandered over to the bottom of the stairwell and listened. Thanks to the quiet of the house and Emma's open bedroom door, he was able to pick up on much of her conversation. He stole a look at the moving kitty clock and saw it was not even seven fifteen. He took a chair and quietly eavesdropped as Emma spoke warmly and giggled back to the caller. He quickly theorized that the call was coming from a man. The conversation went on for about ten minutes before Emma ended it with a closing that sent a painful twinge through his stomach.

"And I love you so very, very much, Scott," she professed in a truly heartfelt manner. This overheard conversation would dampen his spirits on this day. He was unusually quiet at breakfast which Emma attributed to tiredness. In truth, he had already begun imagining a reigniting of their old relationship, except with elevated sexual components. He had viewed Emma as a lonely, vulnerable widow fresh from three months of caring for a dying husband. He had not even considered the possibility that another man could have already slipped into her life in such a short time. On this Friday morning, it was a tired Fin Cromwell who set out to repair the broken window. His understandable drowsiness was also straddled with the disappointment that Emma Lipton's affections were already in the possession of another man.

Fin skipped out for lunch unannounced at noontime and made the short drive to Billy's Chowder House, where he washed down a haddock sandwich with a bottle of Miller High Life. He returned to working on the downstairs window and completed that task a short time later. As far as Fin could discern, Emma was sleeping in on this day. However, at three o'clock, he was called inside to join her in the living room. He took a chair adjacent to her and watched as she jotted details in her checkbook. With her head down, he was able to stare at his friend and admire her pretty delicate features and petite body. It was becoming increasingly obvious to him that his former affection for Emma was returning. A few more seconds passed and she tore a check from the book and handed it to him. He glanced down and saw two thousand dollars and his name on the face of the check. He thanked her, folded it in two and tucked it in his shirt pocket. Emma put her checkbook away and returned her attention to her old friend.

"Fin, as you have no doubt observed, I am a nervous wreck since those dirtbags broke into the house. That's why I want to ask a favor of you. Would you be willing to move down here from Kennebunk for the duration of my project? Based on everything we've discussed, I know your work will probably extend out for the better part of a year. I know what I'm asking is a lot, but it would go a long way toward calming me down," she explained. He fidgeted in his chair and stared deeply into her eyes, but withheld an answer. "If it were anyone else, I wouldn't even think of asking this of them, but we go back a long way." She looked into his eyes and was not encouraged by his expression or body language.

"Emma, I've been in the same place since my wife kicked me out and that's eleven years ago. It's only a lousy room, but I'm not sure it'll still be there when the year's up," he explained apologetically. His words brought tears to her eyes. Her reaction was not lost on him and he let out a deep sigh. She nodded her head in acceptance and rose from her place on the couch. Circling behind his chair, she placed her hands down on Fin's shoulders and leaned forward.

"I understand, Fin. I'll be fine," she said softly in his ear. She walked to the window and glanced out to sea, a look of apprehension etched on her face. He studied his high school love from across the room and again marveled on how well she had preserved her figure from Kennebunk High School. Emma's state of depression weighed on him. Following a full minute of silence, he rose from his chair and joined her at the window. He brought his face down over her shoulder.

"If it's that important to you, I'll have everything moved in by the end of the weekend," he whispered in her ear. She turned and placed her hands on the side of his face.

"It is that important," she replied, and showered his cheek with a flurry of innocent kisses.

It was very late in the afternoon when Emma set out on a walk up the beach to the jetty while Fin drove up to Route 1 to deposit his weekly check. The stroll north was pleasant for her, particularly with the issue of home security resolved. In addition to safety, she liked the idea of not being alone in the evenings. Along with the invigorating walk, Emma also spent some of her time standing at the edge of the ocean considering her relationship with Fin. If she had harbored any doubts about her command over her old friend, then these had been dispersed over the preceding twenty-four hours. For the last couple of days, she had observed how he looked at her and now his actions had confirmed her suspicions. Walking northward, she told herself she would not abuse her power over this good man. She, if anyone, knew the pain from love deprived of anything short of total fulfillment. She reached the jetty in just over twenty minutes and climbed up onto the granite walkway. She proceeded to follow the flat-sided boulders out to the entranceway to Wells Harbor. Taking a seat with her back against the base of the light beacon, she peered out to sea and fantasized about a week with Scott at the house. So engrossed was she in her daydream that she failed to notice the day growing darker around her. Dusk had enshrouded the house by the time she returned. On the table was a note from Fin explaining his absence and promising his return before nine o'clock.

22

By the end of September Fin was completely moved in and progress on the house was proceeding nicely. Work on the porch was largely completed with all rotted and distressed boards replaced and the integrity of the short stairway up to the porch restored. It was early Sunday evening when Fin returned home from working on another customer's Victorian windows. He found Emma relaxing on the ocean side of the porch in one of two wicker chairs kept out for the season. The sun had just set and a half moon appeared above the darkening ocean water. He let out a moan and collapsed into the vacant chair.

"It's such a beautiful night," exclaimed Emma and drew in a deep breath. Fin's response was to throw his head back and close his eyes. He was at the tail end of a seven day workweek and based on all outward signs it was taking its toll. "I really don't want to get up or go inside but I'm getting cold." He rolled his head to one side and opened one eye. "Fin, my feet are freezing. Would my dearest of friends please go up to my bedroom and bring down my heavy afghan? It's draped across the bottom of the bed." To Emma's surprise, he stood up from his chair and proceeded up to her room. His compliance with her request was truly unexpected. She had made the appeal as a joke. A few moments later he returned through the back door carrying the blanket.

"Why don't you stand up for a second and I'll get this thing wrapped all around you?" Emma followed his suggestion and watched as he laid the afghan out over the chair and onto the porch by her feet. He followed this by pushing her back onto the chair and wrapping up her body and extremities, leaving only her head exposed to the cooling, night air. Lastly, he lifted her from the chair with comical ease and took possession of it himself, cradling her in his lap and draping his arms around her petite body. Mildly stunned, she stared at him with a puzzled expression.

"Fin, what are you doing?" she asked.

"I'm not sure. I'm probably just making a total fool of myself," he confessed. He followed his words by pressing his lips against hers and tightening his grip on her. She returned the kiss.

"You're breath is very pleasing," she murmured to him, her voice taking on an intimate tone.

"I found myself in need of a sugar fix on the way home and I stopped for some Junior Mints. My timing couldn't have been better." She slipped her arms out from under the blanket and ran her fingers through his hair. At that instant she was reminded of the night in 1973 when he carried her back from the river. Her response to him set off something inside the man. "Emmy, I get close to you and I lose control over everything," he confided in her ear. "When I'm close to you like this and I smell your hair and skin, I'm lost to the world. You've always had this complete power over me ever since we were kids and I can't seem to shake it. I think God meant me to love you and nothing I do will ever change that," he confessed. Emma became frightened by Fin's confession and grew rigid in his arms.

"I think I want you to put me down," she demanded sternly. He rested his face on the top of her head and breathed in the fragrance of her shampoo. "Fin, I mean it," she insisted. He hoisted himself up from the wicker chair and placed her down. A few feet away, her cell phone rang and she walked to the table where she had left it. Fin listened and heard Emma's voice thaw in the next instant. She turned her back to him and whispered into the device. He circled the porch and walked to his truck. Emma was relieved to hear the engine of Fin's truck turn over at the front of the house. Scott was on the telephone with good news: everything was arranged at his end for his trip up to Wells Beach to spend a week with her. He would arrive on October sixteenth, a Sunday, and stay until the following Saturday. Emma felt her heart race while Scott explained everything that had gone into his grand scheme. Beverly would also take the week off and travel to western Pennsylvania to visit her mother and siblings and leave him free for this grand adventure. Emma's heart was racing with excitement by the time she closed the conversation with Scott a few minutes later. It took a full two minutes before she returned to the here and now and considered the obstacle Fin represented by living and working at the house.

Emma was spread out on the couch in front of the television when Fin's truck motored up the driveway. For the last ninety minutes she had attempted to sort out the mess she faced regarding Fin's occupation of the house. He had left her in a huff earlier and she wondered about his frame of mind on his return. The front door opened and closed and soon after came the sound of his keys dropping onto the dining room table.

"I hope you're not too drunk," she called out to him.

"I don't think one beer at Billy's is going to get me drunk," he answered back. There was no slurring of his speech.

"You nursed one beer for an hour and a half. I'm surprised they didn't toss you."

"I had a scallop plate to go with it. Not to worry, they made a few bucks off of me," he said, appearing in the doorway to the room. He turned to leave.

"Fin, please sit down. I have to go over something with you." He shuffled into the living room and took a chair hallway across the room. "I know this is not going to go down well with you, but I need you to move out of the house for a week. I'm also giving you a week off next month that will coincide with this. It is three weeks away, so you have plenty of time to find a temporary place to stay," she indicated. Fin's mouth literally dropped open as he stared across the room at her in astonishment.

"Are you goddamn kidding me?" he blurted out.

"This is nonnegotiable," she insisted, folding her arms across her chest to indicate there would be no further discussion.

"Where am I supposed to go? Am I supposed to camp out on the beach for a week?"

"Oh, for Christ's sake, stop being so dramatic. Rent a cheap motel room up on Route 1 somewhere. I'll reimburse you for the cost."

"You're really something, you know that, Emma? I move in here so you won't be scared shitless every night and now I get tossed out on the street for a week," he ranted.

"Again, this is nonnegotiable. If you don't like it, then feel free to walk away from our verbal contract. It's up to you," she concluded. Fin wrestled with his male pride for the next few moments. His first impulse was to tell her to stick her contract and her cottage where the sun didn't shine and walk out, but the flow of cash this work represented meant a great deal to him. After a few uncomfortable seconds he stood up and walked out of the room. Back in his bedroom he consoled himself with the thought of how much money he was squirreling away. He gave Emma her little victory, knowing that his long climb out of debt was nearing completion.

23

On a sunny Friday morning in early October, Fin greeted Emma in the dining room with a full coffee pot and pastries from Congdon's Donut Shop on the table. He appeared to be in particularly good spirits. It was early and the sound of *Fox and Friends* was still echoing through the first floor of the house. He poured her a cup and took a seat across the table from her. Her eyes still only half open, she took a sip from her coffee and pointed at a scone from the selection of pastries.

"I'm going to celebrate a wonderful event in my life tonight and I'm hoping you'll join me," he suggested. Emma stared over at him suspiciously. "It won't be a date or anything like that and I'm not putting any special meaning behind it. I just want to share this moment with someone I care about."

"What's the big event?" she asked.

"As you know, I was pretty close to paying off all my debts when I started working for you last month. With today's check, I'll be able to pay off my last creditor. That makes me officially free of all that crap I went through back in the nineties," he explained. "All I'm talking about is dinner at Billy's and a couple of drinks. I know you love lobster, so I'm thinking you might skip lunch today and have a couple of lobsters tonight." Her face brightened.

"Okay, but I don't want us sitting at the bar. I want to be at a table," she insisted. Fin agreed with a nod of the head and attacked a small stack of honey-dipped donuts. They finished breakfast with full stomachs and in good spirits, while a pleasant breeze off the ocean filled the house with a clean, fresh scent. This morning, Fin was about to begin work on the third story of the cottage, where two bedrooms with slanted ceilings were about to be completely restored and revitalized. This included work on the windows, trim, doors and wallpaper. Emma was seated in front of the television when Fin, with toolbox in hand, prepared to climb to the third floor. "We need to talk, Fin," she called out to him. His face appeared in the doorway. "It recently dawned on me that since you gave up your room in Kennebunk you've been saving quite a bit of money on rent. What was your rent up there per week?" His pleasant expression turned serious.

"A hundred dollars a week," he answered. She took a sip from her coffee and paused.

"I see no reason why I shouldn't knock a hundred dollars off of your weekly stipend, given that you're saving that much staying here with me," she theorized before turning her attention back to the panel on Fox. Fin stared at her with a dumbfounded expression spread across his face. She turned back to him and burst into laughter. "God, you're so gullible," she called out. He turned his face to the wall and let out a groan.

"Well played, Lipton, well played," he conceded.

Emma and Fin pulled into the parking lot at Billy's Chowder House at six o'clock. She found an empty space for her Volvo next to the building and they made their way inside. Standing by the front desk, Fin was showered with greetings from an assortment of restaurant employees and they were seated in the back room at a table overlooking the Mile Road Bridge and estuary. Within a few seconds their waitress, Betsy, was at the table delivering menus and taking orders for beverages. She also knew Fin and joked with him about another employee at the restaurant while taking their orders for drinks. After burying his face in the menu for the better part of a minute, he looked up to see Emma staring intently across the room. He turned and observed a man and woman standing over a table while a bus boy hustled to get it cleared and set.

"I hate that woman," said Emma, her eyes focused on an impeccably dressed businesswoman. The female in question was elegantly attractive with blond, highlighted hair and an unmistakable air of superiority.

"I know them. Well, I know him. His name is Brian Kelly and that's his wife," reported Fin. He turned back to Emma.

"I don't even know her and I despise her," she confessed. "She has that arrogant look about her that just makes you want to slap her face." Emma's words and mood change caused Fin to laugh aloud.

"He's a really good guy. He helped me out when my ex tossed me out of the house. I was doing a job for him at the time. He owns a good sized motel and cottage operation up on Route 1. He found out I was sleeping in my truck and let me stay in one of his cottages for a few weeks. She, I have heard, is not as nice."

"What does he see in her?" Emma asked. Fin shook his head in disbelief.

"Come on, Emmy, look at her. You know what he sees in her." She shifted her eyes away from the beautiful Mrs. Kelly and back to her menu.

"You men are so shallow," she stated and shook her head in disgust. "I haven't eaten since this morning, on your suggestion if I remember correctly, and so I'm going to have the twin lobsters," she declared. Fin smiled across the table at her.

"Wow, there goes my food budget for the week. I guess I'll just have to go with the hot dog and fries," he clowned, his words prompting his companion to kick him under the table. Involuntarily, Emma found her attention drawn back to the Kelly's table across the room.

"How old is she?" Emma asked.

"They're both about our age," answered Fin. "I know that because I know they were in high school together like us."

"She's our age! That woman is our age!" exploded Emma in disbelief. "I thought she was some kind of trophy wife."

"No. Actually, she makes most of the money in the family. They're loaded like you. Brian jokes about his wife being rich while he has to pinch pennies but everyone knows that everything she has is half his," explained Fin. Soon after the drinks arrived, Fin excused himself from the table. To Emma's surprise, he did not head in the direction of the men's room but crossed the dining room and stopped at the table occupied by Mr. Kelly and his wife. She watched as Fin engaged the man in a discussion while the woman looked on intently. The conversation went on for about a minute. It seemed to be over when the two men shook hands. However, Fin's departure from the table was halted when the woman suddenly spoke up. Frozen in place, Fin responded to the woman twice before she broke eye contact with him and returned her attention to her husband.

Rejoining Emma at their table, Fin immediately directed the conversation toward his current work on the top floor of the house, knowing she would not let them stay on that topic for very long.

"What was that all about?"

"Oh, I just went over and told Brian how much my friend hated his wife," he replied behind a straight face.

"I'm serious, Fin."

"I just invited them over to the house later for a nightcap," he needled. She sighed and waited on a serious answer. "Actually, Brian owns a little cottage around the corner from you on Deptula Lane. I asked him if it was available to rent in a couple of weeks. It is and I'm going to be staying there when your company comes to visit." Emma processed the explanation and nodded her head.

"What did *she* say to you before you left?" Fin grimaced.

"Brian and I didn't mention what the rent would be. Margaret, that's what her name is, wouldn't let me go until we settled on a price for the week. I suggested three hundred dollars but she insisted on three-fifty," he explained.

"God, what a bitch," snapped Emma. "I'm not going to be able to enjoy my meal knowing that witch cost me that much money." Fin smiled across the table.

"Emmy, relax. I'm sure Brian will give me the hometown discount when we talk about it alone. It'll probably cost you two hundred, two fifty max," he reasoned. Emma shook her head in relief and glared across the room at Margaret Kelly. Following a short lull in the conversation, Fin lowered his voice and grew more serious. "Emmy, I think I may know why you dislike Brian's wife so much." She brought her attention back in from the estuary outside and refocused on her friend. "I think you see a lot of Whitney Crowninshield in Brian's wife. Physically and in their mannerisms, they seem to be cut from the same cloth," he theorized. A frown broke across Emma's face as she considered Fin's words.

"You could be right," she admitted begrudgingly. "I don't think you ever completely recover from the shit I took in high school."

To Emma's surprise, her celebratory evening out with Fin did not end with dinner. For the past week she had been whining about a new film called *Separate Lives*. Reading about it on line, she found the story line fascinating and pertinent to her. It seems it was not going to play anywhere in York County and she found this inexcusable. Fin directed her to turn the Volvo southward out of Billy's parking lot for they were going to the Portsmouth, New Hampshire area. There, *Separate Lives* was playing at a theater that catered to quality films and the people who appreciated them. They arrived in Portsmouth fifteen minutes before the showing of the film and stood in line amongst intelligent, responsible adults. Emma enjoyed the motion picture even more than she had expected. Fin enjoyed the second half of the film more than the first half. During the last hour of the movie, Emma rested her head on his shoulder and provided commentary for her friend. They arrived back at Wells Beach shortly before midnight. Stumbling up the stairs together to the porch, they entered the darkened house. After flipping on a couple of lights, Fin walked toward his downstairs bedroom but was stopped by his employer and landlady before he reached the door. She buried her face into his chest.

"Thank you for a wonderful evening," she stated sleepily. She beckoned him to lean forward and kissed him on the lips. "Sometimes you're too good to me," she added. He pecked her back on the mouth, tasting her lips before she pulled away. He watched as she moved toward the stairs. At that instant, he longed to pounce on her petite body and make love to her until the sun peaked above the Atlantic horizon.

"Emmy," he called out longingly. She turned back to him.

"No, Fin, I love someone else," she replied and disappeared up the stairs.

24

Fin dumped a folded pile of shirts, socks and underwear onto the passenger side of his truck and closed the door. The last of his packing was completed. It was late Saturday morning and all of his other clothing was already hanging in the closet a quarter of a mile away. For the next week he would be living down the road in Brian Kelly's small beach cottage on Deptula Lane. He ambled back into the house and searched for Emma. After climbing the narrow stairway to the second floor he found her pulling bedding from her bedroom storage bureau. She turned and saw her friend leaning against the far wall, his attention focused on her.

"Can I help you?" she remarked sarcastically.

"I need a little spending money for the weekend and seeing that my gorgeous employer still owes me for my rent next week I thought I'd collect it before the banks close," he explained. She raised her eyes in frustration and moved toward the night table where she had left her checkbook the evening before. Sitting on the edge of the mattress she flipped open the plastic covering and began filling out the blank check.

"What did you wind up paying the ice princess and her husband for the week?"

"Brian charged me two hundred and sixty-seven dollars and fifty cents. I told you he'd cut us a break," remarked Fin.

"That's an odd amount," she commented while tearing off the check.

"He's a stickler for paying all his taxes. He told me he pays every nickel so he can look the bastards in the eye and not take any shit from them if he's ever audited," he explained. She handed him the check and impatiently waited on any other matters he might bring up. He took a quick peek at the check and stared back at her.

"Is there anything else?" she asked impatiently. He raised his hands in mock surrender and indicated there was not. "Then I take it you'll be on your way," she added and turned away.

Emma took a sip from her coffee cup and glanced down at her watch. It was almost four o'clock and the shadows were beginning to lengthen over the beach. The days had grown much cooler over the last couple of weeks, but she had left two porch chairs out in anticipation of Scott's arrival. She closed her eyes and felt the cold October breeze whisk over her face. Her anticipation of the forthcoming intimacy with Scott was intoxicating. The sound of an automobile coming to a halt carried over the nearby action of the waves. Jumping to her feet, she raced around the porch and saw Scott emerging from his vehicle. She called out to him and he stretched out his arms in response. She raced down the steps to the yard and was enveloped in his arms seconds later. Emma's tongue explored her lover's mouth for the next minute before she partially disengaged and ushered him towards the entrance to the cottage. She was pleased with his first response to her beachfront home as he walked directly to the dining room window and exclaimed about the superlative view.

The itinerary for the evening, as laid out by Emma, was a simple one. Dinner consisted of homemade chicken and rice soup along with fresh French bread picked up that day at the IGA. The light meal was to be followed by a leisurely walk along the beach. She had consulted her H.B. Provisions tide chart and Mother Nature was on board with Emma's plans. The tide was due to be out and a neap tide was also possible. Her romantic blueprint called for her and Scott to retreat upstairs to the bedroom no later than nine o'clock.

At seven-thirty Scott begged off on the stroll up the beach, explaining that the long drive to Maine and a poor night's sleep on Saturday had done him in. Therefore, it was shortly after eight when the two lovers climbed the stairs and found the comfort of Emma's bed. The sandy-haired academic administrator fell onto his back only to be mounted by Emma. It only took seconds before she was tearing clothing from his body. She laughed when one of his shirt buttons came loose and flew across the room, making audible contact with the window. With his upper body fully exposed, she brought her mouth down on his neck and bit into his flesh. He winced and closed his eyes. She slowed the pace of her sexual onslaught by sitting back on his torso and initiating a slow, methodical massaging of his chest and stomach muscles. He let out a long, appreciative sigh, savoring the pleasure her hands and fingers provided. She continued the massage for another ten minutes and then appeared to have Scott in some sort of sexual stupor. She brought the massage to a close and moved her body down over his. With their bodies aligned she picked up on the cadence of his breathing. She whispered his name into his left ear. There was no response. With this development came the realization that her massage had sent him into a deep sleep. Emma rolled over onto her pillow and stared up at the ceiling in frustration. Sometime after midnight she awoke and found Scott still dead to the world. She played with the idea of using his body while he slept but decided against it. There would be plenty of time in the next six days to rid her body of its demons, she reasoned.

Monday morning brought a procession of showers in off the Atlantic. Emma awakened to the sight of her ocean-facing window speckled with the moisture of a thousand droplets. Lifting one leg over her guest, she rained a series of kisses over the side of his face. He smiled and slowly shed the bonds of his long night's sleep.

"You left your sex hungry lioness starving for you last night. You're lucky you weren't torn to pieces while you slept," she advised her handsome visitor.

"I would have died a happy man," he confessed. He reached his hand behind her head and pulled it to him. A moment later his tongue was exploring her warm, moist mouth. Scott Harrington was a well-groomed man in his mid fifties who still clung to a measure of the good looks carried over from his youth. No longer the lady killer he was twenty years earlier, he nonetheless hoarded much of the self-confidence and pride of his former self. He, like so many other men of similar profile, refused to acknowledge the loss of influence over members of the opposite sex. Emma rolled her body up off of the mattress and remounted her lover.

"Was I dreaming or did you tear my clothes off last night?" he asked. She nodded yes and surveyed her would-be victim with a playfully menacing expression.

"I've waited a long time to be alone with you, handsome," declared Emma. She rhythmically moved her body over his and watched him gradually fall under her power. The smell of the bed's clean linens and the sound of the wind blowing rain against the cottage only heightened Emma's appreciation of Scott's fit body. The lovers dedicated the entire morning to lovemaking, making no concession to breakfast. It was shortly after noontime when they descended the stairs to the kitchen and dining room.

Scott watched attentively as Emma flitted between the kitchen and dining room preparing, and then serving, eggs and sausages. Of principal interest to him was her magnificently thin body. It was this attribute that initially drew him to her years earlier. One of his fellow male employees had commented about Emma over drinks, saying Frederick Lipton's wife had the body of a fifteen year old girl. The observation and the mental image it provoked preyed on his thoughts and erotic daydreams for the next few weeks, causing him to act on his urges. It was then that the long, eight year affair with Emma Lipton began. She had just joined him at the table when he interrupted their ongoing chit-chat.

"I think we've lived apart much too long. I'm going to tell Beverly about us and move out," he declared. Emma froze in place for a moment before slowly placing her knife and fork down.

"That's a very radical move on your part. Are you sure you're ready to turn your life upside down?"

"Yes, I am. It's just a matter of coming up with the proper timing. The holidays mean nothing to me but Bev is quite old fashioned in that way. I wouldn't want to scar Christmas for her from here until eternity, so maybe I'll push it up to next month. Thanksgiving is just so much garbage. I'll make the break and move out in November," he announced. Emma gradually returned to her meal, moving at half speed as she absorbed and processed Scott's decision.

By late afternoon the morning rain had lifted and the two lovers slipped on wind breakers and headed southward on bicycles. They followed the coast by Fisherman's Cove and paralleled Moody Beach until they reached the sand dunes of Ogunquit. Rolling onto a softly graveled road they continued to pedal farther away from Wells until a footbridge allowed them to join Route 1 and the village of Ogunquit. Emma led Scott through the clustered community center and down a roadway cavalcaded by restaurants, hotels and specialty shops until she directed him out onto a narrow finger of land.

"Scott, we're moving out onto some very valuable real estate," she called back to him, her hair blowing wildly over and around her shoulders. Slowing their speed, they coasted down a constricted avenue populated by art galleries and jewelry shops and finally dismounted their bicycles. They had reached Perkins Cove. They were standing by a small, half empty parking lot. A few feet away the lights were on in a gift shop called the Blue Willow. "That's a neat shop. We'll have to go in after I treat you to something warm," she added and flashed Scott a sweet smile. She rolled her bicycle up to a coffee shop perched at the edge of the incoming tide. Emma leaned her bike against the shop porch and instructed him to do the same. To their left, waves of foaming ocean water moved into a constricted, rocky cove.

"I found this place quite by accident a couple of weeks back. It hasn't been open that long from what I understand," she added. They slipped through the front door of Breaking New Grounds, a charming coffee shop in an idyllic location.

The shop was empty except for an elderly couple tucked away in the far corner of the sitting area where, no doubt, they reasoned that the cool draft from the opening and closing door could not reach them. Emma motioned Scott to choose a table with an ocean view and she went about ordering a pair of hot chocolate drinks for them. She paid the man behind the counter and joined her lover at a small table by the window.

"I have it from a reliable source that the hot chocolate here is fantastic…the reliable source being me." She reached across the table and clutched his hands. "You laid quite a bombshell on me earlier with that talk of walking out on Bev. It has me feeling a little guilty but, at the same time, incredibly excited. Bev has been a dear friend and stealing a friend's husband is going to elevate me on the list of all-time backstabbers," lamented Emma.

"We've been stabbing her in the back for the last six years," he added.

"The affair is eight years old, not six," corrected Emma before glancing up and seeing that their beverages were ready. She crossed the room and collected their drinks while Scott stared out the window. His eyes widened when a man in a sea kayak rounded the head of the cove and paddled in their direction. Emma returned to the table and placed the steaming cups capped with whipped cream down. She slid back onto her chair and grew more serious. "There's going to be a lot of logistic and financial details to sort out if you follow through with your plan. My sister went through a divorce seventeen or eighteen years ago, and I couldn't believe the mess that turned into. Like you, she was not the injured party and it wound up shredding her once the lawyers got their teeth into the proceedings," recounted Emma. Scott waved her off.

"The financial end of our mess may not be as complicated as you think. It was Beverly who brought the real estate and stock portfolio into the marriage, thanks to her miserable parents, and they badgered me into signing a pre-nuptial agreement. I'll probably come out of this disaster with precious little except my car and the clothes on my back." Harrington's revelation left Emma's mouth wide open in astonishment.

"How is that possible?" she asked. "You have a darn good job at the university." Scott answered with a boyish grin or what was left of one after fifty-five years on the planet.

"Frugality was never my strong suit," he confessed with a shrug of the shoulders. Emma lifted her cup and licked a portion of the whipped cream off the top of her beverage.

"Perhaps I'll have to be frugal enough for both of us," she answered with a hint of disapproval in her voice.

Emma and Scott pedaled their bicycles up the graveled driveway to the house shortly after six o'clock. The plan was to hurriedly change clothes and drive across town to the Maine Diner for dinner. She thought it best to avoid Billy's Chowder House, where there was the greatest likelihood of running into Fin. They were on their way out to the car when Scott ducked his head into the downstairs bedroom.

"I haven't even been in this room yet," he exclaimed, pushing in the door and looking around.

"Please, Scott, don't go in there," she insisted. He glanced back at her.

"Bad memories from your time here with Frederick?" he asked. She averted her eyes.

"Yes, something like that," she answered and quietly closed the door. She had, to date, made no mention of Fin's presence in the house and had already decided not to share his role in her life with Scott. The couple hustled out the door and made their way up to Route 1 for dinner at the diner.

It was an insistent Emma who pulled Scott out of her Volvo and pushed him toward the beach on the far side of the house. He moved slowly, the victim of too many dinner rolls, a large bowl of seafood chowder and the largest slice of banana cream pie he had ever eaten. Emma used all of the leverage her slender body could muster to yank him onto the beach for a walk northward to the jetty. The walk to the entrance to Wells Harbor and back took over an hour and, coupled with their bike ride, accounted for a full day of exercise.

Arriving back at the house Emma turned aggressor, cornering her lover on the living room couch and taking possession of his lap. It was not long before she was breathing into his mouth while her buttocks moved back and forth over his pubic region. She kissed him seductively a handful of times then leaned back to observe his condition. She smiled at the sight of her lover lost in an erotic fog. She never grew tired of her ability to take possession of a man's free will through this sort of manipulation. She bit lightly on Scott's ear before maneuvering him sideways and onto his back. He offered only token resistance and even that was nonverbal. Seconds passed and she was seated on his chest, his arms and shoulders pinned against the couch under her knees. She leaned down to him.

"Remember how I satisfied your every want and need this morning?" she whispered.

"You were great," he answered, then drew in a deep breath in an attempt to lower his body temperature.

"Well, tonight it's my turn. I'm fairly sure you can guess where I'm taking this, given the relative positions of our bodies," she declared behind a cabaret smile. He grinned and took a series of deep breaths.

"Emma, I literally don't have the strength to stop you at this moment. You've seen to that. But neither one of us have showered since this morning and we've been running our asses off all day."

"I didn't let the lack of a shower stop me from satisfying you this morning," she reminded him. He shook his head in acknowledgement and closed his eyes.

"Fine! I'll go take a shower, but after that there'll be no excuses," she warned. "I want you upstairs and in bed waiting for me when I'm done."

She dismounted him and made her way upstairs. Scott undressed and was waiting on her ten minutes later when she emerged from the bathroom and walked naked into the bedroom. He was true to his word and serviced Emma into the late hours. Finally, it was a totally satisfied and drained woman who called off an exhausted Scott Harrington as a downstairs clock struck midnight. His evening of sex over, he rolled over onto his back and let out a sigh of relief.

"I have never been used by a woman like that in my entire life," he declared. Emma giggled and looked down the bed at him.

"Pardon me, sir, but exactly how many years were you in the monastery and away from the weaker sex?" she joked.

25

Fin had had done everything within his power to stay busy during his week away from Emma. After calling around, he found a day and a half project up in Kennebunkport to keep him busy and make himself a few dollars. He also did some repair work for Brian Kelly at the Deptula Lane cottage in return for the man's rental discount. By Wednesday afternoon Fin ran out of busy work and picked up a case of beer at the store. He was motoring down Mile Road on his way back to his temporary housing when he passed Emma and her houseguest driving in the opposite direction. A man was seated behind the wheel of her Volvo while Emma leaned on his shoulder. Fin felt a pang of hurt pass through his stomach. It was difficult for him to see Emma draped over another man. He had hoped to avoid the sight of her during her visitor's stay. He continued back to the house and slid the beer into the refrigerator. For the next hour Fin attempted to shake off the image of the former Emma Corman and the other man. He walked to Moody Point and back and even out into the estuary in search of relief from the effects of the sighting. Finally, he retreated back to the cottage and attacked the case of chilling beer.

The Miller High Life bottle flew end over end until it made contact with the front lawn and rolled to a stop on the grass. It lay in the midst of fourteen other bottles tossed off the deck by an inebriated Fin Cromwell. Darkness had crept in over the estuary as he sat alone at the end of the quiet, private road. He closed his eyes and attempted to drive the image of Emma seated against the stranger from his mind. Unfortunately, his effort was in vain, just as it had been the half dozen times he had tried earlier. He filled his lungs with cool, autumn air and rose to his feet. He tried to remember the last time he had consumed this much beer, but his memory failed him. Rising from his chair he walked to the edge of the deck and stumbled down onto the lawn. He took another deep breath of fall air and set out down the gravel road. Although lightheaded, he managed to walk in a straight line toward Webhannet Drive and the sound of crashing surf. Fin heard himself talking aloud and cursing the man who owned Emma's affection. He turned onto Webhannet and walked in the direction of Emma's house, the farthest of the 'Four Sisters' from him. The road was quiet at this hour, with most of the oceanfront homes he passed in complete darkness. The driveway leading up to Emma's cottage was shielded from the road by a neighbor's detached garage, but Fin located it after only a few moments of difficulty.

Emma sat perched on Scott's lap in the corner of the living room while classical music filled the air around them. It was good to have her romantic partner by her side, she thought. She loved breathing in the scent of his aftershave on intimate occasions like this. She also enjoyed the warmth and feel of his touch as his hands moved over her body. She was in the early stages of arousal when Scott posed a question that brought her back to the material world.

"Emma, would you mind if I asked you something of a personal nature?" She pulled back from him slightly with a look of curiosity.

"No, go ahead. After all, you are the man I love," she answered. He fidgeted in place for a second before speaking.

"I know that Frederick left you very well off and comfortable. Emma, our lives will be coming together very shortly in a very real way. I was wondering if you would share a few details of your financial situation with me. I was curious to know exactly how wealthy a woman his death has left you," he explained. She stared at him long and hard before answering.

"I feel very comfortable sharing most anything with you, my love, but money and finances are two of the few exceptions," she responded. She raised her hand to his cheek and gazed warmly into his eyes. "Please don't hate me," she pleaded good-naturedly. To her surprise, Scott appeared offended by her response and pulled back. She was about to apply her seductive powers on him when there came the sound of the front door opening.

"Are you expecting someone?" asked her startled guest. Emma sat straight up and turned in the direction of the dining room.

"Hello, is someone there?" she called out. Her words prompted the sound of heavy footsteps moving in their direction. A moment later Fin's six foot, eight inch frame appeared in the doorway and looked down menacingly on them.

"Emma, call the police," called out a flustered Harrington. She looked up at Fin and saw an angry stranger standing in his place. She scrambled to her feet and approached him. He ignored her. His stare was locked menacingly on Scott and he moved toward him in the corner of the room. "Emma, call the police," repeated the man and attempted to make an escape by way of the far door. Fin stormed past Emma, snatched Harrington by the arm and flung him to the floor. Rushing to his aid, Emma jumped on Fin's back and wrapped her arms around his neck. "Emma," called out the man again in a plea for assistance. She tightened her grip around Fin's throat but it appeared to have little effect on him.

"Fin, I want you to stop right now! What's wrong with you?" she hollered from atop his back. Fin's hands had reached Scott's neck and he began to tighten his fingers. "Fin, this isn't you," she screamed into his ear. "You're drunk and making a fool of yourself." He paused and stared down on his potential victim. Sensing a moment of sanity in the man, she lowered her voice and spoke calmly. "Fin, let him go and look at me," she insisted. His grip loosened around Scott's throat and he turned his head. There were tears in his eyes. It was unclear whether they were tears of rage or regret. "Go home, Fin," she ordered in a soft voice. "This isn't you," she repeated and slid down from his back. Fin knelt in place over Scott for another ten seconds before slowly climbing to his feet and turning away from the man. Emma signaled down to Harrington to stay where he was and cautiously walked her friend to the front door. "Are you going to be okay? You didn't drive here, did you?" Fin shook his head no and moved toward the stairs. Holding onto the bannister, he made his way down to the back yard and stopped. Emma stood against the porch railing watching her friend. He turned back to her.

"I'm drunk as hell and totally in love with you," he called out. She dropped her head in acknowledgement of his confession. "Tomorrow morning, I won't be drunk no more," he concluded and began walking toward the road. "Tell the guy in there that I'm sorry," he called out and disappeared into the darkness of Webhannet Drive.

Emma closed and locked the door and rejoined Scott in the living room. She found him seated on the couch, his eyes glazed over from the shock.

"I guess it could have been worse. We could have been naked when he barged in on us," she stated lightheartedly. He looked up at her with confusion plastered across his face.

"How did he get in so easily? I know you locked the door when we got home," observed Scott. Emma rolled her eyes and joined him on the couch.

"He lives here. He has a key. I should have been more open with you. Fin's my contractor. As you noticed, the house is going through a complete restoration. He just spent over three weeks working on my porch," she explained.

"Contractor or not, I hope you're going to fire his ass after this," he shot back, making his statement more in the form of a demand than a suggestion. She sighed and lowered her head onto Scott's shoulder. It was clear she needed to provide her lover with a little more background information.

"Fin is a little more than a contractor. In fact, we go back all the way to high school. I've told you I went to Kennebunk High for three years before moving to Massachusetts. Well, Fin entered my life at a very critical point. I owe him a lot. He singlehandedly saved me from committing suicide and that's no exaggeration. I had the pills and I was minutes away from swallowing them when he happened upon me. I'm not even positively sure he knows he saved my life, but he probably does. So, darling, as you can see, a decision like that is not as easy as it first may appear," she explained.

"But why the hell is he living here?" he asked heatedly.

"That's my fault. A short time after I moved in, there was a break-in while I was home. It really freaked me out. I got Fin to give up his place in Kennebunk and move into the downstairs bedroom for security purposes." Harrington jumped to his feet and walked across the room to the window. He was visibly put out by Emma's explanation and revelations. "For God's sake, Scott, you can't be jealous of the man. You're a good looking guy. No, you're a great looking guy. Do you honestly believe I could be tempted away from you by someone like him? He's not exactly every woman's dream," she scoffed. Scott remained motionless at the window. "He hasn't been educated beyond the twelfth grade, for God's sake," she added. He looked back across the room at her. She read his eyes and body language. He was open for negotiation on the matter of Fin Cromwell.

Emma placated her lover on this night, playing his body like a Stradivarius. By now she knew all of his sexual proclivities and vulnerabilities and quickly rendered him helpless beside her. No doubt, Scott saw through Emma's scheme but in the end, surrendered on any demands involving the massive intruder in exchange for an hour or two of ecstasy. A northerly wind had come up in the last sixty minutes and blew relentlessly against the house, creating whistling sounds in the eaves. It was lost on Scott, who lay quietly on his back beside her in the four-poster bed. She stared at him and then up at the ceiling beams above. Something that had taken place earlier in the evening was plaguing her. She replayed the confrontation between Fin and Scott over and over in her head. She visualized the imposing figure of Fin standing in the doorway and recalled that Scott had made no effort to protect her. Instead, it appeared he had attempted to escape the room by way of the other door. At that moment, he had had no knowledge of Emma's relationship with Fin and that, by all appearances, she was in imminent danger too. These were the thoughts that weighed on Emma's subconscious on this night, realizations that infiltrated her thoughts until morning.

Emma and Scott were careful to savor each and every hour of the next three days. They made a day trip to the Old Port section of Portland and strolled through the antique shops and art galleries when they were not planted at some romantic table in a coffee shop. Blessed with an Indian summer afternoon on Friday, they picnicked on the ocean's edge at Spouting Rock in Kennebunkport in the shadow of the Bush compound. On the morning of their last day together, they remained in bed until noon, each memorizing every line and detail of the other. Finally, it was time to part. Their six days had flown by, but they talked of the better days on the horizon. They agreed that November would bring a state of bliss to their lives. There was no talk of the victim to be left in their wake.

26

A storm brought high winds and a pelting rain up the eastern seaboard and into southern Maine on Monday morning. Emma reached down and pulled a pink quilt up over her bed covers for more warmth. The sky over the ocean was still dark at this hour and she wondered about the exact time. She rolled sideways, burying her face in the second pillow. It had been Scott's just two days before and she picked up on the scent of his cologne. From the floor below came the sound of footsteps. It was Fin returning, she thought. She listened closely and heard the unmistakable sound of coffee being prepared all the way from the kitchen. She climbed out of bed, slipped on a bathrobe and descended the stairs. Emerging from the stairwell, she observed the open door to Fin's bedroom. She approached the sounds coming from his room and found him placing folded laundry into a bureau.

"You're back," she called to him. He turned and nodded. It was evident he was still mortified about the night of the confrontation. "Thank you for staying away for the remainder of my time with Scott," she added sarcastically. He dropped his head and continued unpacking.

"I'm still embarrassed about that night last week. I was pissed out of my head and made a total jackass of myself," he confessed without turning around.

"You're forgiven and that's the end of it," she replied before turning and walking back into the dining room. "I'd like my coffee with cream and sugar this morning," she called back to him. He smiled and emptied the last of his clothing into the drawer. He drove to Congdon's for Monday morning breakfast pastries. This amounted to the only penance she demanded from him for his home invasion a few days earlier.

It was mid afternoon when Fin descended the stairs and stepped out onto the porch. He was half surprised to find Emma there, bundled up and seated in a chair with a book propped up on her knees. She glanced up at him.

"I had to step away from what I was doing and get some fresh air. I've measured and cut the same board three times and it's still not fitting into place," he explained. She closed the book and lowered her reading glasses. "You look cute in them," he added.

"No, I look old in them," corrected Emma. She reached over and patted the chair next to her, inviting her friend to take a seat. He accepted the invitation and flopped into the chair beside her. "You've been quieter than usual today," she observed. "I told you that matter in the living room was behind us," she reiterated.

"I just didn't make a fool of myself in the living room, I think I made a fool of myself on the way out, too." Emma broke off eye contact and looked out to sea. "Did I say what I think I said?"

"What do you think you said?"

"I kind of remember saying something about going home and not being drunk the next day. It's what I could have said next that concerns me," he explained. "Emmy, did I say something else?" Her expression saddened.

"You told me that you loved me," she replied. He shook his head and looked away.

"I was drunk as hell," he reminded her.

"And in wine there is truth," she quoted.

"And maybe in Miller as well," he conceded. The porch went quiet for a few moments.

"What you actually said was one of the most beautiful things anyone has ever said to me. You said that you were drunk and you were in love with me but by the next morning you wouldn't be drunk anymore. It was beautiful in its simplicity, Fin." He reached over and patted her hand before rising to his feet and walking to the back door. He reached for the knob and stopped.

"I would give anything in this world to be him for just one day," he confessed sadly.

"Be careful what you wish for," she answered stiffly and reopened her book of Dorothy Parker poems.

Work on the two third-story bedrooms was proceeding nicely by the second half of the week. On Thursday night, Emma returned from a shopping trip in Biddeford to find Fin in his bedroom prepping for an evening out. What struck her as curious was the new drape hung on the backside of his bedroom door. Until now, the door, comprised largely of individual panes of glass, had provided only partial privacy. Now, a dark, purple drape blocked any view into the room. She loitered in the living room, emptying her bags and laying out her purchases on the table. A few minutes later Fin emerged from his bedroom dressed in a coat and tie.

"What's this all about?" she asked. He responded with a sheepish grin.

"I'm going out for the night," he replied and started for the front door.

"With whom?" Emma appeared stunned by his declaration. "You usually don't dress up for the guys at Billy's."

"Gee, Ma, I've already cleared it with Pop. You don't have to worry," he clowned.

"Fin, I'm serious. Are you meeting a woman?" He leaned down and responded playfully.

"Yes, I'm meeting a woman. The day you come home and find me dressed up and shaved for a man is the day you can take me out onto the beach and shoot me," he jested.

"Does the purple drape on your door have anything to do with your date? I hope you don't think you can bring some trollop here for a fling after getting her boozed up?"

"I'm only expecting a quiet night of dinner and chit-chat," he confessed. He was ready to leave for the evening. It was Emma who was determined to keep the conversation alive.

"I'm curious. How did you manage to meet someone? You spend so much time of the day here with me. Who is she and how did you meet her?" He glanced up to the ceiling in mock frustration.

"If you must know, she's someone I was fixed up with by friends."

"Who? Who fixed you up?" Fin pulled out a dining room chair and sat down across from his curious friend. He stared into her face for ten or fifteen seconds for dramatic effect before speaking.

"If you must know, it was Brian and a couple of his buddies." He watched a smirk materialize on Emma's face.

"What a friend we have in Jesus…and Brian Kelly," came back Emma sarcastically. "He's a married man. How does he know all these women?" Fin folded his hands and rested his chin on them, his eyes riveted on Emma.

"Like I said, it's Brian and his friends. "You know, I'm not sure I really want to fill in the last piece to the puzzle," he muttered. Her eyes widened.

"Well, now you have to tell me," she insisted. Fin rolled his eyes in frustration.

"If you must know, I'm going out with Brian's sister-in-law," he announced. It only took a second for Emma to process his words.

"You're going out with his wife's sister?" He nodded yes behind a timid grin. "I don't believe you," she fired back. He smiled and shrugged his shoulders.

"I can hardly believe it myself. I have to be the luckiest guy in the world. I know she's been divorced a couple of times, but nobody's perfect." He rose to his feet and replaced his chair under the table.

"You're really going out with that woman at Billy's sister?" He shook his head yes.

"According to Brian, she's a real looker, like his wife," he added. He reached over and mussed Emma's hair. She looked disheartened and could only manage a weak smile. Again, he walked to the door and paused with it half opened. He turned back to his friend. "Emmy, don't be so goddamn gullible. Brian's buddies have set me up with a girl that they say has a lot in common with me. They say she's sweet and kind but I'm sure she's no Emma Corman...or Emma Lipton for that matter," he called back to her. He thought he saw a look of relief register on her face.

"You bastard," she muttered back at him. There was no hostility in her tone and gave pause to Fin as he motored to Kennebunk to pick up his date.

Emma spent the majority of Thursday night channel surfing in the living room. At eight-thirty she grew bored and snapped a DVD into the player. She hoped for a call from Scott, but did not expect one. No doubt he was at home with Beverly, caught up in a dreary conversation about the university or perhaps a friend's finances. At ten o'clock she pointed the remote at the DVD player and brought her entertainment for the evening to an end. All night her mind had wandered to thoughts of Fin and his date. Only a week earlier it was she who was enjoying the companionship of a member of the opposite sex. Emma hung around the living room a short time longer before climbing the worn, wooden stairs to her bedroom.

She was still awake, her cheek resting comfortably against her sweet smelling pillowcase, when she heard a truck engine pull into a nearby driveway. Emma listened intently and picked up on the slamming of a vehicle door followed by the crackling of gravel under foot. In the seconds that followed came the sound of the front door opening. She found herself strangely eager to interrogate Fin about his date. She slipped her feet into a pair of slippers and threw a robe on over her pajamas. She eyed the alarm clock next to the bed. It read ten thirty-five. Descending the stairs, she heard movement out in the kitchen. She found Fin with his head in the refrigerator in search of something to eat or drink.

"I take it you've come home alone," she commented. Her words caused him to turn and acknowledge her presence.

"Yeah, it's a work night and Chanel had to get up early for work tomorrow," he explained. Emma giggled.

"Oh, it's Chanel, is it? That's a very exotic name. If nothing else, I'll bet she smelled good," she wisecracked. "So, tell me about Chanel." He shrugged his shoulders and buried his face back in the fridge. "Come on, Fin, it couldn't have been as bad as all that." He reached in and plucked an orange from out of the fruit tray.

"I got this date pretty much because this lady has had a problem finding suitable guys to go out with. She's tall like me. She says she's six foot one, but she looks taller. It was Brian's buddies, Bobby and Perez, who pushed it. Brian had his reservations. It turned out Brian was probably right," Fin concluded.

"Why? What did she say?" He shrugged his shoulders.

"She didn't have to say anything. She was too nice to say anything. I could just read it in her reactions to things and how we left things at the end of the night." He walked to the dining room table and took a chair. Emma followed him into the room and positioned herself directly behind him. His massive hands took to peeling the orange in the room's muted light. She reached down and massaged his shoulders. He stopped peeling and leaned back into the movement of her fingers. The relaxing movement of her hands on his neck went on for a minute or two before he spoke. "Emmy, you're a good, good woman and I'm really lucky to have you as a friend."

"You're very special to me, Fin," she replied and removed her fingers from his shoulders and neck. "Goodnight," she whispered in his ear and followed this with an innocent kiss to the top of his head. He began turning in her direction but she was already scurrying up the stairs to the bedroom.

On the day following Fin's date, Emma found herself alone in the house. Fin was picking up supplies at Aubuchon Hardware and she did not expect him back for an hour or so. On a whim, she wandered into his room and curiously perused some of the paperwork, letters and such, scattered atop his bureau and writing table. An envelope, partially obscured and labeled Kodak, caught her eye and she lifted it from his desk. Inside she found a quantity of dated photographs which she removed and held under the light from his window. The first two pictures depicted the upper village of Kennebunk. They appeared quite dated. However, it was the next half dozen photos that froze her in place. In front of Emma were teenage pictures of her posing somewhere along the coast. Her mind flashed back to a spring day in 1974 when Fin had escorted her to Parsons Beach on a picnic. She vaguely remembered him bringing a camera on that outing. Flabbergasted by her discovery, she stuffed the photos back into the envelope and discreetly returned it to its original resting place. Emma was struck by the realization that the photos had survived in his possession for thirty years, not to mention the years of his marriage. She found it almost incomprehensible that anyone, let alone a man, could be so sentimental.

27

The call came in the middle of the night. Becky pleaded with her sister for refuge for a few days, at least until the end of the weekend. It was not the first time Becky Andrade had turned to her big sister for protection from Josh, her abusive husband. If nothing else, her timing was impeccable. Fin had just completed all structural work on the third floor bedrooms and was about to commence with the wallpaper and painting. Emma would need these bedrooms over the next few days for her niece and nephew. After inviting her sister up for a long weekend, she had set her alarm clock for six and went back to sleep. Now the alarm was clanging by the side of the bed and she reached over to quiet it. Her bedroom was black as pitch as she peeled back her bed covers. When her feet made contact with the cold linoleum floor, she cursed her sister and then her parents for not allowing her to be an only child. She threw on her robe and hustled downstairs. Fin's bedroom was still in darkness. She walked to the kitchen and put on the kettle. She decided to have tea on this morning.

When the tea was ready, she carried a cup into the dining room and sat. At this time she noticed the light from Fin's lamp bleeding around the drape covering his door. It was not long before he emerged from his room and made for the kitchen.

"We're going to have some company for the next few days," she announced to his back.

"Your lover boy?" Fin asked.

"No, it's not anyone I might actually want to visit. Becky is coming up from New York with her two kids. She lives up by Albany," she answered. "You certainly must remember Becky." Fin joined Emma at the table with his tea cup in hand.

"Why did you wait until the last minute to tell me?" he asked.

"I didn't know until late last night myself. Her husband has a history of getting physical with her. She called last night, scared to death and asking for a place to go. What could I do? She is my sister," explained Emma. Fin squeezed out his teabag and added milk and sugar to his drink. "This means putting off any painting upstairs until Monday." He nodded knowingly and took a sip from his cup.

"How old are her kids?" Emma had to think for a moment.

"Tara's fourteen and Kyle is eleven," she replied. Fin smiled down into his cup of tea.

"It's hard for me to imagine little Becky with a teenage kid," he observed.

"As I said, I'm putting the kids upstairs and Becky will go in the spare bedroom across from mine," she explained. Noticing her cup was empty, Fin reached across the table for it and started back to the kitchen. He paused by the front door then turned back to Emma.

"What time did you say your sister was coming?" Emma noticed Fin's preoccupation with something in the front yard and tightened up.

"I didn't. Why do you ask?" He flashed a tenuous smile.

"There's a car parked in your driveway with New York plates, that why," he answered. She folded her arms on the dining room table and buried her face in them.

"The nightmare has begun," she proclaimed dejectedly which triggered a roar of laughter from Fin.

Emma awakened her sister and the children in the car and directed them into the house. Becky had immediately begun recounting her problems when she abruptly stopped in mid sentence. The sight of Fin Cromwell standing in the middle of her sister's kitchen at six-thirty in the morning caught her by surprise.

"Isn't that the ugly guy you knew in high school?" she whispered to Emma while being escorted up to her room.

"Yes, that's Fin Cromwell. He's my contractor and he's working on the house."

"He's as ugly as ever but he has a hell of a body, particularly for a guy his age," observed Becky behind a wry smile.

"I'll see if I can't get him to make you people breakfast. You have to be starving," said Emma before leaving her sister to unpack.

Following breakfast, Fin retreated to his workshop in the cellar, while Emma and Becky brewed a second pot of coffee and prepared for an extended chat. Emma observed that her kid sister had gained a few pounds since Frederick's funeral. By now Kyle was already outside exploring the coastline while Tara was upstairs listening to music and sulking.

"They're missing a day of school, but that won't kill them," commented Becky. "Emma, this time I was actually afraid for my life," confided Becky. "God, this house is old, but what a spot to be in!" Emma bit her tongue and secretly counted the hours before she would escort her sister, niece and nephew to their car for the long ride home.

Fin slipped out for lunch, joining Bobby Copeland and Perez at Congdon's. From there he proceeded up Route 1 to the library in Kennebunk, where he accessed the internet and went in search of wallpaper that reflected the style of the late nineteenth century. He felt bad that Emma was losing a day's work from him and decided to do something productive under the circumstances. Meanwhile, back at the cottage, Emma was isolated, one on one, with her younger sister. After nearly an hour of listening to Becky report on the living hell that was her life, her sister changed subjects.

"Am I misreading something or is that Fin guy living with you?" her sister asked. Emma became slightly agitated.

"He's not living with me in the biblical sense. His room is downstairs here and I'm upstairs," she explained. "Oh, and before you ask, it's for security reasons. I had a break-in a couple of months back that scared the hell out of me."

"But isn't it creepy having someone like him living under the same roof?"

"Who are you talking about, the big, scary looking guy?" asked Tara who had quietly descended the stairs.

"There's nothing creepy or scary about Fin. Fin is Fin. We've been friends since we were kids."

"If I remember correctly, he had a huge crush on you. Mom and Dad used to laugh about how he looked at you. Mom said once that she wouldn't be surprised to see you leading him around on a leash someday," laughed Becky. Emma shook her head in disagreement.

"Becky, now you're exaggerating," she responded.

"No, I'm not. They hid a lot of things from you because you always got so emotional about everything," continued her sister. Emma did not appreciate the sudden tone of the conversation and stopped responding. It took Becky a few minutes to pick up on her sister and hostess's displeasure with her, but she quieted down over the course of the morning. Fin stayed away much of the day on Friday, keeping as much distance between him and Emma's blood relatives as possible. On Saturday, he reached Brian Kelly by phone in New Hampshire and asked if he could rent the little house on Deptula Lane for an additional night. Brian told him where the backup key was and he spent Saturday night a quarter of a mile away from Emma and her guests.

Emma received a heated call on Saturday evening from Josh Andrade. He insisted on speaking to his wife and cursed Emma out when she was reluctant to turn over the phone. Becky eventually took the call and an intense argument ensued. Ten minutes after it had begun the call was over, and Becky sat across the table from her elder sister in tears. Emma spent the next two hours laying out a potential plan to rid her sister of Andrade. She encouraged Becky to get a restraining order and to find an attorney to begin divorce proceedings. For the first time in her sixteen year marriage, Becky seemed prepared to put an end to this abusive relationship.

28

After spending the night at Brian Kelly's cottage, Fin planned to attend services at the Baptist Church in Kennebunk on Sunday morning. Neither he nor Emma was sure what time the Andrades would be packing up and returning to New York, but he was sure he could ride out a few hours more of their company. Emma volunteered to make a ham and egg breakfast for her guests. The morning was unseasonably warm and they decided to dine out on the back porch overlooking the ocean. It was a reasonably jovial breakfast, with even Tara showing a trace of warmth toward her mother and aunt. All of this came to a screeching end at about eleven-thirty with the sound of heavy boots moving over the length of the porch. It was then that Josh Andrade turned the corner of the house and locked eyes on his wife. Andrade was a burly man with thick, muscled arms and a broad back. His round face had a ferocious look about it, made even more menacing by the brush cut of his hair. Becky dropped and broke her coffee cup at his appearance and seconds later he was pulling her out of her chair and dragging her over the new boards that encircled the cottage.

"Did you think it was too fuckin' far for me to come?" he spat out while she called out for mercy. Emma jumped to her feet and tried to defend her sister, but was swept aside and thrown down with comical ease by the man. It was then that Tara burst into tears and ran to the far end of the porch.

The sudden and violent confrontation on her porch left Emma emotionally numb for a moment. She pulled her cell phone from the pocket of her jeans and began pecking out the number of the Wells Police Department. Andrade put a stop to her efforts with a slap to the wrist. The blow sent the phone sailing into the next yard. Presumably under the influence of alcohol, he continued to drag his wife in the general direction of the driveway.

"Get inside and get your suitcases," he hollered at the children. Tara and Kyle scrambled into the house in a mad dash to obey their father. Andrade dug his fingers into the fabric of Becky's jacket before looking around and spotting a tall stranger standing in his path. It was Fin dressed in his church clothes, a charcoal suit and tie.

"Things look a little out of hand here," said Fin calmly. "Why don't you put the lady down and see if we can't talk our way through all this?" he

168

suggested. Andrade released his hold on Becky, sending her sprawling onto the surface of the porch. He took on a conciliatory posture and stepped toward the towering stranger. A second later he lashed out and caught Fin just above the jaw with a vicious blow. The punch sent Fin stumbling backwards onto the porch, the back of his head striking the railing. The contact of his skull against the wooden rail provided a sickening thump.

"Mind your own fuckin' business, numb nuts" roared the brute. He turned back to Becky who lay weeping before him. Emma stood frozen in fear a few steps away. She wanted to run to Fin but feared the response from her brother-in-law. "Stand up, you worthless bitch," he ordered his wife. Apprehensively, she climbed back to her feet. Andrade locked his hand around her wrist and turned. He was astonished to see Fin Cromwell standing back in his path, blood streaming from the corner of his mouth. Josh Andrade was clearly unaccustomed to anyone surviving a sucker punch from him. He tossed his wife aside and confronted Fin for the second time.

"You're a real fuckin' glutton for punishment," he exclaimed. He paused for a moment before rushing across the porch at Fin, attempting to drive him over the railing. Fin countered the attack by stepping aside and raining a flurry of blows off the man's head. One of the blows struck Andrade on the temple and dazed him. He staggered backwards against the side of the house. Fin stepped forward and connected with a half dozen more punches, while the shorter man attempted to clear his head. Andrade's eyes glazed over and he began slumping toward the floorboards but was propped back up and pounded with another series of right hands. Becky and Kyle rushed forward and mounted an attack on Fin. However, their efforts had no outward effect on the angry giant. It was Emma who finally pulled him away from her brother-in-law who promptly slid sideways along the outside wall of the house and crashed in a state of unconsciousness to the porch floor. Becky cried out in anger at the sight of her husband's face, already grotesquely swollen and bleeding.

Emma sent Becky and her children back to New York that afternoon. She underscored her advice to her younger sister and encouraged her to contact a lawyer and the police department on her return. Next, Fin and Emma chauffeured Andrade to the emergency care unit at the hospital in York for an examination. They made a second trip to the hospital that afternoon and left his vehicle in the parking lot. They wanted no more to do with Josh Andrade.

At three-thirty on Sunday afternoon, Fin followed Emma up the stairs to the house. They were both emotionally and physically drained. Emma wandered into the kitchen and poked through the cupboards.

"How about joining me for a cup of tea?" she asked. She looked back and winced at the sight of Fin's swollen lip. He nodded yes to the offer of tea and made his way into the living room where he collapsed onto the couch.

"That is one scary guy," he called out to her. She joined him a second later carrying a bag of cookies.

"If you think he's scary, I can only imagine what he thinks of you," she observed. "He has to have a concussion after all of that," she added. Fin leaned his head back and closed his eyes. "Do you feel okay?" she asked.

"I've got a slight headache but nothing too bad. My problem is whenever I close my eyes I can see that bastard's ugly mug," he confessed.

"And I'm sure whenever he closes his eyes he sees your...handsome face," she answered. "You were a hero today, Fin. I'm so damn proud of you right now," she confessed. Emma stared over at her friend and saw that he looked physically depleted. He closed his eyes for a second and appeared to be on the verge of falling asleep. Oddly, her mind flashed back to 1973 and she remembered the teenage boy who waded out to her in the Mousam River. Emma examined him in profile from the far end of the couch and it released something nurturing inside her.

"Fin," she called over to him. He turned slightly and opened one eye. She patted her hands on her thighs and waited for his response. He lifted his feet from the floor and leaned sideways, bringing his head down onto her lap. He looked up at her and smiled. Emma took to running her fingers through his reddish-brown hair and he closed his eyes, a look of total contentment forming on his face. "I'll bet the work on the house came with a little more garbage than you anticipated," she commented. He smiled but kept his eyes shut. She ran her fingers further back on his head and stopped abruptly. "Is this what I think it is?" She was referring to a patch of dry blood caked onto the back of his scalp. His eyes popped open.

"When pretty boy knocked me down, my head hit the railing pretty hard," he explained. "The edge on one of the posts dug into me pretty good." His explanation further awakened the motherly instinct in her and she ran her fingertips over his forehead and down the side of his face. She stared down and saw nothing short of adoration in his eyes.

"I couldn't believe the way you came to my sister's defense this morning. Would you have done the same for me, Fin?" He shifted his gaze away from her.

"Emmy, I'd die for you," he responded with a degree of intensity that half frightened her. She leaned forward and pressed her lips down on his. He reached his hand up to the back of her head in an attempt to extend the kiss for as long as possible. Thirty seconds passed before she pulled back, prodding him to release her. "Emmy, I want you to know that I'll do anything for you," he whispered. "I don't care if it looks like I'm only being used. I'll surrender my pride and my self respect, whatever that is, if it means getting closer to you." Emma understood his meaning. His declarations were sexual and unconditional. She pecked him a final time on the mouth and slid out from beneath his head. She left him resting on the couch, threw on a warm jacket and headed out up the beach towards the jetty. A long, healthy walk was in order.

Emma had grown accustomed to the chilly Maine air since her arrival in September. It had been a hectic day and the steady cadence of the ocean's wave action was finally calming her. The November days had grown short and darkness fell before her return to the cottage. The beach's main parking area was in sight when her phone sounded from within her pocket. She hurried to answer the call, thinking it might be her sister with an update on her situation.

"Hello," she said forcefully into the phone.

"Emma, where have I found you?" There seems to be noise in the background." It was Scott.

"My love," she replied. The sound of her lover's voice sparked a warm response. "You know me. I love to be by the sea. I'm just getting back from a walk to the jetty," she explained.

"You and your seaside strolls, you're insane."

"You do realize you're going to have to ratchet up your love of the sea once we're together?"

"You know the old truism; women are drawn to the sea and men to the mountains," answered Scott. "However, for you, no sacrifice will be too great."

"God, it is wonderful hearing your voice. This has been a hell of a day, but simply the sound of your voice has gone a long way toward blotting out the bullshit I've been through," she confessed. "It was just this morning that I came downstairs and looked at the calendar. Darling, we will be together in a few, short weeks." Emma's words were followed by a pause at Scott's end of the phone call. His silence did not go undetected.

"Yes, on the subject of our forthcoming happiness, I'm afraid there has been a slight detour placed in our path. It seems, unknown to me, Beverly and her mother have planned a four day Thanksgiving getaway in Newport. She knew I had the four day weekend off and didn't feel obligated to even clear it with me," he explained. Emma stopped in her tracks with the phone pressed close to her ear. Sensing Emma's displeasure with this revelation, he continued quickly. "I know you're probably not too happy with this but it will only delay things two or three weeks," he assured her.

"To say I'm not happy with this is putting it mildly. Scott, I love you, damn it," she snapped.

"And I love you, too. Emma, you have to understand. I'm the one walking away from a twenty-two year marriage and all the bloody guilt associated with it. I'm the one who has to look Beverly in the face and tell her I love another woman. Christ, there'll be hell to pay."

"So now it all comes down to ruining Bev's Christmas as opposed to ruining her bloody Thanksgiving?" She was quick to point out the absurdity of his whole 'bloody' comment. Scott could hear the tone of their conversation growing more acid and softened his tone.

"Emma, my love, I promise it will be all done and over by mid December," he vowed. She let out a scream and cursed into the phone. She had taken her eyes off the incoming tide and a wave washed over her feet and ankles. "Now what's wrong?" he blurted out.

"I looked away from the ocean for two seconds and now my feet are soaked," she complained. Harrington was anxious to divert the direction of the conversation and attempted to do so.

"You said something earlier about your bad day. Does it have anything to do with that goon living in your house?"

"No, it's more to do with my sister, Becky. She came with her kids for the weekend and all hell broke loose."

"In what way?"

"Scott, it's a long and very ugly story and best told in front of a warm fire after a couple of strong drinks."

Emma lingered on the cold beach until the conversation wound down. Most of the talk was romantic in nature. However, Harrington was told in no uncertain terms that a line had been drawn in the sand. He was to move out on his wife and join Emma in Maine by Christmas or she would call off the long running affair.

Fin was asleep on the living room couch when Emma slipped into the house and quietly made her way upstairs. Her walk to the mouth of Wells Harbor and back had taken nearly ninety minutes. She quickly peeled off her wet sneakers and changed into something comfortable. It had been a dreadful day, she thought. Sitting on the edge of her bed, she phoned her sister for an update. Becky reported that the hospital had called and was holding Josh Andrade overnight for observation. She was gladdened to hear that her sister planned to contact a lawyer the next day and begin divorce proceedings. Becky and the children had talked about nothing else over the long drive back to New York and the three were in total agreement. Emma offered her kid sister some financial assistance, not the moon and the stars in her words, but some financial assistance if that proved necessary. The phone call ended on a light note when Becky asked if she could borrow Fin for guard dog services for the next few weeks.

It was an exhausted Emma who retired to bed a short time after eight o'clock on this Sunday night. Fin awakened from his extended nap on the couch just before ten, wondering if Emma had returned from her walk. To put his mind at ease he climbed the stairs and looked in on her. Once convinced of her wellbeing, he made his way back to the downstairs bedroom and retired for the evening.

29

On Monday morning, Fin was taken by surprise by Emma's general mood and disposition. He had fully expected to awaken to the nurturing creature that had rubbed his scalp and cooed over him the evening before. Instead, he was confronted by a figurative stranger who spoke little over breakfast and then distanced herself from him the remainder of the day. He worked until nearly six o'clock and then went in search of her. He found her bundled up on the porch and looking up at the half moon.

"You've been quiet today, Emmy," he observed.

"That's a woman's prerogative," she answered icily. He shrugged and stepped toward her. He was about to speak when a cell phone sounded from a pocket in his flannel shirt. He took the call, stepping down from the porch and eventually out onto the beach sand. It became evident to Emma that he meant to keep the call private. She watched with considerable interest as her friend walked to the edge of the tide line and turned southward. His conversation proved inaudible from her position on the porch except for a few seconds of laughter. She watched with curiosity as he strolled along the moonlit beach with one hand to his ear. After close to fifteen minutes he meandered back toward the house, climbed the private cement steps up to the yard, and rejoined her.

"How long have you had a cell phone?" she asked.

"Just for a couple of weeks. I thought it was time, now that I don't have a land line in Kennebunk." Emma nodded and looked up at him. He could see that she was curious about the call. "The call was personal, not business," he casually confessed, knowing this would only elevate her curiosity.

"So, what did Brian want?" she asked.

"It wasn't Brian," answered Fin and stared up at the arc of the moon. She was not about to relent.

"So, what did one of Brian's two idiot friends want?"

"They're not idiots and they have names…and it wasn't Bobby or Perez." He stared back down at her.

"Stop being a jerk, Fin. Who was it?" she asked impatiently.

"Well, if you must know, it was Chanel. She called to ask me if I'd be her escort to a wedding." Emma gave off a sarcastic moan.

"I hope you told the girl giraffe what she could do with her invitation."

"Actually, I told her that I would," he replied.

"Fin, don't be such a chump. This woman treated you like dirt just a few days back and now you're groveling back to her."

"She didn't treat me like dirt. I told you before, I just didn't think she was interested," he reminded her.

"Please, Fin, don't make a fool of yourself."

"What's it to you if I make a fool of myself? If I come off as a chump, then so be it."

"She's using you," warned Emma. Her tone was childlike and condescending.

"She probably doesn't want to be looking down at her date on the dance floor and nothing more than that," he theorized. "Now, if you don't mind, I'd appreciate it if you kept your opinion to yourself," he insisted. Emma jumped to her feet and approached him.

"Listen to me, Fin Cromwell, you live in my house and, right now, earn a living through me," she roared, pushing her index finger into his chest. "We also go back a long, long way. So, I'll offer you my opinion any damn time I feel like it," she insisted behind a glare that he found both unnerving and seductive. He reached down and framed her face with his enormous hands. Falling to his knees he pulled her mouth to his only to have her rip herself away. She escaped into the house and let the door slam behind her. He waited outside in the chilly November air until the temperature of his blood cooled.

Emma was seated in the living room in front of the television when Fin closed the back door behind him and made his way to her. Joining Emma in the living room, he took a seat within her peripheral vision. She looked adorable, he thought, with her arms folded over her chest and her eyes squinted in anger. He turned to her and got her immediate attention.

"Something you said out on the porch made a lot of sense. You said we go back a long way and we should be able to give each other our opinions," said Fin. She turned her body in his direction and muted the audio on the television. He lowered his voice.

"Emmy, you just lost your husband a precious few months ago. How in the name of God did you get so close to this Harrington guy so fast? I'm just guessing here, but I'm pretty sure he was in your bed every night a few weeks back," he suggested serenely. Emma's brown eyes flared with rage.

"Who the hell are you to play mister high and mighty with me?"

"Emmy...relax," he insisted gently.

"Is it me or didn't you just try to put your tongue down my throat no more than fifteen minutes ago?" He nodded begrudgingly.

"I'm not getting in a war of words with you 'cause you'll cut me to pieces. I just know that Harrington guy had a wedding ring on and something ain't right with you two being so close so soon after your husband's death." She glared over at him with undisguised contempt.

"But it's perfectly okay for you to come on to me before Frederick's cold in his grave. Is that what you're saying?"

"No, I'm just saying that I loved you long before Frederick ever laid eyes on you, so maybe the grieving period wouldn't be the same," he answered.

"That's one pitiful rationalization."

"I'm sorry if it wasn't up to your high academic standards," he sarcastically apologized.

"I guess it's all I could expect from someone born in the shadow of a sardine factory," she countered.

"Don't be so nasty," he insisted.

"Don't be so sanctimonious," she responded. Fin rose from his chair and walked slowly in the direction of his room. "Where do you get off walking out on me? Perhaps you'd like to be jobless and without a place to live tomorrow?"

"Emmy, do what you like," he called back to her and closed his bedroom door.

Fin lay on his bed with a copy of the classified ads opened to the 'help wanted' section when a series of gentle taps sounded on the door.

"It's open," he responded and the glass paneled door swung in. Emma peeked in and winced at the sight of her friend scanning the want ads.

"The nasty fishwife of a woman who you spoke to earlier is gone. I hope you'll ignore everything she said." He smiled and folded the newspaper.

"That was one cute fishwife," he remarked up at her. "Is there any chance of getting her number?" She smiled down on her friend warmly.

"I'm not the little girl from Mechanic Street you loved so many years ago," she confessed in a forlorn manner. He stared back at her, his eyes contradicting her assertion.

There was no communication from Scott during the week, leaving Emma on edge and despondent. When Fin descended the stairs late Friday afternoon she intercepted him in the dining room.

"If you're not doing anything special tonight I would really like someone to go to the movies with. It will be my choice of movies so I'll pay," she stated enthusiastically. Fin closed his eyes and took on a dejected look.

"Emmy, if I had known I would have kept my schedule open, but Chanel called me on Wednesday and asked me out. I think she's mixed me up with another guy she went out with recently. I'm already dreading the look on her face when I show up. You're not mad, right?" Fin watched as the enthusiasm drained from Emma's face. She squeezed his arm to convey her understanding and plodded up to the second floor.

The first floor of the house was dressed in darkness as Emma stepped carefully down the pitch black stairwell. A dry throat had driven her from the bedroom television and sent her in search of a can of soda from the kitchen. Barefoot and dressed only in pajamas, she passed by Fin's bedroom and saw that his light was still on. Of particular note was the fact that the drape that covered the panes of glass framed in the door had snagged, leaving three windows uncovered. Emma noticed this and quietly made her way to the kitchen. Returning from the refrigerator with a can of orange soda she glanced toward her friend's room and saw movement. Hidden in the darkness of the dining room she moved on cat's paws nearer to the door. She peered in just as Fin emerged from the bathroom, a towel wrapped around the waist of his tall body. Pausing in the middle of the room he snatched the towel from around his waist and began drying his hair. This left the entire back of his body exposed to her. Her eyes widened at the sight of his tight, muscular physique. Her attention moved downward and locked on his tight buttocks. It could have been the ass of a twenty-two year old, she thought. She stood spellbound in the dining room until he moved to the far end of the bedroom and out of sight. She heard the sound of a bureau opening and determined he was getting dressed. Slowly and carefully she backed away from the bedroom door and felt her way to the stairs.

Emma flicked off the television set, her first action after returning to the bedroom. She threw herself back onto the mattress, closed her eyes, and conjured up the image of Fin's body as he dried his hair. This was not the first time she had thought of him sexually. There had been occasions over the previous weeks when she had reason to approach him during his work, to bring him a drink or advise him of her feelings on a construction matter. It was then that his muscled arms or strong back raised feelings in her. She thought this odd, for she had never been attracted to alpha males in her life, but Fin was different. The connection, the bond with him from her high school years, was unique. In addition, she trusted him completely, something she felt with few, if any, other men. A pang of guilt came over her and she rolled onto her side and remembered her days with Scott beside her in this bed.

The clack of the front door closing jolted Emma from a light sleep. She shook the cobwebs of fragmented dreams from her head and focused on the noise from the floor below. From the kitchen came the familiar creak of the dated refrigerator door and the sound of something being placed down on the counter. Her mind harkened back to hours earlier, when she had stood in the darkness and watched her friend dry his body in front of the mirror. She had actually caught sight of a portion of his manhood from her vantage point in the dining room. Since that moment, she had pondered on the full length of it. Dating back to her days at Kennebunk High she had theorized that Fin was larger than an average or ordinary male, a fact that both intrigued and intimidated her somewhat. Her glimpse of him earlier largely substantiated her theory. She tiptoed to her bedroom door and analyzed the noise from downstairs. Within seconds she was convinced Fin was alone. She slowly edged back toward her bed, stepping on a floorboard that groaned under her weight. She held her breath and slipped back between the sheets. Fin continued with his activity a floor below, assuring her he suspected nothing.

Time crawled over the next hour as Emma tried in vain to nod off to sleep. The image of Fin's youthful looking body seemed burned into her consciousness as she waged war against her desire. She listened as he briefly turned on the living room television, only to abandon it within five minutes and retire to his room. Emma slid her fingers up the inside of her legs and caressed herself. Her breathing grew deeper and faster as she tormented herself with thoughts of Fin. His was the body of a Roman gladiator or Hun warrior, she imagined. His words from days earlier flashed back to her. He had offered to surrender his pride and self-respect for an hour or two of intimacy with her. She slipped her fingers further inside herself and intensified the passion growing within her. She would be safe with Fin, she reminded herself. Driven by urges deep within her, she sat up in bed and thought of Fin lying in bed in the far end of the house. Regaining her sanity, she fell back onto the mattress and pulled the covers back under her chin. She reached for the glass of ice water on the corner of the nightstand and downed it in one long swallow. She was sure she had survived her extended moment of insanity.

On this night sleep would not come. The relentless cravings of her own body returned and with heightened intensity. She glanced over at her alarm clock and saw it was nearly quarter past one. Again, she sat up on the edge of the bed. Stepping over her slippers, she made for the hallway dressed only in pajamas and quietly proceeded down the stairwell toward Fin's room. Coming to the main floor, she noticed a sliver of light bleeding through the doorway and walked soundlessly toward it. Outside, the ocean washed listlessly over the cold packed sand. Emma turned the handle on the door and pushed it inward. The movement caused a familiar creak. She glanced toward the right-hand corner of the room and saw Fin lying on his back; his eyes shifted in her direction. He smiled up at her affectionately. She stepped into the room and looked down at him. He wore a tee shirt and sweat pants. There was a book balanced on his chest that he rapidly tossed to the foot of the bed.

"I've come down to ask something terribly selfish of you," she confessed. A crooked smile formed on his face. He beckoned Emma to explain herself. "I've awakened in an awful state. Fin, my body is on fire." His eyes remained trained on her.

"Go ahead, Emmy," he encouraged.

"Fin, the other night you said you would do anything for me. You said your pride or anything else wouldn't stop you from doing anything I asked," she recounted. He nodded yes even while his smile disappeared. "I know I'm going to sound like a selfish bitch, but would you do what you did for me back in your apartment on Friend Street so many years ago?"

"You know I will," he pronounced without hesitation. She avoided his eyes, staring down at the floor instead.

"I'm really in the mood for that and I was hoping you still felt the way you did the other day." She brought her brown eyes up and met his.

"Was there anything else I could hope to share with you?" She closed her eyes and appeared embarrassed.

"I think anything else would violate my understanding with Scott," she explained. He reached up and lifted her chin. She opened her eyes and stared back at him. "I've promised Scott not to have sex with any other man," she explained apologetically.

"What you're asking for *is* sex," he maintained.

"In my mind, it isn't," she countered.

"Well, thank you, Bill Clinton," he wisecracked and shook his head in disbelief. Her head sank and she let out a deep breath.

"So…is it yes or is it no?" she asked, wanting to arrive at a decision.

"I still love you as much as I did back in Kennebunk High. So, of course it's yes," he concluded. She leaned down and kissed him on the side of the face.

"I'm a little embarrassed," she revealed. Appearing both hurt and anxious, he sprang from the mattress and slowly dropped to his knees in front of her. Her body went rigid when his huge hands took hold of her hips and gently moved her backwards toward the edge of the bed. He smelled of shampoo and shaving lotion thanks to his date earlier in the evening. She reached down and coiled his hair between her fingers. This was not the same, inexperienced Fin she had seduced thirty plus years ago, she thought. He clearly knew how to frame the moment. He unstrung the delicate, pink rope at the waist of her pajama bottoms and deliberately brought the garment down to the floor in front of her. Emma's body quivered and she locked her fingers around his thick, brown hair. Her breathing was growing deeper by the second. He paused in place before her and planted one kiss after another over and beside the edge of her panties before bringing his warm breath to bear on her tummy. He breathed through the sheer fabric of her undergarment and sent warmth inside of her. On impulse, she leaned down and kissed the top of his head. For a moment he paused in place and inhaled her scent, intoxicated by the essence of his first love. Finally, Fin slipped down Emma's panties and lowered her back onto the bed. Her legs bent at the knee, she lie, arms outstretched and legs dangling to the floor. The body of Emma Lipton was Fin's altar and he knelt before it with no reservations.

Emma thought nothing of time or place or consequence as her body moved closer and closer to its liberating climax. She called out to God and Fin when the glorious moment came upon her. In the final moments, Fin had lost his human identity and, in her mind, was little more than a tool to bring her body to total fulfillment. It was only in her physical and mental journey back to the here and now that she remembered his gift to her. Emma glanced down at him as her mind cleared. His face was beaded with sweat and showed some wear and tear from the grinding action of her lower body. She made effort to cover herself and swung down to join him on the floor. She covered his lips with hers and tasted the essence of her own body.

"Emmy, you taste the same as you did as a girl," he observed. She gracefully rose to her feet and began gathering her clothes. Her time with him was over. Fin's eyes were trained on her nude body as she turned for the door. "Emmy, I'm afraid I'm never going to stop loving you," he confessed. The sincerity imbedded in his voice caused a wave of guilt to consume her. She paused in the doorway and looked back at him. He was still kneeling by the bed. Emma's eyes welled with tears.

"You're more to me than you know," she replied before disappearing into the darkness of the house.

30

Emma chose to sleep in the next morning and did not wander downstairs until shortly after ten o'clock. It was the weekend, but this had little to do with her decision. She was embarrassed by her actions the previous night and hoped to avoid Fin. Her plan proved to be successful and she puttered into the kitchen and found a half pot of coffee waiting for her. She glanced out the front door and saw that Fin's truck was not in the driveway. The house felt chilly and she tweaked the thermostat up slightly. After retreating upstairs for heavier socks and a pair of jeans, she returned to the living room and pulled a copy of *Pride and Prejudice* down from an overhead shelf. She curled up on the couch, hoping Jane Austen could help erase some of the prior night's imagery from her mind. Outside it was clear and very cool, with a strong wind blowing in off the ocean. It was not long before Emma was immersed in the love perils of nineteenth century England and worlds away from her own problems on the southern coast of Maine.

Her eyes remained glued to the pages of her book while she reached over to her coffee mug. A moment later she paused with a mouthful of room temperature coffee and made her way back to the kitchen to brew a few more cups. It took a few minutes for her next pot to brew and she used the time to tidy up the counter and storage shelves. After pouring herself a fresh mug of coffee, she wandered into the dining room and took a chair at the far end of the table facing the front door. She had only rejoined Elizabeth and Mr. Darcy for a few minutes when a truck engine sounded in the driveway and she waited on Fin. Seconds later came the familiar flutter of his engine as it shut down. A knot of anxiety formed in her stomach as he approached the house. The front door opened and he strode into the cottage. She purposely kept her eyes riveted on the book. It was not until he walked up within a couple of feet of her that Emma lifted her gaze ever so slightly. He reached down to her, running his second knuckles across the end of her nose in a gesture of absolute tenderness. Relieved, she smiled up at him and rose to her feet. A moment later she was embracing her long-time friend, her arms wrapped tightly around him.

"I was afraid you hated me," she confessed. She held him tightly for another thirty seconds before falling back onto her chair. Fin moved to the window and peered out at the shimmering blue water without speaking. "Sometimes I think you should have left me in the middle of the river thirty years ago," she added. He answered her with a subdued laugh.

For a week Fin had forbidden Emma from going upstairs, as his work on the third floor bedrooms drew closer to completion. After pouring himself a mug of coffee, he asked her if she wanted to finally view the canvas on which she would decorate her upper level Victorian bedrooms. The question brought her curiosity to life. She put down her book and made for the stairs. Fin followed her up the two flights with a sense of excitement. The upper bedrooms were small with slanted ceilings and a single window. On day one of the restoration they were each furnished with only a bed and a rolled up oriental rug. Emma planned on buying the bulk of the furnishings only after Fin's floor, wall and ceiling work was done. Nearing the top of the stairs, he slipped his hand over her eyes and guided her into the right bedroom. She opened her eyes and let out a gasp. First to hit her was the dark stained walnut trim and flooring that shined from a recent oiling. The walls were covered in floral wallpaper that she had picked out six weeks earlier and then lost enthusiasm for after showing a swatch to Scott. Now, the bright design looked magnificent, framed by the dark wooden floor and window trim. In the far corner stood the brass bed she and Frederick had brought up eight months earlier. Finally, an oriental rug passed down to Frederick from his parents appeared perfectly suited for its positioning in the middle of the room. Emma reached her arm around Fin and pulled him to her. She stood transfixed in the doorway of the room before turning her attention to the second bedroom. This room did not prove to be a disappointment either and benefited from a stream of sunlight that poured in through the south facing window.

"Do you have any idea how wonderful it is going to be decorating these two rooms?" she asked Fin with moistened eyes. "They're like something out of a storybook." The two returned downstairs and Fin asked her if she cared to join him on a walk up the beach. She declined, citing the wind chill factor from the weather for her reason. Anxious for some fresh air and exercise, Fin bundled up and set off for the jetty. Emma returned to her novel but found herself upstairs viewing her remodeled bedrooms less than twenty minutes later. She was standing in the window of the second bedroom when her cell phone rang. She pulled it from the pocket of her jeans and saw that it was Scott calling. There was no one she wanted to share her excitement with more than him.

"Hello, my love," she answered sweetly.

"I've found you in good spirits. That's good news. I know this whole Thanksgiving thing with Beverly and her mother has not gone over well with you."

"Your timing is impeccable. I'm upstairs at the house standing in one of my two newly completed bedrooms. I'm standing in the window of one and staring down to Moody Point. Scott, I can't wait to take you up and show them to you when you return. You're going to make love to me in both of them. That's how we'll christen them," she added exuberantly. Harrington chuckled from his end of the conversation. Emma was careful not to bring Fin's name into the report.

"Actually, I've called with an update and an action plan. I had the distinct impression from our last conversation that you thought I could be cooling on the idea of leaving Bev. Emma, nothing could be further from the truth."

"I'm really glad to hear that," she confessed. "I worry about something going wrong or you falling out of love for me. Now, what, pray tell, is this action plan business you're talking about?"

"Okay, first some background and then I'll talk you through everything. Now, hear me out…no interruptions," he insisted. "I've learned that this Thanksgiving weekend with Bev and my mother-in-law stems from her mother's failing health. The old battleax has had a number of health issues recently and Beverly wants to get in one more holiday weekend with her mom before she can no longer do it. She's been taking her mother on little sojourns like this for the last thirty years, but the old warhorse is just wearing out. Her mother got some unwelcome news at her last checkup, they won't share any of this with me, and Bev decided to act while she still could. Her mother has always loved Newport so that's where we're going. Anyway, that's the whole story behind the delay in me leaving her."

"Scott, it sounds a little sad," injected Emma.

"Sad, my ass, it's inconvenient," he scoffed. "Anyway, it's going to be hard enough on Bev when I break the news to her. We don't need to add insult to injury by blindsiding her before this godforsaken Thanksgiving weekend."

"No, I'm in total agreement," she added.

"Anyway, what I'm planning to do is break the news to her the Monday after our return from Newport. I figure a weekend alone with those two should have me in the right mental state. We can temporarily stay in a hotel down here while I finish out the week at work. I'm asking for a leave of absence from the university and I'm reasonably sure they'll grant it. As I see it, we'll be together back in Maine the following weekend," he assured Emma. There was a short period of silence before she responded.

"I can't believe it's really going to happen," exclaimed Emma blissfully. "This isn't going to be easy, Scott. You really must love me."

"This is going to be hard. Word will get out fast among our friends and

I'm going to be blackballed by the whole lot of them. I don't care because I'll have you," he explained. "However, this is where I could use a little help from you."

"I'll try to be as supportive as I can," she assured him.

"I'd like you to be there by my side when I break the news and the whole thing hits the fan," he proposed.

"You want me in the room with you?" she blurted out.

"Emma, this is nasty business and you're a strong woman. I could really use you there for moral support."

"You want me, the other woman, to be there with you when you tell Beverly you're leaving her?" she repeated in astonishment.

"Emma, I'm the one throwing myself on my sword for you. I'll need you there by my side. She's going to come apart and I'll need you there to keep me strong and on message." Emma, shocked by his request, stood speechless for a full thirty seconds by the window. "Emma, I'm asking you to do it for me," he added.

"Scott, I'll do it, but only because I love you so very, very much," she finally conceded.

"Thank you, you've taken a weight off my shoulders. Also, there will be the matter of getting that Neanderthal out of the house. We are going to have to have the house to ourselves and I'm going to have to insist that another contractor be brought in to finish the work." Emma felt a painful knot grow in her stomach, causing her to hesitate. "Emma, you have to know that he can't stay," insisted Harrington.

"I know, you're right," she conceded. Her concession brought a wave of sadness over her, erasing the exuberance from only moments earlier.

Emma's phone conversation with Scott was long over when Fin bounded onto the back porch and strode into the house. His face was reddened by the November air as he blew on his hands for warmth.

"Emmy, I'm making myself an Irish coffee. I've got some Jameson's Whiskey in my room and the rest we can improvise," he suggested. She looked up at him somberly and signaled that she would join him for a drink. She watched as he marched into the kitchen and began preparing the coffee. She was already considering the best time to reveal her future plans with Scott to him. She quickly decided to wait until sometime over the long Thanksgiving Day weekend. Fin would need little time to pack his minimal belongings and vacate the downstairs bedroom. It was the shock of hearing of Emma's personal plans and of his loss of the project work at the house that she most dreaded springing on him.

Emma withdrew from her accustomed level of conversation over the next hour and Fin was quick to pick up on it. Returning with a tool from his cellar workshop he found the first floor of the house empty. He searched for her with no success until he reached the newly restored top floor of the cottage. It was there he found her seated quietly on the edge of one of the beds, her mind seemingly light-years away from her surroundings. She looked up at him sadly and then looked away. He joined her in the room, seating himself next to her on the mattress.

"I have a hunch I know what's getting you down all of a sudden," he remarked and dropped his long arm across her shoulder. She made no reply to his statement. "The holidays are coming closer and Thanksgiving will be your first big one without Frederick." She shook her head no. "Are you going to be doing something with that guy? My guess is that you won't," he theorized. Emma turned to him then dropped her eyes to the floor. He read her response as a no. "I've been talking to my daughter, Vicky. She's a freshman up at the University of Maine in Machias. My plan was to go up there and rent a motel room and do some catching up with her over Thanksgiving and the weekend. The important thing is for me to see and be with her. Her and her mom had a major falling out and I'm what's left of her family right now. I actually feel a little guilty about being happy about it. What if I invited her to spend the long weekend here with us? Would you have a problem with that?"

"Isn't Machias pretty far away?" she asked.

"Yeah, it is. She wanted to be as far from her mother as possible." Emma turned back to Fin and peered deep into his eyes. "Emmy, I don't want you to be alone...and I'd love you to meet Vicky," he added. "We could put her in one of the two new bedrooms," said Fin enthusiastically. Emma's head was swimming with the conflict between her own guilt and the desire for company at Thanksgiving. There was also more than a small amount of curiosity about Fin's daughter.

"I wouldn't put her up in the old servant's quarters," she replied, casting an eye around the room. "She could have the guest bedroom across the hall from me," she promised. Happy with this response, Fin was on his feet and moving toward the door in the next instant.

"I'll ring her right now and see what kind of plan we can work out," he called back to her.

It was growing dark when Fin vaulted up the stairs and found Emma standing at a top floor bedroom window. He walked up behind her and placed his hands on her petite shoulders.

"Vicky says she has a half dozen friends driving home to Massachusetts for Thanksgiving. She's going to hitch a ride with one of them and have me pick her up at the train station here in town. I'll just have to drive her back on Sunday, which is no problem," he exclaimed. She tilted her head sideways, making contact with his left hand. He leaned down to her and inhaled.

"You smell like an angel," he whispered. She responded with nervous laughter.

"It's called patchouli and every dirty, little hippie girl in the sixties wore it," she explained.

"Then I was born too late for my own good," he answered lightheartedly and drew in an extended, second breath.

For reasons she could not yet share with Fin, Emma decided against moving the progression of restoration work down to the second floor from the top story. Instead, she directed him to resume work in his first floor bedroom. He did so over his own objections. This sent Fin and his meager collection of belongings up to the third floor. For the next week he and Emma shared a bathroom and managed to coexist within the constraints of a single, showering bathtub and toilet. Meanwhile, Emma watched Fin grow more and more excited as his daughter's arrival date drew closer. At long last, it was the twenty-third of November and he was working on the east window of his bedroom when the cell phone in his pocket rang. He answered the call and learned that his daughter, Victoria, was standing with her duffle bag at the Wells train terminal. Throwing on an overcoat, he dashed from the house and out to the truck while Emma made her way to the kitchen to put on a pot of tea. She had not so much as seen a photograph of the college freshman and was incredibly curious to lay eyes on the product of Fin's ill-fated marriage.

Emma was standing on the porch, bundled up against the cold Atlantic air, when she heard Fin's truck roll up the driveway on the other side of the house. She felt a flutter of anticipation pass through her stomach as she pried open the storm door and made her way back into the informal dining room. She felt self-conscious standing awkwardly in the room and waiting to meet this teenage stranger. She picked up on Fin's voice as he directed his daughter up the stairs to the porch and to the front door. The door swung open slowly and then, amid a flurry of foolish laughter, Victoria Cromwell appeared across the room. Emma did everything in her power to remain placid but her mouth, nonetheless, dropped open. The teenage girl turned in her direction and smiled warmly. Even from nearly twenty feet away the girl's eyes seem to penetrate her own. Victoria Cromwell was tall, probably over six feet, with straight, dark, chestnut brown hair that cascaded down onto her shoulders. She walked toward Emma behind an engaging smile. Emma scanned the teenager for traces of Fin. The hair color was a near match and, of course the height, but little else. Then, she thought back to the story he had told of his mother, the young girl with magnetic beauty who came out of an extremely rural area of Washington County and latched onto his father. There was something quite extraordinary about the appearance of this girl and it probably came through genetically from Fin's mother, she thought. Reaching Emma at the far wall, the tall, slender girl embraced and thanked her for the invitation for the holiday weekend.

"My father has spoken glowingly about you," she whispered in Emma's ear. The beautiful girl sounded far more educated than her father.

"I have some tea steeping in the kitchen. You have to be half frozen, standing up at the train depot waiting for your dad," contended Emma. "First though, let me take you upstairs and show you your room." She grabbed onto Vicky's slim wrist and escorted her upstairs to the second floor. The girl was more than happy with her accommodations and thanked her hostess no less than two more times for the invitation. When Emma returned downstairs, she found Fin preparing the tea in the kitchen and beaming with pride. "What a beautiful, beautiful girl," she said to him. "I can picture her walking down a runway as a model," she added.

They may not have been a traditional American family but Emma, Fin and Vicky shared a festive holiday in each other's company. Emma's house was the only of the 'Four Sisters' beach cottages to be occupied this Thanksgiving Day weekend. Fin and Emma prepared the turkey together, while Vicky sat in front of the television set and watched the Detroit Lions host their traditional game. Vicky, Emma learned, was an avid football fan and hooted loudly from time to time from her chair in the living room. However, her father called her out to the kitchen at one point to mash the potatoes. It was about one-thirty when they all sat down at the dining room table. Emma was taken aback somewhat when Fin lowered his head and said grace, thanking God for the abundance of food and for everyone's good health at the table. It was not the gesture that caught Emma a little off guard, but the degree of sincerity in his voice. By this time she was very comfortable in Vicky's company and the two dominated the conversation for the better part of the meal. Over and above the table conversation, Emma found herself staring at the teenager. The uniqueness of her beauty affected her in a way that she could not fully comprehend. On a handful of occasions, her mind would revert back to times spent with Fin from their youth in and around the upper village of Kennebunk. Strangely, the father and daughter also conjured up memories of her family on Christmas and Thanksgiving and she privately relived moments spent with her father and mother at the kitchen table around a festive feast. The recollections were agreeable and poignant. As the meal wound down, Emma was happy with the knowledge that both Cromwells would share her house for another three days. When Emma began apologizing to Vicky about her humble dessert, Fin interrupted and brought a large white box from the back of the refrigerator. Cutting the strings surrounding it, he unveiled his surprise, a homemade strawberry custard pie. The women let out a unified moan, but promised to sample it later in the afternoon. They kept their promise during the day's second televised football game.

Thanksgiving Day was winding down at the Lipton house. The turkey had been carved and put away for a future meal or sandwiches and the sun had long set behind Mount Agamenticus when the conversation drifted to motion pictures. It was then that Emma learned that Vicky had never seen *An Affair to Remember*. Fin let out a cry for mercy while Emma scanned over her collection of DVDs and eventually snatched the film from her wall display of movies. From there it was only seconds before the introduction credits were flashing onto the television screen and the haunting musical score was filling the room.

"The chick flick to end all chick flicks," complained Fin as he marched from the room. His exit brought on laughter from the two women as they found comfortable spots on the couch.

"Are you saying you have no idea of the basic plot or anything?" asked Emma in astonishment.

"None. I've heard the movie mentioned in passing a thousand times but I have never been exposed to the plot, let alone seen it," responded Victoria.

"My dear girl, hear me out. You will never forget the first time you saw *An Affair to Remember*. I remember watching it with my father on Mechanic Street. Oh, and by the way, you're about to fall in love with Cary Grant," promised Emma as the opening scene flashed onto the screen.

Fifteen minutes into the film, Fin returned carrying a punch bowl of egg nog and a few slices of pie.

"The egg nog has just enough brandy to give you a glow," he disclosed and joined the women, at least temporarily, in front of the television set.

Fin insisted on going back to work on Friday while Emma and Vicky set off to Portland for a frantic day of shopping. After parking down by the waterfront, they climbed and explored the narrow streets of the Old Port, searching out the trendiest of shops and the most high end art galleries. Eventually they came upon a coffee shop half hidden on a side street and laid claim to a table by the window. Emma treated her young friend to a latte and listened while Vicky Cromwell described life at home with her dad before the disintegration of her parent's marriage. Emma thought she picked up on the natural animosity between adolescent girls and their mothers during Vicky's accounts of things at home, but withheld comment. In addition to listening, Emma would bookmark the teenager's stories from time to time and point out young men who, by their actions, showed interest in the eighteen year old. Her observations always brought forth a burst of laughter from both females. Vicky returned the favor on one occasion when a prematurely grey, middle-aged man lingered on the sidewalk outside the shop and stared trancelike at Emma for no less than five seconds before moving on. Emma immensely enjoyed her time with her teenage companion, sampling what a healthy mother-daughter relationship had to feel like. When Vicky inquired into how her father managed to forge a friendship with her some thirty years earlier, she relayed the story involving the Mousam River but left out the sleeping tablets and dire purpose behind being stranded out in the middle of the waterway.

By late afternoon, both women had accumulated half a dozen bags of Christmas gifts. Vicky was visibly humbled by Emma's generosity and apologetically asked to repay her over the next few months. Emma waived her gesture off and insisted it was her pleasure. However, in the back of her mind was the issue of her upcoming permanent union with Scott and the impact it would have on the girl's father. On the ride back to Wells, Emma played with the idea of informing the teenager of her plans and asking her to break the news to Fin on their ride back to Machias on Sunday. In the end, it was self-interest that stopped her. Her time with the Cromwells over this holiday weekend had been magical thus far and she feared putting the remaining two days in jeopardy by informing the girl of her plans with Scott. They arrived back at Wells Beach with Emma still harboring her secret and Fin having no idea of the emotional and economic bombshell soon to be dropped on him.

Emma lay in bed on Saturday morning, tucked warmly under the covers and fantasizing about Scott. She was still struggling with the notion that he would be hers in less than three days. It was practically too wonderful to be believed. Her stare was hypnotically fixed on a bank of clouds suspended out over the Atlantic when there came rapping on her door.

"I'm awake," she called out and watched as Vicky shouldered open the door and entered carrying a tray.

"I made you breakfast," announced the girl, as she brought the food to the edge of the bed. "I made you breakfast because I love you and I love my room and I love spending time with you and my dad," she confessed with youthful exuberance. Momentarily speechless, Emma reached out for the tray. "Dad said you liked your eggs boiled for two and a half minutes and that you were partial to raspberry jelly on your toast." Emma poured a cup of coffee from a carafe and beckoned her young friend to join her. A second cup rested on the corner of the tray, presumably for this purpose.

Sitting at the foot of the bed, Vicky sipped on her coffee while her dark probing eyes peered at Emma. Victoria Cromwell had a mystical quality in her appearance and Emma, time and again, found herself falling prey to it. She wondered to herself how any heterosexual male could resist the charms of this striking girl if she, a middle-aged woman, could feel the teenager's influence under the most innocent of circumstances.

"Vicky, you are such a beautiful girl. Do you take after your mother?" She shrugged her shoulders.

"I guess I'm okay. I don't look like my mother. Daddy says I look a lot like my grandmother. I've seen pictures of her when she was young and there is some resemblance." From overhead came the sound of weight pressing on floorboards and soon after, footsteps descending the stairs. Within seconds Fin was standing in the doorway.

"Should I have stayed upstairs and waited on breakfast?" he asked.

"Only if you plan going on a hunger strike," joked Vicky behind a broad grin.

"Wait a minute. I seem to recall a certain young woman who inherited her height and nice thick hair from me offering to make me pancakes this weekend. Well, string bean, we'll be leaving too early tomorrow morning for any pancakes, so this must be the day," reckoned her father. Vicky rolled her eyes but immediately rose from the bed.

"Thank you for the thoughtful gesture," said Emma as the girl made her way toward the door. "Your father is a very lucky man to have a daughter like you," she added.

"I'm pretty lucky myself," she replied and shuffled out of the room.

31

The weather forecast for Sunday, November 27th called for overcast skies in the morning, to give way to rain, with wind gusts of up to twenty five miles per hour. Emma had tossed and turned for the first half of the night, kept awake by thoughts of her pending confrontations with Fin and Beverly Harrington. Her bedroom was as dark as a grave when she awoke to the sound of a female voice.

"Emma, I wanted to say good-bye before Dad and I left for Machias," whispered Vicky into her ear. She opened her eyes and made out the outline of the girl kneeling by the bed.

"I'll get up and make you breakfast," blurted out Emma. The girl's hand came down on her and held her in place.

"It's six o'clock and we've got to head out. We'll eat on the road. I'm just here to thank you a final time for having me as a guest in your home." The Cromwell girl was close to her, so close she could feel the eighteen year old's breath on her face.

"Again Vicky, the pleasure was all mine."

"One last thing, in the unlikely event you don't realize it, I firmly believe my father is in love with you. For this reason, I'm asking you to tread lightly on all matters dealing with his heart. Please, for me," she asked. She ended her visit with a kiss to Emma's cheek and retreated from the room like a phantom. Two minutes later, Emma heard Fin's truck engine turn over and the joyous portion of Emma Lipton's Thanksgiving weekend came to an abrupt end.

Fin's pickup cut through the drizzle and motored north on Route 1. To passenger and driver alike, the journey to Maine's Washington County had felt like an eternity. They passed a 'Welcome to Machias' sign then drove on past Bad Little Falls, a span of river rapids that culminated in a gorge. Finally, the two travelers turned into the parking lot of Helen's Restaurant. En route, they had decided on having a light brunch before separation. They entered the restaurant and were instantly seated at a small booth in the far corner of the dining room. A young waitress brought menus to the table and inquired about coffee. The girl appeared to recognize Vicky and tossed out a comment about school. A brief conversation ensued before a customer in the adjoining booth beckoned to the waitress.

"So, all and all, the weekend wasn't too painful, was it?" Fin asked, reaching across the table for a creamer for his coffee.

"Daddy, Thanksgiving was wonderful, Emma was wonderful and, most of all, you were wonderful. It was so much better than what Thanksgiving at Higgins Beach must have been like."

"I can't remember the last time I had my little girl to myself for four days. I just hope you didn't miss seeing your brother, mother and stepfather too much."

"I would have enjoyed seeing Trevor and I can still take Mom in small doses. But I certainly didn't miss seeing Mel this weekend," she confessed. Fin took a sip from his coffee and searched his daughter's face for any unspoken concerns.

"Has he been up to anything I should know about?" Fin asked, a serious expression suddenly written over his face. Vicky shook her head laughingly and placed her hand on her father's massive forearm.

"Mel has never touched me or said anything inappropriate to me. I think he's too afraid of Mom for that. But, during my last couple of years at home, I'd catch him inadvertently staring at me. It wouldn't be in any creepy way…just not the way my Daddy looks at me," she explained. Her father nodded knowingly and let the matter drop. They placed their orders for brunch and Fin spent a few minutes catching Vicky up on her family history up there in Washington County, Maine, history on her paternal side of the family. The informal lesson held her interest, evidenced by the follow-up questions she tossed out at her father. Then, he grew slightly more serious.

"I know this may be jumping the gun, but have you made any plans regarding your Christmas vacation?" he asked.

"Well, if my father is kind enough to invite me back to Wells, I'd love to spend the majority of it with you and Emma. I'd have to spend at least a couple of days with Mom and Melvin, but that would only be for two or three days, maybe." Fin's face lit up with joy.

"Your mom's going to be pissed," he warned her.

"I'm a big girl now and able to make my own decisions." Her father leaned back in the booth with a broad grin covering his face just as brunch was delivered to the table.

Fin dropped Vicky off within the campus walls of the college shortly before noon with a prolonged hug. He took great consolation in the idea that he would spend Christmas with his daughter, a holiday visit that would be measured in weeks and not days. On the return trip to Wells, Fin detoured off Route 1 and drove through his hometown of Jonesport. He made no effort to connect with his mother or siblings, but merely cruised through town along Route 187 and updated himself on the many changes in the community. His mouth dropped open when he passed a huge open lot where a large business and residential building once stood. He had not heard of the fast moving fire that had burned the structure to the ground fifteen years earlier. He did not stop his vehicle at any point, but simply cruised quietly through town like an apparition and updated himself on the many changes. The side trip added thirty minutes to his journey home but, in the end, he considered it time well spent. Every building and street corner conjured up memories, good and bad, and he found himself mentally in a more spiritual frame of mind by the time he rejoined Route 1 in Columbia Falls.

The stormy weather intensified as he motored southward. He met the leading edge of the worst weather just south of Bangor. The driving rain and strong winds were blowing in from the west and kept him under the speed limit. His journey from the northernmost to the southernmost coast of Maine took over five hours. The dinner crowd was just starting to arrive at Billy's Chowder House as he cruised down Mile Road on the final leg of his journey. He spotted Perez and Bobby Copeland's truck in the parking lot and was tempted to stop for a Miller High Life. However, he shook off the temptation and continued toward the house. He could already hear the ocean pounding up against the seawall half a mile away and decided Emma might be a little fidgety at the cottage. In addition, he had missed her exclusive company and hoped to spend some quality time with her on this miserable evening.

Fin pulled his rain slicker over his head and made a mad dash for the porch while windblown rain pelted down on the house and yard. The cottage was in darkness except for a single light bleeding out from the dining room. He burst in through the front door and found Emma seated thoughtfully at the table. She cast her eyes up at him and he immediately picked up on her somber mood. His first thought was that she had received grave news from her sister.

"We have to have a serious discussion and I'm afraid you're not going to take it well," she suggested and motioned him to the table. Caught totally off guard, Fin moved guardedly into the room and seated himself next to her. She seemed withdrawn and distant, he thought. She bore no resemblance to the woman he had spent the holiday weekend with at the house. "I'm about to make a very big move in my life and it will have a major impact on you," she informed him. His eyes opened widely and stared deep into hers. "I would appreciate it if you didn't say anything until I am done speaking," she said frigidly. He felt a shockwave of anxiety pass though his body as Emma Lipton, now seemingly a complete stranger, prepared to dictate the new terms of their relationship and perhaps even his life. "On Monday morning I'll be driving down to Massachusetts and joining Scott. We've decided to be together full time." Her words tore though him and sent his mind reeling and unable to process the full effect of the implications. He broke eye contact and stared blankly at the far wall. "You don't have to move out today or tomorrow. Scott and I will not be back until Friday night. You will have to be out by then. I'm sure you can understand that," she added, almost condescendingly. Fin's eyes scanned back to hers. From the porch, the gonging from the cast iron wind chimes seemed to lend a baleful backdrop to the proceedings inside. If anything, the weather was growing worse. "Fin, I'm sorry everything had to come down like this, but it just has to be this way." She reached down, pulled her checkbook from an adjacent chair and began writing. "Naturally, given your history with Scott, I'll have to find another contractor. I realize this is coming at a bad time, with Christmas just a month away, so I'll be giving you a generous severance. I'm under no legal obligation to do this, but we go back a long way," she explained. She tore off the check and handed it to him. It was made out for eight thousand dollars or four weeks severance. She handed it to Fin and felt a measure of guilt leave her body. He quietly stared down at the check for five or six seconds. He had complied with her wishes and remained silent since returning. Now, he would respond. He stared down at his stipend and began tearing the piece of paper, first in half and then into smaller and smaller pieces. Finally, with Emma's check reduced to little more than confetti, he threw it in her face.

"That was stupid and shortsighted," she remarked with the remnants of the check speckling her hair and shoulders. He rose from his chair.

"I'll be out of the house long before Friday," he informed her while slipping his arm back into his yellow rain jacket.

"You're not going back out in this, are you?" she asked in astonishment. He stared down at her with visible contempt.

"Trust me, you don't want me around you," he snarled and walked for the door. After descending the porch steps, he proceeded past his truck and down the driveway. He needed to work off some of the stress and anger, but there was no beach to walk on owing to the tide and storm surge. He turned onto Webhannet Drive and headed northward. He passed Folsom Avenue and caught sight of the incoming waves breaking on the seawall. The force of the Atlantic sent water spouting fifty feet into the air. The driving rain made contact with Fin's skin, stinging his face and causing him to believe there could be hail as well as rain pellets in the air. He continued his trek as the wind blew precipitation against the side of his face. Reaching Mile Road, he huddled beneath the Beachcomber's overhang at the front of the store and re-buttoned his jacket for a small measure of added protection. The storm remained relentless. Still stunned by Emma's demands, he resumed his journey northward along Atlantic Avenue in the direction of the jetty.

Atlantic Avenue runs approximately one mile to the border of Wells Harbor and ends at a parking lot. The walk from the Beachcomber to the Wells Harbor channel took Fin fifteen minutes. Reaching the end of the roadway, he glanced up at a floodlight. It was here he was able to appreciate the velocity of the wind as it blew the downpour of rainwater by the light. Upon leaving the house it had been his intention to walk to the end of the jetty, but the force of the wind was giving him second thoughts. Dispirited, he turned toward the ocean and listened as the sea roared its warning. Fin reminded himself of the purpose behind this endeavor. He planned a rendezvous, of sorts, at the far end of the jetty. The floodlight perched over the parking lot temporarily robbed him of his night vision. He hesitated for only a moment before plodding through the downpour. He located the sandy path adjacent to the jetty walkway and strode in the direction of the pounding surf. For the first one hundred yards his path was partially illuminated by the parking lot lighting, but soon after he found walking more treacherous. He left the packed sand and scrambled up onto the irregular, granite boulders that constituted a sidewalk. Looking eastward into the driven rain, he spotted his destination. A single green light blinked on and off at the southern edge of the harbor channel about a half mile away. When he nearly stepped into a deep gap between two boulders he briefly questioned his sanity. Even under ideal weather conditions and a full moon, walking to the end of the jetty was an ambitious undertaking, he thought. However, on this night and in his frame of mind, Fin knew he was literally putting his life in danger.

By the time he reached the midway point of his trek he was already physically depleted. He stopped briefly and rested, his eyes locking onto the green light anchored at the end of his pathway and out in the raging Atlantic Ocean. He looked across the channel and made out the red light at the far end of the corresponding northern jetty, the boundaries of the Wells Harbor entranceway. His night vision was returning, he thought. This would allow him to better discern the breaks and gaps in the granite slabs laid out in front of him. Again, he wrestled with the option of turning back. He reminded himself of the purpose behind the risky undertaking, a purpose that most would label nothing short of insanity. He persevered and moved forward. He kept his eyes focused on the next boulder, and then the next, until he glanced up and spied the green beacon no more than ten yards away. With the drenching wind pushing at his back he stepped off the final few yards before grabbing hold of the steel brace supporting the light. Around him the ocean roared furiously as wave after wave heightened on its approach to this rocky fingertip of granite before breaking on both sides of his position, driving past him toward the sand dunes and harbor. He circled the steel stand cemented deep into stone and moved to the easternmost point of the manmade trajectory of rock. Finally, he looked out into the black, violent sea.

"Lord, I've come out to speak to You because I'm angry and disappointed," he hollered into the wind, and rain and darkness. "Once again, my life is falling down all around me and I'm not sure I can take it or even want to take it anymore. Why am I always on the losing end of life? Just once, why can't I have what other men have? I didn't ask to look like this," he cried out with increased intensity. With his pants completely drenched and plastered against his legs, he lowered himself down onto the granite piling and rested his back against the steel tower. "You gave me a mother who turned her back on me and a wife who walked out on me...and I took it and never turned my back on You. My faith in You has never wavered. I'm a decent man and a good Christian." Fin gritted his teeth while tears welled up in his eyes. "Why did You send Emma back into my life? How much fucking suffering must I do before You're satisfied?" His head dropped in shame. "I'm truly sorry for that but You've pushed me past my limits." The fury from the wind, rain and ocean seemed to only increase as the cold penetrated his clothing and sent shivers through him. Thanks to the glow from the blinking green light, Fin picked up on an unusually large wave building fifty feet from his position. He watched the swell grow and grow, then begin to break near the base of the jetty. The cold, ocean water exploded all around him, literally shaking the rocks beneath him and sending a surge of foaming sea over the top of the granite block where he sat. The frigid water poured over his folded legs, then receded. Fin remained stoically in place. "Lord, I know You can crush me like a bug...and I don't care," he responded, his voice dropping off as if in despair. "If You love me You'll send a rogue wave up to wash me off this forsaken pile of rocks and put me out of my misery."

Fin sat positioned in the mouth of the storm for twenty minutes. He wished he had worn heavier clothing or at least an additional layer or two. Eventually his mind drifted back to Vicky. He envisioned her receiving the news of his death and the thought of it tore at his conscience. Finally, he lifted his frozen body from the granite slab and cautiously made his way back to the harbor parking lot and Atlantic Avenue.

Fin had lost all track of time when he turned into the driveway and staggered toward the house. The lights on the first floor were still on. He pushed in the front door and was rewarded with a rush of warm air. From the living room came the sound of the television set. He walked to his bedroom and disappeared behind the door. He peeled off his raincoat and hung it in the bathroom where it could drip harmlessly on the tile floor. Next, he stripped the remainder of his rain-soaked clothing from his body and tossed it in the shower stall. The storm had penetrated every layer he wore. He pulled dry clothing from his drawer and dressed himself. Less than ten minutes after returning to the house, he made his way to the refrigerator and removed four bottles of beer. Returning to his bedroom, he twisted off a cap and downed the beer in one continuous swig. Forty-five seconds passed and a second beer was in his stomach. Sitting atop his bed, he assured himself that the beer was going down rapidly to preserve its coldness. He opened a third brew and tortured himself with thoughts of Emma sitting in the living room in front of the television. She was about to fulfill her fantasy, he thought, while he faced at least a few weeks of little or no income. He guzzled his third beer in five minutes and thought he felt some lightness in his head. He leaned down and rolled all three empty bottles across the room. Outside his window a gust of wind whistled through a gable on the house, giving off a forbidding sound. Scoffing at any thoughts of moderation, Fin twisted off another cap and polished off the bottle of beer in two swallows. He threw his head back against the wall with a thud. His newly emptied bottle fell onto the floor with a loud thump. It prompted an agitated knock on his door.

"I'd appreciate not finding any damage in that room in the morning," warned Emma. He stared at the far wall of the room and withheld his anger. Thirty seconds passed and he made out the sound of her slippers shuffling through the dining room and back to her chair in front of the television. Awkwardly, he rose from the bed and made his way into the dining room. The effects of four beers in just over five minutes affected his balance as he plodded toward the living room door. Glancing across the room he spied one piece of luggage lined up against the wall and by the front door. Emma was not only planning to leave for Massachusetts the next morning, she was chomping at the bit, he thought. He reached the far doorway and leaned against it for support. A few feet away Emma sat in the corner chair. She looked somewhat ridiculous with her feet up, a few remnants of the torn check still clinging to her hair. She glanced up at him and immediately returned her eyes to the television. Staggering slightly, he walked across the room and stopped beside the chair. He peered down at her, imagining her clean, petite body beneath her pajamas and robe. He wrestled with the thought of taking her before she moved out of his life forever. The desire to paw her and mouth her soft flesh became almost unbearable. "You're making me very uncomfortable standing over me like that," she snapped. Her leg, calf to ankle, lay exposed beneath him. Again, her skin looked soft and warm and perfect, he thought. He reached forward and grabbed hold of her body. Lifting her up from the chair like a doll, Fin cradled her with one arm against his upper body and made for the door. She called out in protest and pounded on his back with both hands. Reaching the stairwell, he climbed up on unsteady legs while Emma went into a series of hysterical screams. He stopped halfway up the stairs and brought his mouth down over hers. "Put me down, you animal," she called out as she continued pounding on him. He resumed his climb and soon was moving across Emma's room toward the bed. Fueled by her unfulfilled promises and commitments, he regarded her as an object of sexual desire and nothing else. He lowered her from one shoulder and dropped her onto the bed. She scrambled to get away but he snatched at her robe and pulled it from around her body. She cried out to the empty houses surrounding hers and the wind driven rain pelting against the building. There was no one and nothing to rescue her. He grabbed the collar of her pajama top and tore off the garment in a single motion. Emma squealed in horror only to have the bottoms ripped off a second later in the same, violent manner. Determined to defend herself, she kicked at Fin's groin. He deflected the blow and it only seemed to inflame his rage. Kneeling over her nearly naked body, he slipped a single finger under her panties and ripped them down the length of her legs, pulling them and her slippers off at the same time. It was done. Emma lay naked beneath him and at his complete mercy. He paused and stared down at her. She was perfection, he thought, and for the next hour she was his. She closed her eyes and felt his huge hands grab hold of her wrists. A great fear took hold of her. Emma could see she had touched off something inside of Fin that she had not seen before and could not control. An image flashed before her. She saw Scott climbing the stairs and finding her dead in her room. She began to weep. These were the final seconds of her life, she thought. Her weeping grew more pronounced. She could not bear to open her eyes and see Fin's anger. Ten seconds passed before she felt his lips come down on her nipple. The gesture was gentle and unexpected. His lips broke contact with her left nipple and moved to her right. He repeated the gesture. She opened her eyes and saw him hunched over her. He moved his body downward and placed a kiss on her navel. He did not make eye contact with her. She let out a deep breath. The storm within Fin had passed. He grabbed a blanket and covered her naked body.

"Emmy, I'm sorry," he muttered and clumsily made his way to his feet. She was afraid to respond, fearful of awakening the darkness that had guided his actions only moments earlier. She pulled the blanket up to her chin and watched Fin leave her alone with the wreckage of the evening.

Fin returned downstairs burdened by the weight of his actions, his circumstances and the effects of too much alcohol in too short a period of time. He grabbed his rain jacket and stumbled to and out of the door. He was met with the same extreme weather he had escaped from only twenty minutes earlier. His first impulse was to drive away but he quickly realized the danger in doing so and set off on foot. He checked his pocket for the lump of his wallet. It was there and so was about one hundred dollars in cash. He set off for Mile Road. He decided to make the walk to Route 1. He prayed the Atlantic Coast Lodge was open on this tail end of the holiday weekend. He would rent a room from Brian Kelly and perhaps have an ear to listen to his account of an evening in hell. The trip up Mile Road sent him into the teeth of the wind and rain and now the rapid consumption of beer was making him sick to his stomach. He passed Billy's Chowder House where the lights were being dimmed for closing. He continued his trek westward to Route 1, all the time running his cash balance in the bank through his head to come up with a plan for the next few weeks. Arriving at the lodge, he saw few cars on the grounds. However, there were lights illuminating the office. Fin walked to the door and looked in, hoping to spot Brian. The office was empty except for a blond woman seated at the computer behind the front desk. He pushed in the door, causing her to turn away from her work and focus her attention on him. She was a pretty woman of about thirty with a pair of reading glasses propped up at the end of her nose. She surveyed him and took on a look of apprehension.

"I was hoping that Brian was in. I'm a friend of his and I needed to rent a room for the night," he explained.

"I didn't hear you drive in. Brian's not working tonight," answered the woman in a thick, Maine accent. Fin let out an audible sigh. "Do you have money or a credit card?" she asked.

"My truck broke down so that's why you didn't hear me come in." Fin decided to lie in an attempt to normalize his situation. The pretty blonde stared at him warily.

"A motel room will be fifty nine dollars plus tax," she informed him. Her accent sounded vaguely familiar. He reached in his pocket for his wallet.

"Where are you from? I think I know that accent."

"That will be fifty nine dollars plus seven percent Maine sales tax," she repeated. "I'm from Beals, Maine." Fin's face lighted up as he laid four twenty dollar bills down on the table. She slid a registration form across the desk for him to fill in. He stared at the name plaque on the desk. It read: Mary Porterfield.

"I grew up in Jonesport. I went to high school there, at least for a while," he added. The woman seemed to relax as she counted out his change.

"Brian will be here in the morning. He went home to New Hampshire for the long weekend," she informed Fin while passing him over his key. "Now, your breakfast in bed will be served at seven thirty sharp. Tall Barney's Restaurant is our caterer, so I'm sure you'll be satisfied with it," she added straight-faced. After a moment of complete bewilderment, Fin broke out into a hearty laugh. Her Down East humor and Washington County restaurant reference struck a chord and had him shaking his head all the way to the door. He had not smiled, let alone laughed, since leaving Vicky nine hours earlier. "There'll be pastries and coffee in the lobby here in the morning," she added, correcting herself.

"Goodnight Miss Porterfield," he called back to her and shuffled back out into the rain.

32

Fin opened his eyes to unfamiliar surroundings and extended his arms outward. He let out a yawn and scanned the room for a clock. He sat up and saw he was in a king-sized bed. That, at least partially, explained why he had slept so well, he thought. Taking a second to clear his head he remembered it was Monday morning. If he harbored any ideas about lying in bed and meditating on this morning they were quickly dashed. In the next instant the quiet of his room was interrupted by the sound of heavy-handed pounding on the motel door.

"Yeah," he called out.

"Are you dressed? The last thing I want to do is barge in on you naked, Cromwell." It was Brian Kelly.

"Just a minute," he called out and rolled out of bed. Within seconds he was wearing pants and a shirt. He opened the door and let his friend in. Fin retreated to the far end of the room and collapsed onto a chair. His visitor, one of the few people he trusted outside of his daughter, meandered in and took a seat at the bottom of the bed.

"Mary told me I had a friend staying at the lodge. I couldn't believe my eyes when I checked the registration and saw who was staying in my motel," confessed the man. Fin shook his head in disbelief.

"Brian, you wouldn't believe the shit I've been through in the last twelve hours," he confessed. "Emma's ended everything, my work at the house, our pathetic relationship, everything." Kelly invited his friend to join him back at the main house for coffee and some pastry. He assured Fin that they would have more than adequate privacy in and around the office at this time of the year. Fin agreed to join him across the yard at the house in thirty minutes. He knew he needed to unburden his problems on someone. "If it's available, I wouldn't mind renting the little cottage down on Deptula for a week or so…just until I can find something permanent." The trace of a smile broke across Brian's face.

"I'll put you in touch with the lovely, kind and generous Mrs. Kelly. I'm sure you two can negotiate something in the way of rent," he suggested.

"For the love of God, don't do that to me," blurted out Fin, causing Kelly to break out into full blown laughter.

Fin's time spent in the company of Brian Kelly proved therapeutic. The two friends polished off an entire pot of coffee while Fin recounted every detail of his twelve hour ordeal. Brian consoled his friend and attempted to lift his spirits by suggesting that he may not have seen the last of the love of his life, Emma Lipton. He theorized that, over time, Emma would become more and more aware of Scott Harrington's faults and weaknesses. He also praised Fin for his restraint up in Emma's bedroom, particularly under the circumstances and in his condition. In the end they agreed that Fin would move into the yellow cottage on Deptula Lane immediately. It was just after noon when Fin set out for Emma's house to pack his things and depart from her life.

Packing did not take long. Fin filled a suitcase and duffle bag with his things and piled them onto the passenger seat of his truck. He brought the front door key back into the house for the final time and looked around. The cottage had been his home for just over a couple of months, but it had made an impression on him. He loved it because he saw his Emmy in every corner and in every doorway. He took a last walk up the stairs to the second floor. He remembered how Vicky had taken to her bedroom across the hall from Emma's and it pained him. Finally, he crossed the hallway and stepped into Emma's bedroom. It still showed some of the fallout from the incident the previous night. He felt the shame from fifteen hours earlier return. His eyes dropped to the floor where Emma's pajamas lay strewn beside the bed. Fin took three steps, reached down, and lifted the pajamas to his face. He inhaled her scent, probably for the last time, and thought back to happier days. He stood frozen in place for nearly five minutes before placing her garments back on the bed. It was time to leave Emma to another man, a man she desired.

Fin backed his truck down the driveway and out onto Webhannet Drive. He surprised himself by turning the vehicle northward. Crossing Mile Road, he steered the pickup onto Atlantic Avenue and headed toward the parking lot by the harbor. He decided to return to the jetty and apologize to his Lord for words spoken in a state of total despair. He drove the length of the road and coasted into the parking lot. He would not be alone on this visit, he thought. An RV with Florida plates and a rusting Chevy with Maine plates were parked facing the channel. He climbed out of the driver's seat and made his way down the sandy path toward the sea. In the distance, the sea foamed and broke against the side of the jetty. He marveled at the positive change in the weather from the day before. Already, he felt the first wave of inner peace begin to return to him. He needed to set something straight and it had to be done in the right place. Scrambling up onto the granite boulders he glanced eastward to the mouth of the harbor. He asked himself how he had ever made it out to the end of the jetty the night before under such godforsaken conditions. Fin began the hike to the eastern tip of the walkway, dodging the pools of water left behind in the crags of many boulders. Alongside, the swells of ocean water plowed down the channel and harmlessly lapped against the side of the jetty. In ten minutes he was standing beside the green light at the far end. Fin took a seat with his back against the base of the steel tower.

"Lord, I'm back from last night. You probably noticed I didn't get to church yesterday. I'm sorry about that. It couldn't be avoided. Of course, that's not why I'm here. Last night, like an idiot, I came here and ran my mouth off pretty good, blaming You and questioning You for everything that's pathetic about me and my life. You should have washed me off this pile of rocks and let me freeze to death in the water. Thank You for not doing that. I'm just here to say that I'm truly sorry for that whole performance and I beg You for forgiveness. There are a hell of a lot of things wrong with me and my life but You gave me Vicky and no man could hope for a finer daughter. Also, thank You for the strength to not do anything really bad to Emma. I still don't know how I had the strength to turn from her lying there and leave the house. It had to come from You. Lord, You have to help me get over her and stop loving her. You know everything so You know how much it hurts when I think about not seeing her anymore and knowing another man is with her. I remember hearing this song once with a guy singing about a girl. The words that stayed with me were that *she may be my treasure…or the price I have to pay.* Lord, it's beginning to look more and more like Emma's the price I have to pay. All I can hope is that You have a plan for me. Maybe that fine-looking woman from Beals that I met last night is in that plan? She seemed really nice and she had the face and the smile of an angel. Anyway, I'm sorry for all of that garbage I threw at You last night and I ask You to forgive me," whispered Fin. Feeling the burden from his actions the prior night dissipate, he folded his arms and stared out to sea. He reminded himself of his sudden lack of work, but was immediately consoled by the cash balance in his checking account. His project working for Emma had allowed him to wipe out all business and personal debts in a short time and build enough of a nest egg to cover the cost of his next six months of living expenses. He thought of the coming Christmas holiday and Vicky's intention to spend most of it with him. This meant that he would not go back to living in a room but would search out a small house or cottage that could accommodate him and an overnight guest.

Fin rose from his seat on the boulders and became aware of dampness on the backside of his pants. He looked up and down the coastline and was reminded why he lived in Maine. The late morning sunlight glistened off of the surface of the water while the line of the horizon was broken by only a single lobster boat just south of his position. He turned from the open ocean and began the walk back to the parking lot. His prayer and meditative time spent in isolation had buoyed his spirits. He glanced across the channel and saw that the corresponding jetty along Drake Island Beach was void of humans. Fin took a deep breath and felt at peace with his life and the world. A ring sounded from his cell phone. He plucked the phone from inside his jacket and brought it up to his ear.

"Yeah," he answered, slightly miffed by the timing of the call.

"Fin, I'm calling to ask a favor of you." It was Emma. Angered, stunned, shocked, excited, he froze with the phone pushed against his ear. "I need you to come and get me," she informed him. He stopped and stared out toward the ocean. A gust of wind sent a swirl of beach sand blowing up onto the jetty and by his feet.

"Why…are you calling me?" he asked, unable to process her request or this unexpected turn of events.

"I never got out to Amherst or western Massachusetts. I got as far as Lowell and I got off Route 495 and called Scott. I couldn't go through with it. I just couldn't go through with it," she repeated. "I told him that before we screwed up Beverly's life and our own, we had to call this off." The news and just the sound of Emma's voice sent his mind swirling.

"But why do you need me? Did you break down or something?"

"No, the car's running fine. I just need you to come and get me," she repeated. Her words set off a ten second period of silence. "Fin?"

"Emmy, with everything that happened yesterday and what I almost did to you, why are you calling me? Have you completely lost your mind?"

"I don't think you understand. I didn't change my mind because I suddenly felt guilty about Scott walking out on his wife or about the turmoil that decision would bring down on all three of us."

"I'm not following you," he said.

"I changed my mind because the thought of going back to the house and not having you there was too much to bear. I've come to love having you around in the morning…and at night."

"I think it'll take a little more than that to make you happy and I've never been able to satisfy you along those lines," he reminded her. "I saw the way you reacted when I carried you upstairs to the bedroom. You cried, Emmy, you literally cried like a frightened child."

"Fin, I actually thought you were going to kill me. You appeared that angry. I cried because I thought I was going to die," she explained.

"How could you think that? After everything we've been through together, how could you think that?"

"I know. After you stormed out of the house I just laid there and thought about everything. You've never hurt me, no matter how unfeeling or cruel I was to you. You're also the only man who has ever said that he would die for me," she added, her voice going soft. "Do you have any idea what those words mean to a woman?"

"It's true. I would die for you. Hey, what's that sound where you are? Are you still down in Lowell?"

"Fin, come for me," she repeated. "Save me, Fin."

"Save you from what? How can I come for you when I don't know where you are?"

"You know very well where I am…you know very well," hinted Emma.

"No, I don't," he insisted, raising his voice.

"What you hear in the background is the sound of moving water," she added. Leaving the phone pressed against his ear, he turned and looked northward back across the channel.

"Are you already back from Massachusetts?" he asked.

"Yes, I am. And it's time for you to come and save me from myself…again," she stated.

"Oh, my God, you're up in Kennebunk and down by the river," he exclaimed.

"I'm not down by the river, I'm in the middle of the river and I need to be rescued. Fin, it's cold and it's wet. Come and rescue me. Please tell me you'll come." He shook his head in disbelief.

"You know I'll come."

"And I want you to walk out to me through the water the way you did back in high school," she insisted.

"Emmy, it's goddamn November. I'll catch pneumonia."

"Fin, if you love me and if you'd still die for me, then you'll do it."

"I'm in love with a woman who is totally out of her mind," he barked into the phone. "Okay, I'll do it all. For you, I will do it all."

Fin ended the conversation and stuffed the phone into his pocket. He scurried back to the parking lot and headed north toward Kennebunk. Traffic was light on Route 1 and he caught two green lights. This had him coasting down the driveway to Rogers Pond and the Mousam River in near record time. He jumped from the pickup and scrambled down to the embankment of the river. Just as promised, Emma sat perched on the same rock he had saved her from in their days at Kennebunk High. She was huddled against the cold air, her arms wrapped around her folded legs and her head propped up on her knees. From ten yards away he could see that her teeth were chattering as the frigid water flowed past. Fin stood frozen on the lip of the river embankment for the next half minute and stared down on his friend. How kind the years had been to her, he thought. His heart raced, just as it had more than thirty years ago when he had spotted her there on a late afternoon in October. At long last, she turned in his direction and their eyes met. Her facial expression brightened.

"Aren't you on the wrong side of the river?" she called out over the sound of cascading water.

"I can save you equally well from either side." Emma rose cautiously to her feet and extended her arms. He shook his head in mock fear.

"God, that water looks cold! What is it with you and this rock?" he asked playfully. She smiled and gestured to him again.

"I've had very good luck picking up men on this rock," she replied, her arms still extended. Emma began to shiver while tears formed in her eyes. He jumped down into the current of frigid water and let out a howl.

"And you couldn't find a rock in a dryer place?" She continued to stare warmly into his eyes and shook her head in the negative. He made his way the twenty feet out to her position and scooped her up in one motion. "God almighty, the water is cold!" Fin cried out. He gazed down at Emma and saw her face lit up with what appeared to be uncompromising love. Ignoring the water temperature, he lifted her head and brought her lips to his. He held the kiss for nothing less than ten seconds.

"Fin, there is one last thing," she whispered with the parting of their lips. "When we get back to the house, I want you to carry me up to the bedroom the way you did last night. I also want you to rip my clothes off the way you did last night...minus the anger." Her request brought a roar of laughter from him as he sloshed his way back to the river's edge. Fin made no attempt to put Emma down but instead carried her out of the river and in the direction of her car. The parking lot was void of any other people. Reaching her Volvo, he looked down at her with a sophomoric grin plastered across his face.

"Emmy, do you realize how long I've dreamed of lying with you?" confessed Fin with almost childlike sincerity.

"And just think, it only took you thirty plus years to realize your dream. I'm just going to have to make sure you're not disappointed with your little Emmy."